... of an Alpha Male

"Sizzling! Jessica Clare gets everything right in this erotic and sexy romance . . . You need to read this book."
—*Romance Junkies*

"What a treat to find a book that does it all and does it so well. Clare has crafted a fiery, heartfelt love story that keeps on surprising . . . matching wit and warmth with plenty of spice . . . This is a book, and a series, not to be missed."
—*RT Book Reviews* (4 ½ Stars)

The Girl's Guide to (Man)Hunting

"Sexy and funny."
—*USA Today*

"A novel that will appeal to both erotic romance fans and outdoor enthusiasts. Set in the small town of Bluebonnet, Texas, this rollicking story of a wilderness survival school and a couple of high-school sweethearts is full of fun and hot, steamy romance."
—*Debbie's Book Bag*

"Clare's sizzling encounters in the great outdoors have definite forest-fire potential from the heat generated."
—*RT Book Reviews*

"A fun, cute, and sexy read . . . Miranda's character is genuine and easy to relate to, and Dane was oh so sexy! Great chemistry between these two that makes for a *hot* and steamy read, but also it is filled with humor and a great supporting cast."
—*Nocturne Romance Reads*

"If you like small-town settings with characters that are easy to fall in love with, this is the book for you."
—*Under the Covers Book Blog*

Berkley Sensation titles by Jessica Clare

THE GIRL'S GUIDE TO (MAN)HUNTING
THE CARE AND FEEDING OF AN ALPHA MALE
THE EXPERT'S GUIDE TO DRIVING A MAN WILD

THE EXPERT'S GUIDE
TO DRIVING
A *Man* WILD

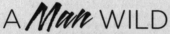

JESSICA CLARE

BERKLEY SENSATION, NEW YORK

THE BERKLEY PUBLISHING GROUP
Published by the Penguin Group
Penguin Group (USA) LLC
375 Hudson Street, New York, New York 10014

USA • Canada • UK • Ireland • Australia • New Zealand • India • South Africa • China

penguin.com

A Penguin Random House Company

THE EXPERT'S GUIDE TO DRIVING A MAN WILD

A Berkley Sensation Book / published by arrangement with the author

Berkley Sensation Books are published by The Berkley Publishing Group.
BERKLEY SENSATION® is a registered trademark of Penguin Group (USA) LLC.
The "B" design is a trademark of Penguin Group (USA) LLC.

For information, address: The Berkley Publishing Group,
a division of Penguin Group (USA) LLC,
375 Hudson Street, New York, New York 10014.

ISBN: 978-0-425-26236-8

PUBLISHING HISTORY
Berkley Sensation mass-market edition / January 2014

PRINTED IN THE UNITED STATES OF AMERICA

10 9 8 7 6 5 4 3 2 1

Cover photo © iStockphoto.
Cover design by Lesley Worrell.
Interior text design by Tiffany Estreicher.

THE EXPERT'S GUIDE
TO DRIVING
A *Man* WILD

ONE

Brenna whistled to herself as she left her cabin. She headed to the ATV shed on the far side of the main lodge that served as headquarters for Wilderness Survival Expeditions. She was alone, which meant it was the perfect time for sabotage.

After glancing around to make sure the coast was clear, she closed the doors and clicked on the overhead light, fanning herself. With the doors shut, it was stuffy in the damn shed, but she didn't plan on being in there long. Brenna moved to the first ATV—her favorite, the cherry red one— and squatted next to the front tire. She took the cap off the valve stem and then pressed her key into it until she heard the hiss of air. Humming to herself, she let out about half of the air before replacing the cap. Moving to the back tire on the same vehicle, she repeated it.

All done. Beaming to herself, she dusted off her hands

and re-opened the shed doors, glancing at the empty parking lot. It was still early in the morning, the birds chirping and a breeze swaying the tall trees in the distance. Her gaze landed on Grant's immaculate Audi gleaming in the parking lot.

A naughty smile curving her mouth, she moved to the hood, popped it, and surveyed the engine. She found the switch casing, opened it, and reviewed the list of switches until she identified the fuel pump switch. With careful fingers, she plucked it out of his car, closed the casing, shut the hood, and tossed the switch into a nearby garbage can.

Some days, she just loved her job.

Recently, their small business had expanded to include Colt's aging father, who everyone called Pop. He mowed the lawns and did repairs, but there wasn't normally enough to keep the man busy. Colt wanted his dad to feel needed, though, so Brenna was tasked with finding stuff to break for Pop to fix. She was great at it, too, though pretty soon she figured he'd be on to her flushing the tampon down the toilet trick. It was time to switch up her game a little, and a bit of vehicle maintenance would do the job just fine. Whistling again, she headed around the front of the main cabin and paused on the front steps.

Two male voices inside were arguing. *Huh.* She glanced at her watch. Six thirty in the morning. Too early for Pop to be up, or Grant, who was a late sleeper. She tended to get up with the sunrise, just like Colt and Dane. Habit from Alaska for them, she supposed, and habit for her from years of living in the backseat of a car.

Like any good nosy busybody, she pressed her ear to the front door to listen in.

"You can't leave right now." Dane sounded almost betrayed. "What am I supposed to do while you're gone?"

"Same thing you always do. Hold classes. Keep Brenna out of trouble. Keep Grant from killing Brenna."

"But we have classes booked every week for the next three weeks."

"Then we'll go in four weeks."

"But what if we have classes then?"

"Dane, Beth Ann and I are going to have our damn honeymoon, whether or not it fits into your precious schedule. Now you're starting to sound like Grant."

"Fuck off, man. I'm just thinking of the business."

All right, time for her to step in and distract them before things got ugly. Brenna opened the front door and yawned loudly, alerting them to her presence. "Morning, boys."

They both nodded at the sight of her. Dane sat at the wooden desk that he shared with Colt, which was a pretty nice desk when it wasn't covered with magazines, books, old coffee mugs, and various other crap. Colt, naturally, was seated on the couch, staring at the Xbox. And both had stopped talking.

Screw that. She smiled brightly at them. "So what's up? I heard something about a honeymoon?"

"Romeo here wants to abandon us for a few weeks and take his new missus up to Alaska and visit the cabin," Dane said, crossing his arms over his chest. "I told him we had to be responsible adults because of the job."

Colt glared at Dane. "Not my fault you've been roped into a big church wedding, buddy. Don't take it out on me."

Dane rubbed a hand down his face, looking frustrated. "God, don't remind me."

"You can still back out," Colt pointed out.

"No, he can't," Brenna said cheerfully, moving to her chair and curling up cross-legged. "Then Miranda and Beth Ann will never talk to either one of you again."

"Miranda wants a big wedding, so that's what she'll get," Dane said, though he sounded a little weary at the thought. "Who'd have thought I'd end up with the high-maintenance girl?"

Colt snorted.

Dane just smiled that silly, lovesick expression he had on his face every time someone mentioned Miranda.

Brenna put a finger to her mouth and pantomimed gagging. "You two are pathetic."

"You're just jealous," Dane said cheerfully.

"Nope. I just feel sorry for any women who have to put up with you two clowns." She pulled a box of Pop-Tarts out of her desk and sighed when she realized it was empty. "Who was supposed to buy groceries for the lodge?"

"You," Colt said.

"Oh crap. That's right. I forgot." Brenna tossed the box over onto Grant's immaculate desk and shrugged. "Anyone for a donut run?"

Two male hands went up.

"Okay. I'll get my keys." She dug through the messy drawer of her desk until she located her keys, held them aloft, and then bounced out of her chair. "Be back in ten minutes."

"Hey, Bren," Dane called. "Aren't you forgetting something?"

She turned and snapped her fingers. "Right. If Pop asks, one of the four-wheelers looks a little low on two tires. Can you get him to take a look at it?"

"I think he meant your pants," Colt drawled.

She glanced down at her legs. She wore a pair of men's boxer shorts. SpongeBob SquarePants. "What's wrong with my pants?"

"They're missing," Colt pointed out dryly. "Along with your shoes."

4

She rolled her eyes. "I'm going to the donut store, not the prom. Like I said, I'll be back in five." And she made sure to wiggle her bare feet as she left.

By the time she returned with a box of fresh donuts and a tray of hot coffees, she was disappointed to see that Grant was up. He frowned at the sight of her bare legs and boxer shorts and ratty T-shirt. Hey, at least she'd brushed her hair. She gave him an arch smile as she entered the room, setting the donuts down in front of Colt on the coffee table and snagging a coffee.

"Morning, boss," she said in her sweetest voice, because she knew it would drive Grant crazy. She grabbed a donut and headed back to her desk.

Grant frowned over at her as she sat down. "Don't eat that at your desk, Brenna. You'll get crumbs into your keyboard."

She deliberately took a messy bite of donut, half the food falling out of her mouth, dribbling crumbs all over her desk.

He sighed and turned away, his hands going to the pockets of his slacks as he paced before the fireplace. It was before nine and the man already looked immaculate. *Sheesh.* She gave him an annoyed look as she ate, noting his dark gray slacks with a pleat pressed into them, the lighter gray sweater he wore over a black collared shirt. Even his hair looked perfect. Tousled, perfectly styled waves that probably wouldn't look that way without a ton of product. He was perfectly shaven, not a hair out of place. And he was frowning as the two other men attacked the donuts as if they hadn't eaten in weeks.

"Have you two looked at the schedule for today?" Grant asked them.

"Schedule?" Dane said in a deliberately blank voice, then scarfed half a donut in one bite. "We have a schedule?"

Colt shrugged.

"I have a schedule today," Grant said. "We have a carpenter coming out to look at the area we've roped off for the paintball course so we can see what needs to be built. I need one of you to be here."

"I can't," Dane said. "Miranda wants to go in to Houston so we can talk to someone about flowers for the wedding."

Colt raised a hand and made a noise that sounded like a whip, but Dane only gave them the same good-natured, lovesick grin.

"So you'll do it, Colt?"

"I can meet with him," Brenna volunteered, putting down her coffee. "Just show me what needs to be done and I can get with the carpenter."

Grant glanced over at her and then turned back to Colt. "So you'll do it, Colt?"

She was tempted to throw her donut at the back of Grant's immaculate head. *Jerk.*

Colt shrugged. "Fine."

"Good. I have to be at the airport this afternoon to pick up family, otherwise I'd take care of it."

Brenna choked on her coffee. She began to cough, grabbing a wad of napkins and covering her mouth as she struggled to get her breath. Dane came over to her side and began to pound on her back with one of his big meat hook hands, nearly knocking her back off the chair again.

So now was probably not the best time to mention to Grant that she'd sabotaged his car.

Without the fuel pump fuse, it wouldn't start. She'd figured it'd be a lot of fun to see him get all flustered and irritated, and then Pop could spend the afternoon trying to figure out what was wrong with the car. It was two birds with one stone, really. She'd keep Pop busy and annoy Grant at the same time.

Except, well, she hadn't looked at the calendar, either. She glanced over at it. Sure enough, it was circled in red and said very clearly, AIRPORT.

Oops.

"Something wrong, Brenna?" Grant's frown was directed at her, as if he could sense what she'd done.

She decided to take the heat off her. Between coughs, she said, "I think we should have a company meeting to discuss what we're going to do when Colt leaves for two weeks."

Grant immediately turned his frown to Colt. "You're leaving?"

Colt glared at Brenna. "You suck."

She gave him a thumbs up between coughs. *Right back atcha.*

"Where are you going?"

Colt leaned back on the couch until he could see Grant's head. "Beth Ann wants a honeymoon and we're low on cash, so I thought I'd take her up to the cabin in Alaska for a few weeks. Just the two of us. She likes alone time."

"But what about classes?"

"Dane can do 'em. This is our slow period anyhow."

"That's why we're setting up the paintball course," Grant said, frowning and moving to snag the last coffee. "So there wouldn't be a slow period. We've already advertised it in all the nearby papers that it's going to be live as of December first. I'm already getting calls about it. I need you here."

"It's paintball," Colt said patiently. "Can't Pop handle it?"

"Pop's already pretty busy," Dane said, earning him a scowl from Colt. "Don't look at me like that. He *is* always busy. Brenna keeps him hopping."

Colt glanced at Grant. "You going to run it for us, then?"

"My family's in town, so I'm going to be occupied with them for the next few weeks." Grant tugged at his collar as if it were too tight. That was impossible. The man probably had his clothes tailored so he could look perfect at all times. Brenna rolled her eyes at the thought and wiped the crumbs off her keyboard. "And Dane's going to want some time off around the holidays, too. It's like we need another set of hands."

"Maybe you should take over some of the classes," Brenna said to Grant.

This time, three sets of eyes turned to glare at her.

Brenna hid her smile behind a look of mock-innocence. "What'd I say?"

Grant shook his head, dismissing her comment. "I'm needed in the office to organize things since my assistant is so very lacking."

She stuck her tongue out at him.

He ignored her and turned back to the two guys. "Do you think Pop can handle an extra workload?"

Dane shrugged. "Why *don't* we hire another trainer? I'm getting kind of tired of having back-to-back classes. Throw in the paintball and it doesn't sound like we're ever going to get a day off."

"Where are we going to find another survival expert?" Grant asked.

"I'll do it," Brenna volunteered. When they turned to look at her again, she shrugged. "I'm the assistant. Let me assist."

"We need someone with certifications," Grant said, warming up to the subject. He stalked over to Brenna's desk. "Write

8

this down, Brenna. We need someone physically fit, preferably in top condition. Someone who's personable and good with all kinds of people, from kids to businessmen. Someone with a lot of background in survival training. We'd need a list of what classes they've taken and what teaching skills they have. And we'll pay for relocation."

She nodded, and then took another sip of her coffee, watching Grant.

"You could probably put an ad in one of the Outdoor magazines. I—" He stopped and turned back to her. "Are you writing this down?"

She fluttered her eyelashes at him. "Oh, did you say to write this down? I must not have heard that."

"Write it down," he said between clenched teeth.

She took out a green notepad from under a pile of papers and wrote notes. "Young. Hot. Certifiable. Outdoorsy."

"Maybe we should look for a new assistant, too," he said in an unpleasant voice.

"Time for a vote," Brenna said, ignoring Grant's tone. "All those in favor of hiring someone new for classes, raise your hand."

All three men's hands went up.

"All those in favor of firing Brenna?"

Only Grant's hand went up.

She stuck her lower lip out at him, mock-pouting. "Sorry, Grant. You lose."

"I'm the one who writes the checks here," he said in an annoyed tone, moving back to his desk.

She shrugged and glanced back at Dane and Colt. They were her yardstick that she went by. If they were frowning, she'd gone too far. If they were laughing and smirking, she was just giving Grant crap like one of the boys, and it was tolerable. And both were still grinning with amusement.

Good enough for her. She wiped the crumbs off her desk and then moved to go grab one of the few remaining donuts. "I'll go wake up Pop and tell him that breakfast is here." As she walked to the door, she added, "He's going to be so upset, though, once he finds out that Grant drank his coffee."

As she shut the door behind her, she heard Grant protest. "How was I supposed to know it was his drink? She only bought four damn coffees!"

Brenna grinned to herself. Whistling, she skipped over to Pop's cabin.

Later that afternoon, she found herself working alone in the main cabin with Grant. This was normally enough to make Brenna want to run screaming for the hills. Or better yet, to find a task—any task—that would get her out of the building and away from his nitpicking. *You're doing this all wrong, Brenna*, he would say. *You need to catalog the receipts in date order, and then alphabetically. You can't just throw them all into a big pile.*

She made a face just thinking about that. Nothing she ever did pleased him and his anal-retentive ways.

"Do you have the flight info?" he asked her for the third time that day.

Resisting the urge to roll her eyes, Brenna glanced over at him and kept her voice neatly controlled. "For the third time, yes. I printed them out and put the arrival and gate information on your desk."

"Thank you."

"Do you want me to print it out again?" She gave him an innocent look. "You know, just in case one copy isn't enough?"

Behind his designer glasses, Grant gave her a sharp, narrow-eyed look. "One is fine. Thank you."

She nodded and went back to emailing one of her friends. Email was really her best friend when she was at work. It made it look like she was busy and if she was busy, then Grant would leave her alone. Theoretically.

He sighed heavily. "I'm sorry, Brenna."

She froze. That did not sound like Grant. Glancing over, Brenna kept the frown off her face and managed to look only mildly concerned. "Sorry?"

Grant took off his glasses and ran a hand down his face. "I know I keep asking you for the same information over and over again. I'm just a little . . . out of sorts with family coming in to town."

"Oh," she said, and then added, "no sweat."

Okay, he was officially weirding her out. Grant never apologized to her. Like, ever. She typed a moment longer, then fired off the email.

"You put in the ad for the new instructor?"

She nodded and lifted a piece of paper without looking over at him. "Do you want to review it again?"

"Huh? Oh. No, that's okay." He lifted the picture on the corner of his desk and then sighed heavily. "Are you going to get dressed at any point today?"

This was more like Grant. She felt a little better. Brenna glanced down at her T-shirt and SpongeBob boxers. "I'm pretty sure all my body parts are covered. Did we get a dress code that I didn't know about?"

"No. It's just that my family's coming in."

"Should I hide under my desk so I don't appall them with my hideousness?"

"Very funny. No, just straighten up while I'm gone,

please." He grabbed a stack of envelopes and began to arrange them into a neat pile. "Make sure the magazines are all lined up and if you could dust, that would be terrific."

"Oh wow." Brenna mockingly touched her shirt. "I didn't realize I dressed up as the maid today."

"Ha, ha, Brenna. You're an assistant. You occasionally will have to do *some* sort of work. Today it just means cleaning up." He ran a finger along the fireplace mantel. "And dusting."

She saluted him. "Whatever you say, boss."

He gave her an exasperated look as he headed back to his desk. Grant picked up his keys and paused, glancing around the main lodge. "You think they'll be proud of what we've accomplished here?"

"Why are you asking me?"

A wry expression twisted Grant's mouth. "Good point. Like I said, it's just nerves."

She stared at him. He'd almost just smiled at her. "You feeling okay?"

"Yeah." He ran a hand down his face again and tugged at his collar once more. He was clearly nervous. "Just a bit distracted."

"You'll be fine once you see them," Brenna said, and then almost bit her tongue. Why was she trying to soothe him? "Shouldn't you be going soon?"

He nodded and turned to the door, then turned back to her again. "I don't suppose you can get rid of the purple in your bangs?"

Her purple Bettie Page bangs? She loved them. Brenna glared and pointed at the door. "Go."

Grant nodded. "Sorry. I shouldn't have asked. They look nice."

As she sat there at her desk, mouth hanging open, Grant turned and headed outside just as Dane bounded through the door, coming inside. The big athlete shook rain from his hair, grinning cheerfully. "Looks like it's going to be a downpour soon."

Brenna ran to him, dragging him away from the front door and to the back of the main office. "What's up with Grant?"

Dane looked confused. "What do you mean?"

"He's being weird," she hissed. "He apologized to me earlier. Twice. And he seemed nervous. And when he was leaving, he *complimented* me on my hair."

"Huh." Dane looked just as surprised as she was for a moment there. "Your hair's cute, Bren. In a Suicide Girls sort of way, that is. Kinda not Grant's thing, though."

Well, that stung, and she didn't even know why it bothered her. "I could care less if I'm Grant's kind of thing," she said, irritated. "What's eating him?"

Dane shrugged, then moved to the swag counter, pulling one of the complimentary shirts off a stack and switching it out with his damp one. "Oh, that. He probably just has his feathers ruffled because of his parents visiting. He hasn't seen them in two years."

"Aren't they rich? What's the matter with them? They don't like flying or something?"

"Yeah, but it's more like Grant avoids them. They always ask him about the wife."

"The wife?" Brenna thought for a moment. "You mean, his dead wife?"

"Yeah." Dane ripped the tags off the new shirt and tugged it down over his muscular chest. "His dad's convinced he's wasting away from missing her, and his mom's convinced that all he needs is someone new in his life to make him forget her. When Mama Markham shows up to visit, she constantly throws women in his direction, trying to set him up. It drives Grant crazy."

Brenna thought for a moment. She'd been working with the Expeditions group ever since they opened, and though it had only been a few months, she couldn't think of a single, solitary time that Grant had gone out on a date. For that matter, he never seemed to get many personal calls, either. It was all work for him.

For some reason, that made her sad, and she felt a twinge of pity. "How long ago did his wife die?"

"Five years ago."

"Five years!" That was a really long mourning period. He must have been positively flattened by her death. Poor guy.

"Yeah." Dane's face was grim. "I wasn't here at the time but I knew Heather. She and Grant were high school sweethearts. From what I heard, it was pretty bad and Grant was devastated as hell. He's probably not ready to move on, but his mom won't let up. She thinks he'll never jump back into the waters unless she gives him a little push."

She chewed on her lip. "Parents are kind of jerks like that." Poor Grant. No wonder he was so flustered at the thought of his parents arriving. A memory flashed through Brenna's mind and she went to Grant's desk. She'd recalled seeing a picture there, but thought it was a sister or a friend—or girlfriend. But no, it was a photo of a pretty, perfect blonde posing on skis. It must have been his dead wife. "His parents should just leave him alone."

"They're family. Family never leaves anyone alone."

She kind of disliked them already. Sure, Grant was an uptight douche, but he was *her* uptight douche to harass and annoy. She didn't want to feel *sorry* for the guy. Ugh. What was next? Getting all hot and bothered because he liked her bangs? Please.

The front door opened and Grant came in, keys in hand, glasses speckled with rain. His perfect hair was soaked and his shoulders were wet from big, splashing drops of water.

"My car won't start." He sighed, and then threw the keys down on the nearest table. "Un-fucking-believable."

Brenna winced. "Yeah, about that . . ."

Grant turned to her, his jaw clenching. "What?"

She shrugged. "I might have disabled the fuel pump switch so Pop could have something to work on this afternoon."

He looked like he was ready to reach across the desk and choke her. Well, that was an improvement at least. This Grant she knew how to handle. "Brenna," he said, his tone warning. "Give me the switch."

"I might have thrown it away."

"Brenna."

"What? Like I knew you were going to the airport."

"It was on the calendar, damn it!"

She spread her hands. "Sorry. You can take my car. I don't know how much gas it has, though. I pretty much only go to the station when the little red light comes on."

He stared at her.

"Oh, and if it chokes when it turns over, you have to pump the brakes a few times. It's a little persnickety."

He continued to stare. Dane ran a hand over his mouth, a sure sign he was trying to smother a laugh.

"And actually, while I think about it, the tags might be expired, but they never really pull you over for that sort of thing anyhow—"

She broke off when Grant pointed at her.

"You're driving."

Brenna pointed at her chest. "Me?"

"Yes, you. You are driving me to the airport. Call the carpenter and reschedule for another day. Get an umbrella." He looked her up and down, and then added, "And put on some damn pants."

TWO

Two hours later, Brenna was in jeans, the car was pulling into the airport parking lot, and she was ready to boot Grant out of the car the next time he made a crack about her 1992 Sunfire.

"We're here," she said in a falsely cheerful voice, pulling up to the first available spot. "You can get out now."

"I don't know if I'll be able to," he said in a low, almost pleasant voice, glancing over at her. "I might be stuck to the gum on the seat."

"Nonsense," she told him. "I throw all my gum on the floorboards."

To her immense gratification, he lifted one of his expensive leather shoes and grimaced. "Lovely."

"Isn't it? Now come on. I can't believe I'm the one telling you this, but you're going to be late for their flight."

They got out of Brenna's car and didn't speak as they

entered the airport, searching for the correct gate. There were dozens of people already milling around the baggage claim, and none of them had the same sour look that Grant did, so she didn't know if his family were here or not.

"The next time you decide to disable my car, do me a favor and check with me first." Grant moved to her side and touched her elbow as he spoke in a low voice, through clearly gritted teeth. He was pissed.

"Oh come on. What fun would that be?" She shrugged out of his grip and put her hands on her hips, glancing around. "I don't see them anywhere."

"Don't change the subject, Brenna." He stepped in front of her, wearing his best It's Time for a Lecture face. "I don't relish the thought of driving my family back to town in that rust bucket that you call a vehicle. When was the last time you had it washed? Or detailed? There's an inch of dust on the dashboard."

Picky, picky. "Your family won't care. They're probably nice people who won't comment on something like that."

He snorted. "You don't know anything about my family. For all you know, they could be a homely pair of Siamese twins."

She smiled sweetly. "Well, that explains where you got your looks."

Grant looked ready to choke her. "Brenna, I—"

"Grant?"

They both turned at the sound of the voice. A trio of adults stood nearby, suitcases in hand. Their faces were lit with smiles at the sight of him—his family. A woman with a smooth gray bob and dangling earrings stepped forward. "Grant, honey! It's so good to see you." Her voice was sweet and cultured, and she set down her suitcase handle, opening her arms for a hug.

Grant obediently moved forward, hugging the members of his family, and Brenna observed them. His mother was tall and slender, and she wore a coral jacket and matching skirt, and low beige heels. An elephant brooch was pinned to her breast. She looked more like she was heading for lunch at the country club than visiting family. To her right was Grant's father, an equally gray-haired man in a dark sweater and slacks that could have been plucked from Grant's cabinet. Standing behind them was a shorter young woman with a curvy frame and long, incredibly straight light brown hair that hung in her face. She might have been pretty if she didn't seem so darn shy. Grant hugged her, too, so Brenna guessed she was a sister or a cousin or something.

"It's so good to see you guys," Grant said, smiling at each person in turn.

Grant's mother's gaze went to Brenna, and she gave her a questioning look. Brenna wiggled her fingers in response, acknowledging the woman's stare.

"Grant, sweetheart," his mother said in a curious voice. "You haven't introduced us to your friend."

"I'm Brenna, his assistant," Brenna said in a cheerful voice, sticking her hand out. "Grant asked me to drive today. He was having car trouble and I was just hanging around, so I got the honor."

"I see," Grant's mother said in a curious voice. "I'm Justine Markham. This is my husband, Reggie, and this is our daughter, Elise."

No one took Brenna's hand. She turned it into a friendly wave. "Nice to meet all of you."

Elise smiled at her. She could have been Brenna's age. Well, that would be fun. She'd take Elise out drinking and get all the good gossip about Grant from her. This could be interesting after all. Brenna rubbed her hands together.

"Should we get your suitcases and head back to the car, then? We've got a fair drive back to Bluebonnet."

"The car's a bit small," Grant told them, picking up the handle to his mother's suitcase and then grabbing Elise's tote. Brenna picked up Elise's other bag, just to help out. "I hope you don't mind."

"Not at all," his father said easily. "We appreciate you coming to get us."

"You could always rent a car," Brenna pointed out.

"Nonsense," Reggie said. "Grant has a lovely car and depending on him for a ride means that we'll get to spend that much time together."

Yeah, about that . . . Brenna thought, but said nothing. She just kept smiling.

"How are things with the business?" Elise asked.

"Things are great," Grant said enthusiastically. "We're really on track to have a good year, and we're making a name for ourselves. We get inquiries about classes every day."

They chatted a bit about the business as they walked across the parking lot to Brenna's car. Justine and Reggie didn't look thrilled, but a smile quirked Elise's mouth at the sight of the car, which made Brenna like her all the more. Grant popped the trunk and grimaced at the sight of the jumper cables lying scattered across the back, along with a pair of grubby sneakers.

"Oh, those are just junk," Brenna said, grabbing the shoes and tossing them under a nearby car. "All better now."

Grant gave her his favorite disapproving look and then began to heft suitcases into her car's small trunk while the others stood around.

"So," Justine said after a long moment. "How are you doing, Grant? How's the social life? You keeping busy? Getting out?"

He gave Elise's bag a shove, trying to make it fit into the small trunk. It wasn't working, so he paused, sighed at the stack of suitcases, and turned back to the others. "What do you mean, Mom?"

Justine exchanged a look with Reggie. "I was just asking, darling. We worry about you and how alone you are."

The look on Grant's face became shuttered. "I'm fine."

Yowch. His tone had gone positively arctic. Dane had been right—he sure was touchy about this sort of thing. Elise gave Brenna a quick, apologetic look.

"But darling, you need to get back on the horse. Get out and see new people again. You're too young to be spending your life a widower. I know it's hard but you can't go through life moping."

Grant glanced over at Brenna as if chagrined that the conversation was taking place in front of her. "Now is not the time, Mother."

"I've invited Bonnie's daughter to dinner with us, son. I wanted to let you know before we all got to the restaurant."

Wow, that was bold of the woman. Brenna had to give her props for being on the ball . . . if it wasn't such a dick move to pull on Grant. He needed time and space, something his mother clearly didn't understand. Brenna felt oddly protective of Grant in that moment. It was clear that he was still wounded from his wife's death.

"You invited her to dinner?" Grant asked.

"It's just a little hello, son. Nothing to get all worked up about," Reggie interjected, taking his wife's side. "We both think it'd be good for you."

"Mother." Grant's tone was a warning.

Justine ignored it. "She's a lovely girl. I think you'll like her. And she's a marketing major, so you'll have so much to talk about. She's very pretty and career driven and very understanding." His mother stressed the last word. "She won't rush you."

That was really a low blow. Outraged, Brenna pushed forward. This was rude and cruel and thoughtless of them. And if someone was going to be thoughtless and obnoxious to Grant, it was going to be her, damn it. She was never cruel, at least.

"Don't," Elise told her in a soft voice as Brenna pushed forward. "They always do this."

"Not today," Brenna said cheerfully.

She stepped between Grant and his parents. "You can't invite this chick to dinner tonight."

"Brenna," Grant said, now turning the warning voice on her.

Justine regarded Brenna for a long moment as if sizing her up, and then smiled. "I'm afraid it's too late, my dear. She's already been invited to dinner."

"Then uninvite her," Brenna retorted. "Having her there is rude."

Elise covered her mouth, her gaze flicking to Justine.

"Uninviting her is even ruder," Grant's mother replied, the smile on her face still. Her voice had gone a little brittle, as if remaining polite were testing her patience.

Now Brenna was getting angry. Grant put a hand on her shoulder, trying to pull her backward and separate her from his parents. Why was he defending them when they were harassing him? An idea struck, and she gave Justine a little smile. "I guess this ruins the surprise, then."

"Surprise?" Reggie asked.

Brenna turned and put her hands on Grant's collar, tugging him down and kissing him full on the mouth. She turned back to Justine, Reggie, and Elise. "Grant didn't want to tell you guys until after dinner. He likes to keep people guessing."

"He does?" Elise asked, clearly shocked as her gaze flipped between Brenna and Grant and then back to Brenna.

She glanced up at Grant, but he was still standing there, his mouth slightly agape, staring down at her. She leaned up and bit his lower lip, tugging on it in a sensual move of ownership. "So shy. It's adorable." She looked over at Justine and smiled again, this time a genuine smile since she now had the upper hand. "That's why you can't invite this girl. She's just going to see me and my boo being affectionate all night."

And just to make her words have punch, Brenna gave Grant a slap on the ass.

The car ride back to Bluebonnet was rather silent. Only two suitcases were able to be squeezed in the trunk of Brenna's car, so Elise sat in the middle of the backseat, her legs tucked close, suitcase in her lap. Her parents were sandwiched on each side of her, and all three looked extremely uncomfortable. Brenna was pretty sure they were wishing that they'd rented a car after all.

And no one was talking. Occasionally, someone would bring up a safe conversation subject—the weather, the business, Dane's engagement, Colt's shotgun wedding, Bluebonnet—but then the conversation would quickly die again. Brenna suspected that it was partly due to the fact that she kept reaching over and toying with Grant's hair at the nape of his neck in a possessive gesture.

It really was fun to infuriate people. And today? She'd infuriated a whole car full of people.

Of course, Grant could sell her out with a word and a look. He didn't have to be part of this charade. The fact that he wasn't speaking up told her that he liked her plan at some level and was going along with it because it benefited him. It was strange to be on the same side as Grant for a change, but she didn't like the way his parents had hounded him.

Plus, he wasn't a bad kisser. It probably would have been better if he'd responded, but his breath had been fresh and sweet, his lips firm, and he was just the right height. She could have done a lot worse for a fake boyfriend.

She drove them to the only bed and breakfast in Bluebonnet—the Peppermint House. Grant said nothing while she let his family out of the backseat, simply grabbing bags and carrying them up the walkway of the red-and-white Victorian.

"We'll be back to pick you up in a few hours for dinner," Grant finally told them, kissing his mother and sister on the cheek.

"I have reservations at a nice sushi place in Huntsville," Justine said. "Is that okay with you and . . ." she trailed off.

"That's fine with us, Mother." He gave her a tight smile. "We'll be back to pick you up at five."

Grant said nothing to her on the drive back to the Daughtry Ranch, which told her that she was probably in trouble. They pulled into the parking lot of Wilderness Survival Expeditions, gravel crunching underneath them. "Hey, there's Pop," she exclaimed cheerfully, then honked her horn at Pop, who was under the hood of Grant's Audi. She rolled down her window and stuck her head out. "How's it going, Pop?"

A hand tugged on her arm, dragging her attention back inside. "Turn off the car, Brenna. We need to talk." Grant's voice was reserved and utterly polite. It was a sure sign that he was furious at her.

Brenna shrugged and turned off the car, waving at Pop. Grant moved around the car to her side, grabbed her by the arm, and began to pull her toward the main lodge. Pop looked at them in surprise, and Brenna allowed Grant to drag her into the cabin. Best to have him yell at her without Pop wondering what was going on, at least.

They stormed inside together, Brenna trailing after Grant. As soon as the door was shut, Grant whipped her around, turning her to face him. That made Brenna roll her eyes at all the dramatics. You'd think she'd done something wrong, with the way he was acting.

"Brenna, what the hell were you thinking?" His green eyes were frowning at her through his glasses.

She plucked his fingers off her arm. "Your mom's kind of a beast, dude."

"I am not a dude, and she is my mother. Show some respect."

"I'll show some respect when they respect you," Brenna told him. "Inviting some chick out to dinner as soon as they got here? So they can hook you up? That's just plain rude. They're not thinking of your feelings. They're tired of you being in mourning because it harshes their parental buzz or something. It's awful and they had no right to do that to you."

He looked surprised at her vehement defense of him.

She was a little surprised at herself, too. Crossing her arms over her chest, she shrugged. "I was just trying to help you out."

"Thank you," he said quietly. "I'm not used to people defending me."

She didn't know how to respond to that. "You're welcome, I guess."

Grant rubbed his chin, then glanced around the room, as if he wanted to look anywhere but at her. "Well, now it's turned into an even bigger mess. They're going to expect you at dinner, and they're going to expect us to act like a couple."

"Pfft. Are you kidding? That's a piece of cake."

Grant stared down at her. "How is that a piece of cake?"

She leaned forward and straightened his collar, then brushed a lock of hair off his forehead. For some reason, he got a soft look in his eyes, and she felt a shiver of desire race through her. "See? That right there was a total girlfriend move. I just act like you belong to me, and they'll buy it."

"I see." He appeared to think this over for a minute. "I hate to deceive them."

"I don't. You want them to stay out of your hair, don't you? To quit pushing dates on you that you don't want? Because if you *do* want them, I'm more than happy to break up with you in the next thirty seconds and you can go to dinner a bachelor."

"No," he said thoughtfully. "Your plan could work. I don't suppose there has to be much kissing. We can just hold hands."

"Oh, there'll be kissing," Brenna said. "You were pretty rusty at it."

"I was not."

"You were. And they're not going to find it believable if we're not all kissy on each other." She fluttered her eyelashes at him.

He looked at her as if she'd suddenly sprang another head. "And you're okay with kissing me?"

She snorted. "It's just kissing, Grant. It's not a marriage license. Don't you ever kiss people you don't give a shit about?"

"Of course not."

"Oh." Well, it seemed like they were two different creatures, then. "Huh."

He shook his head. "You don't have to do this."

"I'm your assistant. I'll just think of it as assisting you."

He considered her for a long moment, and then sighed. "You'll have to change for dinner."

She gave him a mock-lascivious look and ran her hands down her front, over her breasts. "Want me to wear something slutty?"

The look he gave her could have peeled paint. *"No."*

Grant paced in the living room of the main lodge, his thoughts in turmoil. When he was mulling through a problem, he liked to pace in front of the large stone fireplace. It was the feature he'd liked best about the cabin, and he often walked back and forth in front of it to work through a problem. Exercise always cleared his mind.

Normally it helped. Today? Not so much.

In one afternoon, it seemed that his calm, ordered life had been completely torn open and upheaved.

His family was here. That was a pain in the ass, but an expected one. He enjoyed seeing his sister, Elise. She was quiet, gentle, and wouldn't probe on painful subjects. She seemed to know instinctively the kind of company he needed and was happy to just be quiet moral support for her brother. Elise wasn't the problem. It was his parents. Or rather, his mother, since his father tended to give in to everything his mother wanted. Justine Markham was not used to hearing the word *no*.

She'd flown to his side the moment he'd returned home for Heather's funeral. She'd been sympathetic and caring and handled all the details while Grant wallowed in his grief. It was only after the first anniversary of Heather's death had passed that she'd started to press him a bit.

You should date.

You're too young to be a widower, Grant. Get back out there.

I can introduce you to a few lovely girls, Grant. I just hate to see you so lonely and unhappy.

You'll want children someday, Grant. I want grandchildren. It's not going to happen if you keep mourning a woman who's been dead for years.

His mother's arguments had gone from sympathetic and understanding to annoyed and frustrated. So he'd been grieving for a while. So what? He'd loved Heather. Why shouldn't he miss her? Why did his family insist on pushing him toward other women? It wasn't as if he had a biological clock that was ticking. He wasn't even thirty yet. Plenty of time to meet someone new and start over again.

People just needed to back the hell off.

Of course, that was what made Brenna's absurd defense of him so bizarre and out of left field.

He'd been simmering with irritation when his family had started in on their favorite subject, though he hadn't been surprised that his mother had invited a girl to dinner. He expected that sort of thing from Justine.

But he'd been shocked as hell when Brenna had grabbed him by the collar and kissed him, and then pronounced them as a couple. His parents' stunned looks of astonishment probably echoed his own, but Brenna had taken her lie and ran with it. She'd been incredibly believable, too, reaching over and playing with his hair as they'd driven back to town, acting affectionate and silly toward him. He imagined that would be how she would act in a relationship normally.

He should have nipped her lie in the bud. He didn't like deceiving his family. Elise had looked hurt that he'd never mentioned things to her, and his mother had looked briefly furious, then just confused.

And yet for some reason, he didn't correct Brenna. He'd let the lie stand, let his parents think that they were an item. Why? He had no idea. Brenna's defense of him had surprised him. And even though it was a ridiculous concept, she had a point. If they pretended to have a relationship, his parents would back off their continual persistent attempts to find him a new wife.

It was just surprising that this had come from Brenna, of all people. Annoying, careless, rebel without a cause Brenna. The perpetual thorn in his side. The worst employee ever. The most infuriating and useless woman he'd ever known.

The only one who had come to his defense this afternoon.

He should point out to his parents that it was just a joke. That he wasn't dating Brenna at all and that she would be the last person he'd date, with her purple hair and loud ways and her complete lack of respect for him. He'd just bring it up casually before dinner and send Brenna on her way. She wouldn't be hurt in the slightest. She had an iron hide when it came to him. They bickered at each other all day long at work.

Grant adjusted the collar of his shirt, frowning. He'd changed into a jacketed suit that wasn't too formal, but his parents didn't care for casual dining. He hoped Brenna realized that. With a grimace, he realized he probably should have given her more instructions on what to wear.

Hell, and now *he* was thinking like he was going to take part in this charade, too. He needed to make up his mind, and soon.

The front door to the lodge opened, and Grant turned

around. His tongue stuck to the roof of his mouth as Brenna entered, a soft smile on her mouth. She lifted her arms and twirled a little. "Will this do? I had to borrow it from Miranda."

Brenna's dark, wavy hair had been parted down the middle, the thick brown locks brushing against her shoulders. Her heavy fringe of purple bangs had been carefully arranged and curled, and they hung in a perfect line at her eyebrows. Her hair didn't look careless and untamed today—it looked beautiful, thick, and healthy, and just a bit quirky. The dress she wore was a dark blue sheath with thin spaghetti straps and a bit of lace under the bust. It was pretty and demure and wasn't something Brenna would normally wear, but now that she was in it, he couldn't take his eyes off her. Her figure was usually hidden in the bizarre clothing choices she normally wore, but tonight she was an hourglass. When she turned, he could see two small bluebirds tattooed over each shoulder blade. His parents wouldn't approve of that.

He didn't care. She looked gorgeous. And that stunned him.

Her smile widened as he said nothing. Her hands went to her hips, the small clutch purse in her hand a bright spotted-leopard print. "That good, huh? I thought so, too."

Grant rubbed his chin. "You look nice."

"I know! My tits look amazing in this." She cupped her breasts and jiggled them at him, grinning.

His astonished gaze went to that cleavage and he couldn't help but stare for a moment. When had Brenna, the pain in his ass, gotten so built? *Stacked like a brick shithouse*, as Dane would say.

"Are your parents going to flip out?"

He was still staring at her breasts. "Huh? What?"

"Your parents? Are they going to be upset that we're

'dating'?" She released her boobs and made air quotes as she said "dating." "And better yet, do you care?"

"You were right—it is a good idea, if an unorthodox and deceitful one."

"Such flattery," she said with a grin, not offended at his words at all. "So, if we're going to do this, and I think you just said we are, I need you to do one more thing for me. Well, two more things."

"What's that?"

"One," she said, and moved past him to his desk.

He couldn't help but watch her, admiring the lines of her legs. She wore high heels, too, and she looked amazing in them. He'd never seen Brenna dolled up, and he felt as if he'd been suddenly missing out. She was gorgeous. He couldn't stop staring at her.

Brenna picked up the picture on his desk and held it out to him. "You can't have this sitting out on your desk while they're here. They'll know something's up."

It was like a punch in the gut. Heather's smiling picture stared up at him. She'd been so alive, so vibrant in that photo. And now she was dead, and here he was, five years later, pretending he'd moved on and wasn't holding on to feelings. He gazed at the photo for a long moment, not saying anything.

"I know it's rude of me to point it out," she told him softly. "But it's only for a short time. I promise. We'll put it back up as soon as they're gone."

We'll put it back up. As if they were in this together. Funny how he and Brenna had been at odds from day one, and the moment she'd felt he was threatened, she'd latched on to him and declared them a team. Funny . . . and appealing, really.

He nodded, opened a desk drawer, and very carefully laid Heather's picture in there and then closed the drawer. His throat clenched for a moment, as if in protest, and then he was fine. Grant glanced back over at Brenna. "What was the other thing?"

She grinned, looking far more mischievous and like her old self. "You can't look so freaked out when I kiss you."

"I didn't look freaked out."

She gave him a wide-eyed, startled expression, pantomiming him receiving her kiss.

"Bullshit. That wasn't me."

"I'm afraid it's true," she said with a fake sigh. "You're not a very good actor."

Grant gave her a challenging look. "Do we need to practice?"

She gave him an impressed look and, hell, he was impressed at himself for saying it, but now that it was out there, he was curious to see how she'd react.

Brenna gestured for him to close the space between them. "Wouldn't hurt to have a bit of prep before dinner."

All right, then. He moved closer to her, noticing that she smelled a bit like a light, flowery perfume. Did she always smell that sweet and he'd never noticed? Or was this more stuff borrowed from Miranda? Grant stood in front of her for a moment and gave her an expectant look. "Well?"

"Well, what? You're the one who suggested practice. *You* need to kiss me." She exaggerated her face into a pucker and tilted it up for him.

This sounded like a challenge. He'd kiss her, and he'd kiss her until her toes curled. Grant put an arm around her waist, tugging her close against him. Her arms wrapped around him to catch herself and while she steadied her feet, he leaned down and lightly brushed his thumb over her lips. "Be serious, Brenna."

Her mouth relaxed and she got all soft-looking, her lips parting as she glanced up at him. Ah hell, she was great at this pretending shit. She really looked as if she wanted nothing more than for him to kiss her.

Good. He'd oblige her, pretending or not. He leaned in and tilted his mouth over hers, ever so gently kissing her mouth. It'd been five years since he'd kissed a woman. He was probably rusty. She tasted sweet, her lips hinting of cherries, and he gently sucked at her upper lip, nipping at it with soft, gentle kisses as if she were the most delicate, most precious thing he'd ever held in his arms. Over and over, making love to her upper lip.

Kissing Brenna was incredible. He loved how she felt in his arms, all soft and pliant. He could get used to this, he decided. And when she made a soft noise in her throat that sounded like pleasure, he decided he needed more than just a little lip-brushing.

That was when he decided to deepen the kiss. His tongue slicked over her parted lips, darting into her mouth, waiting to see if she'd resist him. She felt amazing in his arms, warm and curvy and so fucking pretty that he wanted to clear off the rest of his desk and drop her up there and see how far they'd take this pretense.

Her tongue flicked against his in response, and he felt her arm twine around his neck.

Hell, yes. Grant's kiss became harder, deeper. His tongue stroked into her mouth with possessive ownership. If this kiss was a battle between them, he was unquestionably the conqueror. Over and over he stroked into her mouth, kissing her with all the passion he could muster, and she was responding to him, making soft little noises in her throat, her hands digging into his hair.

And then he pulled away from her, panting. "How was that? Better?"

She stared up at him, her parted lips still wet from his kiss. "That," she said, and her voice sounded breathy and sexy as hell, "was pretty damn good."

"So do you think I need more practice?"

Her gaze went to his mouth as if she were considering it hard, and he felt a surge of masculine pride at her dazed expression. "Nah, I think you're okay."

"Great." He released her and was gratified when she stumbled, just a bit, as if she'd lost her balance without him propping her up. "You all right?"

"I'm fine," she said in that same breathless voice, then reached over and grabbed some Kleenex, offering it to him. "And you're wearing my lip gloss."

"Maybe I should leave it on. Part of the charade and all."

She shook her head and moved forward to wipe it off him herself. "There's a difference between charade and cross-dresser."

"Very funny." He held still while her fingers moved over his mouth, the small gesture oddly intimate between the two of them.

She winked at him, all mischief again. "I know. I'm a funny girl."

The moment was over, and gone with it, any awkwardness. "Shall we go to dinner, then?" He offered her his arm.

She put her hand into the crook of his arm. "We taking my car?"

"No, we're taking mine. I told Pop that I'd misplaced the fuel pump switch. He got it fixed this afternoon."

"Misplaced, huh?"

34

"Yeah."

"Did he believe that?"

"Not really."

She laughed, as if pleased with her sabotage. "It was either that or sugar in your gas tank."

"Brenna," he said warningly.

"I wouldn't," she said in a light voice. "Promise. Now, dinner?"

THREE

He was unable to stop staring at her all through dinner. The Brenna he normally worked with might have been a huge pain in the ass, but she could be charming when she wanted to be. She'd sat across from him, between his mother and his sister, and had dominated the conversation, telling everyone quite enthusiastically about the business and the number of clients they had, and some of the funnier stories that had come out of Wilderness Survival Expeditions so far. She'd even name dropped a little, detailing out some of their more successful and high-profile clientele, which his mother had been impressed with.

And Grant had simply watched her in surprised pleasure. That Brenna would be easy with his family wasn't so unthinkable—she didn't have an unfriendly bone in her body. But that she would chat about the business and its success as if proud of it and him? He didn't understand it.

"I'm just glad you're happy, son," his father said in a low voice to him, and patted Grant on the back. "That's all your mother and I have ever wanted."

"Business is going great," Grant said, relaxing as they fell back on an easier topic. "We're expanding what we offer so we can keep busy year-round, and I'm looking forward to what next year brings."

Reggie glanced at Brenna. "I meant her, son. But I'm glad the business makes you happy, too."

"Oh." He nodded at his father, because he wasn't sure what else to say. "Yes. Her also."

"So how did you two finally get together?"

Grant took his eyes off the laughing, smiling Brenna and glanced back at his father. "Hmm?"

The elder Markham grinned at his son. "She's your secretary, right? How'd you two finally go from working together to dating?"

"Oh. Uh." Grant reached for his drink, his throat suddenly dry. He hadn't given this much thought. Shit. They should have discussed this earlier, but instead, he'd been goading her into kissing him again. "It's kind of a boring story."

The women's conversation came to a lull as dinner plates were cleared and they turned to focus on the men. "What are you boys talking about?" Justine asked with a smile.

"I was just asking him how he and Brenna got together," Reggie said. "He's being a little cagey about it."

"Maybe we should ask Brenna," Justine said with a small smile.

Brenna shrugged her shoulders as Grant took another sip of his drink. "I got him drunk."

He choked on the mouthful of water and began to cough.

Elise gave a quiet giggle and his mother looked appalled for a long moment. "You what?"

"I got him drunk. I don't know if you've noticed, but your son's a little bit uptight. I needed to loosen him up so I could have my way with him, so I gave him a few jiggers of whiskey and seduced him."

They all stared at her.

"I'm kidding," she said gleefully. "It's nothing too special, actually. He asked me out after work one night and that was the end of it. No great story, other than he's a little shy at times."

Relieved laughter echoed around the table, and Grant shot a glare at Brenna, who gave him her sweetest smile. She lifted the cherry out of her mixed drink and bit down on it seductively, then winked at him.

That made him think of the kiss they'd shared earlier and the soft noises she'd made in her throat as she'd molded her body against him. Ah hell, now he was getting hard. He shifted uncomfortably in his seat, then took another long drink of water.

His sister smiled over at him. Elise was always a little quiet, and tonight she seemed even more so, content to let the vivacious Brenna steer the conversation.

Grant scooted his chair closer to his sister. He hadn't talked to her in a while and didn't realize until now how much he'd missed her. "How are things with you, Elise?"

She smiled, her expression a little shy. "I'm good. Nothing exciting going on with me."

"You seeing anyone?"

She shook her head, her long hair falling in front of her face. "Of course not."

Poor Elise never dated. She seemed shy to the point of painfulness around most men, and had never had a date until long after high school was over. He didn't know if she'd ever dated anyone seriously. He'd been too wrapped up in his own life. It was a shame—his sister was one of the most generous, most loving people he'd ever met. She was pretty, too. Just really damn shy and self-conscious. "You'll find the right guy," he told her.

She gave him a half smile. "I'm not wasting away from loneliness, if that's what you're trying to imply. I keep busy with my photography."

"How's that going?"

"Great," she said, and her cheeks flushed with enthusiasm. "I have a friend who's on the editorial board of a women's magazine, though, and I wanted to talk to you about doing a pictorial on the men who work for you. It'd be good publicity."

"Through a women's magazine?"

"Women can go on survival trips, too, can't they?" She arched a brow at him. "And women have husbands and boyfriends. It's just to get your name out there—"

"Oh my God," Brenna interrupted, leaning in toward Elise. "Did he say yes yet? Because he totally wants to say yes. Is this a pictorial where we get to rub the men with leaves and mud and watch them flex their six-packs? Dane has the most amazing six-pack."

Grant frowned at Brenna.

"Oh, don't look at me like that," she said in a light voice, and reached over to pat his hand. "You look very nice without your shirt, too. But I don't know how you'll feel about getting all muddy for this."

"She didn't say anything about mud, Bren."

"Actually, it'd be fun if we could do something along those lines," Elise said with a smile. "We could do some test shots and I could send them off to my friend and see if it's something the magazine would be interested in."

He shook his head. "Dane might be up for it, but Colt would kill me if I even suggested it."

"It's a good thing that Beth Ann can be on hand to do hair and makeup," Brenna said. "If Colt wants to supervise her getting these men all dirtied up, he'll have to participate."

"These men? It's me, Colt, Dane, and Pop."

"And whoever the new guy is," Brenna said. "I'll pick someone pretty, don't you worry." She winked at him flirtatiously.

"We need someone who can actually conduct survival classes."

"Fine. We can pick someone pretty and just fire them after the photo shoot," Brenna said easily. "I'll just tell them that pretty people can't be qualified for the job we need them for, and they can take it up with you if they have a problem."

"Brenna," he said in a warning tone.

Elise looked back and forth at them and edged her chair out a bit, seeming amused. "Should I move? Do you two want to sit closer together?"

"We're just arguing," he told his sister.

"Sure you are," Elise said smoothly. "Seems more like foreplay to me."

"Elise!" Justine gave a scandalized gasp. "I can't believe you just said that."

Elise rolled her eyes. "I'm twenty-five, Mother."

"We're not arguing," Brenna added. "And if anything has to be settled, we'll settle it at home." And she gave Grant a rather meaningful look.

And damn it all if he didn't get hard all over again. *What was with him tonight?*

By the time the dinner had ended, Grant was convinced that his parents believed he and Brenna were an item. He'd seen his mother eyeing Brenna's purple hair and tattoos a few times, but they'd seemed to like her well enough. And as the evening had worn on, Brenna's flirting had become more and more audacious. He'd flirted back, though he was reserved where she was bold and brassy.

When they got back to the Peppermint House, Elise came running back out to the car before they could pull away. "There's a leak in one of the upstairs bathrooms and my room is flooded. Can I stay with you guys tonight?"

Grant exchanged a glance with Brenna. "There's not an extra cabin."

"She could sleep on the couch in the main lodge," Brenna said in a reasonable tone. "No one will bother her there."

He looked over at his sister and nodded. "Get your things. We'll wait here." As soon as she disappeared, he glanced over at Brenna. "We should just drive her to another hotel. You realize we're both going to have to go into the same cabin now? To keep up the pretense?"

She shrugged at him, yawning with a little pat of her hand over her mouth. "She's family. She can stay with us. I can just head to your cabin with you, hang around for a few minutes and then sneak out the back to my cabin."

Elise returned a few minutes later, smiling, her tote over her shoulder. "Thank you."

"Hey, no problem," Grant said, but he was feeling more tense by the minute. What was Elise going to expect from them when they got to the ranch? Were he and Brenna supposed to be affectionate and all over each other in front of her again? Elise was reserved, but if she thought something was going on, she'd mention it to the other Markhams.

They pulled into the parking lot of the Daughtry Ranch, and Elise exclaimed in surprise as she exited the car. "Oh wow. Is this the ranch? The cabins are so pretty. I love this. It's so picturesque." She glanced around at the scatter of cabins. "There's five cabins? I thought you said there wasn't an extra cabin?"

"My old one doesn't have a bed in it," Brenna said quickly. "It's empty. We're waiting for the new guy."

"Oh." Elise seemed to accept that and shouldered her bag as they went inside.

Brenna took the lead with Elise, showing her around the main lodge and into the kitchen, where they kept extra food and drink, since most of the cabins had only portable refrigerators. Grant went to his desk and immediately began to go through his email while the women talked, trying not to think about their upcoming exit. Would he have to kiss Brenna again in front of them? Why was that making him aroused just to think about? Damn it, he really needed to get his cock under control.

While Elise explored the lodge, Brenna disappeared and returned a minute later with a blanket and pillow. She plumped them on the couch and then gestured at the makeshift bed. "Home sweet home."

"Thank you." Elise glanced around at the room, then at the two of them. "Are you sure it's not an inconvenience?"

"Not at all," Brenna said lightly, moving to his desk and leaning over his shoulder to turn off the power to his monitor. "Grant was just going to bed anyhow, weren't you, boo?"

Boo? The fuck? But as she'd leaned over, her breast had brushed his shoulder, and he'd forgotten everything but his ever-stiffening hard-on. "Yeah," he said after a moment. "We're off to bed."

His sister sat down on the edge of the couch. "What time should I be up in the morning?"

"I'll come wake you up," Brenna volunteered.

Elise glanced at the front door. "Do we need to lock it?"

"Nah," Brenna said, running a hand along Grant's shoulders that was making him crazy with lust. It was an easy, casual motion of possession, but it was also driving him mad. He hadn't had sex in five years and he hadn't noticed the lack until now. Before today, any sexual thoughts had been mixed up with memories of Heather—and most of those memories weren't pleasant. But today? He could think of nothing but Brenna and her lithe body and enticing smile. "No one will be by first thing in the morning except one of us or Pop. It's no big deal."

"We should go," Grant said to Brenna before his dick got any stiffer. "Elise needs to sleep."

"Night, Elise," Brenna said. "See you in the morning."

Grant smiled awkwardly at his sister and then grabbed Brenna's arm, dragging her in front of him as they headed toward the back exit of the lodge. His rising erection would be hidden if they left that way, which was good.

As soon as they got outside, Brenna yawned and clung to his arm, resting her cheek there as they headed the hundred feet or so back to his cabin. Grant's was the largest of the five cabins, and the most elaborate. The others were cabins, but his was a home, and he had it wired with all the fixings, including motion lights. One clicked on as they went up the path, illuminating them as they walked. If Elise were to look outside, she'd see the two of them snuggled close together, heading for his cabin. Like a regular couple.

He pushed the door open and put a hand to the small of Brenna's back, guiding her inside. When the door was shut behind them, he leaned on it, exhaling deeply. It felt like he'd just walked off stage. He was tenser than he realized with this relationship charade. *Jesus*. Weeks of this pretending was going to wreck him.

Once inside, Brenna immediately slipped her high heels off and padded around his living room in bare feet. She glanced around the cabin, as if seeing it for the first time. Maybe it *was* the first time she'd seen it; he'd certainly never invited her in before tonight. He tried to see it through her eyes. The main wall of the living room was an enormous panel of windows that looked out into the heavy trees. Across from that was his big fireplace, and a few well-chosen couches added to the homey cabin decor. His kitchen was state of the art, and the loft upstairs was his bedroom and bathroom. He'd paid a decorator to kit out the place in artful decor, since he wasn't good at that sort of thing. Whimsical forest paintings decorated the walls, and the tables and counters were covered with matching knickknacks to evoke the woodland feel.

"You sure do like, um, stuff."

That didn't exactly sound complimentary. "You don't approve?"

"How can I not?" She looked over at him and gave him a wicked smile. "My cabin's kind of shitty compared to yours."

"I'm the boss," he said easily. "You're the employee."

He could have kicked himself for saying something so ballsy and rude, but she only laughed and turned back around again, then moved to the ladder of the loft, going upstairs. He watched her pert, rounded bottom flexing as she moved up the ladder, and then he frowned and followed her up. "Brenna? Where are you going?"

She smiled at him from over her shoulder and then kept moving toward his bed. "Checking out the digs for tonight."

"Tonight?" He followed her up the ladder, puzzled by her comment. What exactly did she mean, tonight?

"I gave your sister my blanket and pillow. We're going to have to bunk together."

Grant stared at her in shock. "You what?"

"We have to make this look good anyhow, right?" Brenna pressed a hand on the edge of his mattress, testing it, and then flopped down on the corner with a grin. "I gave your sister my blanket and pillow. It's going to be cold tonight, so I thought I'd bunk in here, with you. That okay?"

What was he supposed to say to that? Her bunking with him would mean he'd have a hard-on the entire night. But he couldn't exactly kick her out, either. So all he said was, "Why don't we have more blankets?"

"Because we're a survival school? Duh. Besides, the other guys raided our stash when Beth Ann and Miranda moved in, and Pop took the last ones. I've been meaning to get some more but . . ." She shrugged. "I forgot."

Brenna pretty much forgot everything that wasn't tattooed on her forehead. He gave her a frustrated look. "I don't really have a choice, do I?"

Her playful expression turned wounded. "I don't snore, Grant. I'm a very good roomie. Now come and unzip me." She jumped up and turned around, presenting him with her back. When he didn't get up right away, she bounced in place. "Come on."

Was this another one of Brenna's torments? Had she guessed at his erection and decided it was time to antagonize him a bit more? She did love to harass and annoy him. This could definitely qualify as torture. Cruel, sweet, sadistic torture.

He moved forward and grasped the tab of her zipper and then paused. Did he want to do this?

She wiggled again, prompting him.

And he was suddenly stricken with the desire to see her unclothed. It was odd to think of Brenna in that way, but he wanted to see what she looked like without the dress, without all the shapeless, cast-off clothing she normally dressed in. So he unzipped her.

And sucked in a breath when the dress fell to the floor.

The panties she wore were a mere white scrap of lace between her firm, rounded buttocks. Over her left buttock, a trail of stars curved around her hip. On the right hip, it was a trail of small red hearts. More tattoos to match the bluebirds on her shoulders.

She turned to look at him, hands on her hips. Her breasts were cupped in girlish white lace, but the sight of it mixed with those tattoos was enough to make him groan with need.

"Grant?" Her voice was low and husky.

"I think I'm going to touch you now, Brenna."

He watched in fascination as a shiver rippled over her skin. Her lips parted and she licked them, her gaze fascinated. "I wish you would."

His hand moved to the side of her neck and he pulled her closer, drawing her in for another kiss. Her lips parted under his and the kiss deepened, highlighted by a flicking of tongues against one another. It wasn't his imagination, then. She wanted this as much as he did. He drew his arm around her waist, holding her against his body, feeling her warm skin under his hand and pressed against him. She felt small and fragile in his arms, which was strange given that she was such a forceful, vibrant personality.

Her kiss became hot, hungry, her tongue stroking against

his. She pulled away to catch her breath and whispered one quick word, "Condoms?"

Grant groaned in dismay. "I . . . no. It's been five years." He was an idiot. A complete, unprepared idiot. Of course he should have condoms. "I didn't think—"

She patted his chest in a comforting motion. "Stay here. I'll be right back." Brenna stepped past him and moved down the ladder. She grabbed the decorative throw off his couch and wrapped it around her body. "When I come back," she said playfully, "I want to see some skin."

And she stepped out his front door and into the night.

He stared at the door for a minute, dumbfounded. *Was this really going to happen? With wild, annoying Brenna?* Except she hadn't been so wild and annoying tonight. She'd been vibrant and funny and charming, and if she was a little offbeat, it hadn't bothered him. And she hadn't harassed him once.

He didn't trust it. Was this another game with her, then? Maybe she'd gone back out to her cabin to have a good laugh at him. What if this was another one of her pranks, all designed to make him look like an ass when she told the others about it in the morning? *Yeah, Grant sat there with a boner all night and I never went back. Isn't that funny?* His scowl darkened and he crossed his arms over his chest, sitting on the edge of his bed and waiting.

Just to see if she was really going to come back.

A moment later, she returned, holding up a strip of condoms. "Success. And you're not nearly naked enough."

Relief shot through him. It wasn't a joke. "You keep those in your cabin?" He never heard anything and she was next door to him. Maybe she was having wild dates that he didn't know about. A bolt of jealousy shot through him. To disguise it, he pulled off his jacket and began to neatly fold it on the edge of the bed.

She tossed the blanket on the couch, down to her lacy white bra and thong, a sight that made him hard all over again. "Nah. I knew there were extra condoms in the main cabin. I had extras when I was prepping the survival kits. Your sister says hi, by the way."

He turned and gave her a horrified look as she climbed up the ladder. "Elise saw you?"

"Well, yeah." Brenna shrugged. "I wasn't exactly quiet. It just adds a bit more cement to your story, doesn't it?"

Grant stared at her as she reapproached him. "Is that what this is? Cement for the story?"

She rolled her eyes at him and put her hands on the front of his shirt, then tugged hard enough to make buttons pop off. "It can't be because you're a good kisser and I really want to get laid?"

Was that how most women thought? He'd only known Heather, and while she'd been adventurous, it hadn't been adventurous quite like this. Her adventurous spirit had been saved for mountain climbing and challenging sports . . . and meeting other men in clubs. When they'd first gotten married, their sex life had been pleasing, but tame. Later on, it had changed. Still, she was the only yardstick he had to judge by. "And you want to have sex with me?"

"No," she said in a sarcastic voice. "I thought I'd rip your shirt off and then force you onto the bed and make you watch while I fingered myself."

Even as she said the cutting words, her hands stroked under his loose shirt and over his chest, and her gaze went there, as if fascinated.

She was still entirely too lippy. He grabbed her and hauled her against him, enjoying the widening of her eyes.

"Is that so?" His voice was low and dangerous. Grant rather liked that mental image of her fingering herself, but he thought he'd turn the tables a little. He pushed forward until her legs were pinned between him and the bed, and leaned in to kiss her again, bearing her down onto his mattress. Then he lifted his head and glanced at her, enjoying the soft, dazed look in her eyes. "I have you in my bed. Does that mean you're going to finger yourself now?"

"If we're doing a reversal, shouldn't I be fingering you?" she asked huskily and reached between his legs, grabbing his crotch. "Ooo, I like."

He groaned at the gentle touch of her hand. "God, Brenna, don't—"

She pulled away as if scalded. "You okay?"

"Just . . . it's been a while." He looked down at the smooth, pale skin under him, highlighted by her delicate lacy underthings. "Let me be in the driver's seat."

She grinned and raised her arms up over her head, clasping her hands together. The motion made her breasts high and firm, and almost popping out of her bra. "I'm all yours. Do what you will."

He leaned in to kiss her again.

"Be gentle," she said, fluttering her eyelashes. "It's my first time . . . with you."

"Are you ever serious?"

"Rarely ever. Serious is no fun."

Grant kissed her lightly, tasting her full lips, and he felt the tremble that moved through her body.

"I know," she said when he raised his head again, her eyes gleaming with excitement. She pulled his glasses off his face and tossed them aside. "We can play a game."

"Game?" he murmured, kissing along her jaw toward her ear.

"It's called Guess Brenna's Piercing. You can explore me until you find it."

She had a piercing somewhere? His thoughts went wild, picturing that. *Holy fuck*, his dick was so hard that he'd nearly come in his pants just then. Grant groaned, burying his face in the curve of her neck, trying to find the willpower to make this last longer than thirty seconds. God, she was sexy. "Piercing?" he managed to choke out.

She gave a bit of a wiggle underneath him, her body rubbing against him, her voice breathless as she answered. "Guess where."

Grant leaned in and nibbled on her bare earlobe, his cock growing harder with every passing moment. She kept making these breathy little gasps when his tongue touched her skin, and it was driving him wild. "No earrings," he observed.

"Nope," she replied with a small sigh. Her fingers went to his hair and raked through it, messing it up and digging into his scalp. "Keep guessing."

He leaned over her face again and lightly kissed an eyebrow, playing along with the game. "No earring here."

She pinched his arm. "You knew that already."

"Hush. You quit talking. This is my guessing game."

Brenna made a zipping her lips motion and went silent, watching him.

He leaned down and lightly licked at her closed lips. "No piercing here."

She shook her head, her eyes dancing.

His fingers went to one of the tiny white shoulder straps of her bra. Very slowly, he lifted it off her shoulder and skimmed it down her arm, glancing over at Brenna to see her reaction. Her gaze was intent, riveted to his fingers on her skin, as if fascinated. As if nothing else in the world existed.

Lovely. She was lovely. Tattoos, purple bangs, even the girlish white lingerie—they were all completely and utterly Brenna. He'd never noticed before how totally arousing the package could be.

He tugged the bra cup down on one side, exposing her nipple. Small, pink, tight. With one hand, he massaged the globe of her breast, then tweaked the nipple between his fingers, rolling it back and forth.

She moaned in response, arching under him. Her fingers dug into his scalp and then raked down his arms in response.

"No piercing here," he said in a low, husky voice, and released her. "I should probably double-check, though." And he leaned in and lightly licked the tip of her breast, sending a breathy moan through her again. He liked that reaction, so he continued to nip and kiss that tiny, tight little peak, making it stiff and slick and leaving her hopefully as aching with need as he was. His cock was so hard at the moment that he thought he'd bust in his pants at any moment. He could feel the pre-cum on the head of his cock, soaking it and making his clothing stick. She was driving him mad with need, but he wanted to savor this. Savor her.

"Grant," she whispered. "Please."

"I should check the other breast, just in case," he told her, and very slowly repeated the action. He could do this. He could keep control. It was simple. Slide the bra strap down the arm. Tug down the bra and reveal her pretty breast. He was in charge, not her. Her nipple was already stiff and pointing, and when he slid down to take it in his mouth, her choked cry of response sent a bolt of lust rocketing through him. "No piercing here, either."

"You're pretty good at this game," she panted, then mewed as he bit lightly on her nipple. "Keep guessing."

Oh, he was far from done. He'd only gone to her breasts

and she was quivering in his arms, his dick hard as iron. Of course, he was running out of known areas for piercings. Maybe she had one of those wild ones that he'd never expect, like between her toes or some such.

Because if it was anywhere below the belt? He'd probably come at the sight.

His hands continued to massage her breasts in time, rolling her nipples against his thumbs with each motion. Her eyes closed in ecstasy and her lips parted as she gave herself over to him completely, the look on her face utterly abandoned. He knew she'd be like this in bed—somehow, he'd known. Brenna wasn't someone who went through life half-asleep. She was wild and fierce, and in bed she was completely and utterly responsive.

Grant's gaze went to her bare belly button. No piercing there, but he had to taste it anyhow. Lifting his hands, he slid down the bed to press a kiss there.

She made a pleased sound in her throat, and then chuckled. "No piercing there either, huh? Maybe I was lying about the whole piercing thing."

"Mmm. I've still got plenty of ground to cover." He slid an exploring hand down the gentle curve of her belly, then laid it flat above the waistline of her tiny panties. "Should we take these off?"

"We should," she said in response, and lifted her hips off the bed so he could slide them down her body.

He did, fascinated by the reveal. Her tattoos were exposed to him and he paused to examine each one more closely. The stars were a sprinkle of tiny dots that started small mid-thigh and got bigger as they spread across her pelvis in a scattered fan. On the opposite side, the design followed the same subtle design, as if someone had spilled drops of brightly colored paint across her legs. "Do they mean something?" he asked, lightly tracing wondering fingers over her hips.

"No," she told him. "They're just pretty and they make me happy."

They made him rather happy, too. They were completely invisible in normal clothing, and it was like he was peeling away layers to find a secret Brenna underneath, who was just a bit more unique with every passing moment.

His fingers stroked over her hip bones and then slid toward her apex, to the dark vee of her pussy. And he hesitated, because even though he was leading this exploration, he wanted her approval first.

"Don't get shy on me now, Grant," she said, teasing. "We'll never finish our game if you do." She spread her legs for him in invitation, knees bent, and that sight would go down in Grant's mind as one of the most mind-blowingly sexy moves he'd ever seen.

He groaned, his cock jumping at the sight. He wanted to bury his face in her thighs and make her scream and come in the next moment, but he had to keep playing this tantalizing, maddening game. So he took his hand that was resting on her belly and lightly stroked his thumb down the wet slit of her pussy.

And his fingers touched something hard and metallic.

He froze.

She made a low sound of pleasure, flexing her hips.

"You're pierced . . . here?"

"Ding ding ding," she said breathily. "Give that man a prize."

He had to get a closer look. Grant parted her flesh with his fingers, staring down at her perfect pink pussy. Nestled below the dark curls, in the hood of her clit, was a vertical silver piercing with a tiny ball on the end.

Now *that* was the fucking sexiest thing he'd ever seen. "Damn. I . . ." He didn't know what to say except the obvious. "Does it hurt?"

She laughed and rolled her hips a bit, as if trying to rock against his fingers. "If it hurt, it wouldn't be in. It just makes everything more . . . sensitive. In a good way."

Well, now he had to test that. He touched the piercing with his finger and stroked the flesh around it.

Brenna sucked in a breath.

He dipped a finger to the well of her pussy and felt how slick and wet she was. He took some of that wetness and moved back up to her piercing and began to press with gentle fingers, rubbing the ball of the piercing against her clit.

She groaned, her eyelids fluttering shut again, her fingers digging into his shoulders. "Use your tongue."

The visual of doing that to her nearly flattened him and he ran his other hand over the hard ridge of his cock. He was barely aware that he was still in trousers and wearing most of his shirt. Meanwhile, the woman beneath him was naked and wriggling and slick with need.

He stood up, intending to strip out of his clothing, and was gratified by her disappointed whimper.

"Save that for me," she told him breathlessly. "We're not finished with our game."

He didn't have to be told twice. He knelt between her thighs again, lowering his face toward the sweet tangle of curls, and he felt the tension rising in her body. He wanted to make this good for her. For some reason, it was important that he not fuck this up.

Grant placed a hand on one of her thighs and slowly lifted it to his shoulder, then repeated the motion with her other leg, until he was cradled so close to her damp flesh that he could practically breathe in her scent. Then he grasped her hips with his hands and tugged her the rest of the distance, bringing her to his mouth.

She was delicious. Salty and wet, her pearly skin flushed with heat. He nuzzled through the curls and searched out that piercing with the tip of his tongue again. When he found it, he began to roll it back and forth over his tongue in sweeping strokes, paying attention to her clit, and making sure that his movements set the little ball rolling over it, back and forth.

He barely heard the sounds of her moans, lost in his own world between her thighs. That piercing fascinated him, and he couldn't resist playing with it, flicking it with his tongue, and then using the hardened tip of his tongue to seek out the nub of flesh underneath. Her fingers dug into his hair and she yanked, but she wasn't telling him no, so he continued to tease her. Her hips bucked with need and the piercing banged against his teeth, startling him.

"Need you inside me," she breathed. "Deep."

But Grant wasn't done playing. He'd give her a little more of what she wanted, though. He continued to tongue her clit and her piercing and placed two fingers together at the entrance to her core and thrust.

She jolted, keening her desire. The hands in his hair became more frantic. "Yes," she moaned, the sound almost triumphant. "Oh God. Please, Grant."

He thrust again, and then began a slow and steady rhythm, working his fingers in and out of her pussy, feeling the excited little quivers running through her. He changed the rhythm of his tongue, moving to slow little circles around her clit, then lapping at it again. Then circles. Then more tonguing.

Brenna was writhing in his arms, breathing his name

over and over again, her hips trembling against him. He felt a spasm jerk through her body, and then she clenched around his fingers, sucking them deeper and holding him as her body stiffened in an intense orgasm. She made a soft choking sound, as if she'd lost all the air in her lungs, and her hips rose off the bed, pressing hard against his constantly working tongue, milking the orgasm. He watched her even as he continued to pleasure her, fascinated by her reaction. She was so incredibly abandoned and unselfconscious. It was stunning to watch her lose control.

And when it was over, she stiffened and collapsed on the bed, gasping and panting heavily. "Oh. Wow. Just wow," she laughed, the sound breathy and satisfied. "That was a fun game. Fun for one of us, anyhow."

He had to agree with that. While it had been pleasurable for him, too, his cock was so hard that it was almost painful. "I'll get the condoms."

She grabbed a handful of his shirt before he could move away. "Not yet, naughty boy. It's my turn to play a game."

He groaned and moved back toward her, kissing her fiercely. "I'm about past the time for games, Brenna. Feel how hard I am." He took her hand and guided it to his aching cock, resisting the urge to start grinding against her hand. "I need this."

"Oh, I plan on satisfying you, Grant Markham," she said in a throaty, pleased purr. Her fingers tugged at his shirt, and she found a button still in its hole and ripped it free. "But now it's my turn to play Guess the Piercing."

"I don't have any piercings," he said, his voice rasping and harsh.

She shrugged. "Half the fun is the game. Don't ruin it for me with spoilers." And she gave his shoulders a push, indicating that he should lie back on the bed.

He was in agony, his cock so hard that his entire body ached. But he was fascinated by how self-assured and take charge she was in the bedroom, and damn it all if he didn't want to play this game, too. The thought of Brenna exploring his body with her mouth? He almost came in his pants just thinking about it. "I'll come if you touch me. It's been too long."

"Don't tell me you haven't jerked off in five years?"

"Brenna."

"Is that a yes or a no?"

"What do you think?"

She gave him a sultry look and ran a finger down his cock. "I think it's a no, because you usually seem like you need to loosen up. I guess we need to take the edge off then, hmm? Because I know I'm not done playing." She rubbed him again and then grinned. "What's your recovery time been like in the past? Does your cannon normally fire a single shot?"

He stared at her, almost speechless.

"You don't know? That makes you a single-shot kind of guy after all. Pity." Her fingers wrapped around his cock, flexing around the hard length. "I bet we can break that record for you."

He was about to come in his pants if she kept touching him. And she was talking but he was having a hard time following the conversation.

But then she unzipped his pants and hauled them down his thighs, dragging his boxers with them. His cock sprang free, engorged, the head dark red and wet with pre-cum.

"Mama like," she said again in that breathy, pleased tone that made goose bumps move down his arms. He was literally a hair-trigger away from coming. The smallest touch and—

She leaned down and grasped him firmly, wrapping her

fingers around the length of his cock and sucking the head into her mouth. She stroked once, hard.

He came. A hoarse groan ripped from his throat and his entire body clenched with the force of his release, his eyes squeezed shut. He was suddenly spurting into her mouth, unable to stop the flood of come as his body jerked and shook.

Embarrassing. He was as bad as a teenage boy. She'd never let him live this down.

Brenna stroked him again, her movements slow, and he felt her mouth rise off his cock. He slowly opened his eyes to see her swallowing the last of his release, and then she daintily wiped the corner of her mouth and gave him a sensual smile. "All better?"

"Sorry." He felt fucking stupid.

"I'm not," she said easily, tugging his pants down all the way to his ankles and then tugging at one of his shoes. "Now I get to explore you at my leisure."

Her pose as she leaned over the side of the bed raised the curved moon of her bottom into the air. He was fascinated by that sight, watching it flex as she removed his shoes and socks, and then tugged his slacks off. Her fingers ran up his calves and then over his thighs. "You're in good shape," she said, sounding impressed.

"I exercise when I can't sleep." Which was just about every night. "It helps quiet my mind."

"Mmm. Rock-hard legs." She sat up and moved to his arms, running a hand along his bicep. "Are these hard, too?"

He flexed to show her, and she grinned at the sight, leaning down to bite the muscle. "Very nice. You're just as built as Dane and Colt. You should be out there doing trainings with them."

"I don't belong in the field," he said in a curt voice. Just the thought made him anxious. He wasn't worried about himself inasmuch as he was worried that he'd be a danger to Dane and Colt. And speaking of those two . . . when was she checking out Dane and Colt, damn it? She'd never looked at him twice until tonight. Had she been ogling the other men the entire time?

Her exploring fingers lightly trailed over his chest, tugging at the light sprinkling of chest hair and then dipping to his belly button. "No piercings," she said playfully, grinning up at him.

His cock stirred at her smile, as if he hadn't just come mere minutes ago. "Keep looking," he told her, and was surprised to hear the command come out of his mouth.

It wasn't like him to play back.

But it had been the right thing to say. She lowered her mouth to his chest, leaning in to nip lightly at both of his nipples and then kissing a path back down to his belly button. "Still nothing here. Perhaps I should go lower."

"Perhaps," he agreed, reaching to twine his fingers in her hair and pulling back at the last moment. It seemed too intimate a gesture. She might have been comfortable with the new immediacy of their relationship, but he was still reserved in some aspects. Too much history in his head, maybe.

She brushed her lips down the trail of hair that led to his cock, which was half-erect again. Her playful touches and smiles—plus the skimming graze of her limbs and breasts against him when she moved—were making him hard already. Her fingers gently cupped his sac, and she lightly rolled his balls back and forth, watching his reaction.

He groaned and his head fell back to the pillows. *Damn.* She knew how to touch a man.

"No piercings here," she whispered. Her fingers skimmed

over his half-erect cock and then moved down, delving between his thighs and stroking the skin there.

To his surprise, she slid a finger lower, moving between his buttocks to press at the pucker of his ass. "Anything here?"

"Don't you dare."

She wiggled her finger against his skin, daring him.

He sat up and grabbed her, bearing her backward down to the bed again. Brenna fell with him, her laughter pealing through the room.

"You think that's funny, do you?"

"I guess a prostate massage is a bit much for a first date?" Her voice was sweet and innocent.

"Don't you have any boundaries?" he growled, reaching forward to cup one of her breasts simply because he couldn't help himself.

"Very few."

"Let me guess, boundaries are no fun."

"Something like that," she said, and sucked in a breath when his thumb grazed her erect nipple again. "How's your cannon?"

"Getting harder with every moment," he told her, leaning forward and pressing his cock at the wet junction of her spread legs to prove it to her. She rose her hips against him in response and tilted her face for another kiss. He licked and sucked at her full lower lip, knowing that she liked that, and every time she gave one of those sexy, breathy little gasps, he got a bit harder.

When she rocked against him again, it was his turn to groan. He tweaked her nipple again, pinching and rolling the tip between his fingers as he rocked against her pussy once more, the head of his cock sliding between the slick folds and then rubbing up against the piercing he'd almost forgotten about, which left both of them gasping.

"Condoms?" she asked, her hips raising again.

"Condoms," he agreed, and moved to the edge of the bed to grab one, ripping it off the strip and tearing open the packaging. He fumbled with it for a moment, and then he was rolling it down his engorged cock, as thick and throbbing with need as he had been before.

He turned back to look at her and she raised her arms, her eyes glazed and wild with passion.

She was beautiful.

Grant moved over her, kissing her with languid expertise, savoring the feel of his tongue thrusting slowly into her mouth, mimicking the stroke of his cock. He slid a hand between them, deliberately skimming it down her pussy before taking his cock in hand and guiding it to her opening. She was scorching hot, wet with need, and her fingers were digging into his shoulders in encouragement.

He sank into her, one hand clenched against her shoulder, pinning Brenna against him. She was tight around him, the walls of her pussy sucking him deep, holding him within her.

Brenna made a little whimper in her throat, biting her lip. Her fingernails dug into his back again, and when he didn't immediately move, she smacked his shoulder blade. "Go, go."

He'd stopped because he was savoring the feeling of being buried deep inside her far too much. His entire body ached and throbbed with pleasure, and she was clenched around him, the sensation exquisite. Five years had been too long . . . and somehow not long enough.

A mental image of Heather flashed in his mind and guilt suddenly flooded him.

Brenna wrapped her legs tight around his waist, squeezing with her knees. "This is the part where you're supposed to move inside me, Grant."

He leaned in and kissed her again, and she responded with a sexy, needy flick of her tongue. She arched her chest, letting her nipples skim against his chest. Any thoughts of Heather vanished and he was lost in Brenna again. She was so abandoned. He'd never met anyone like her.

Grant thrust, hard. She gave a triumphant shriek in return and rocked her hips, egging him on. He thrust again, the motion hard and rough, their bodies sawing forward with the force of their movement. Her groan of response was thrilled, and he continued to thrust into her—not quick or steady, but hard and brutal and lacking rhythm. Primal. Wild.

Fierce.

"Oh God, yes," she breathed in his ear, and he felt her pussy clench around him, rippling around his cock. "Fuck me like that."

A dirty talker? That was sexy as hell. He thrust even harder, not noticing when the pillows went flying to the side. Her pussy clenched around him again, and she gave a little gasp, as if surprised. He pounded into her, his entire body shoving forward with the motion, and she clung to him desperately.

"Yes! Yes! Fuck me just like that. I'm so close." Her voice broke in a tiny sob. "Keep . . . please . . . keep going."

With a primal roar he didn't know he had in him, he hammered into her, his thrusts suddenly as quick and frantic as they were wild. She screamed his name in his ear, and he felt her entire body clench, her pussy tight around his cock with the force of her orgasm. Grant roared his own release, coming so hard that he nearly saw stars, slamming his body into her own and feeling her shuddering underneath him. When he'd finished coming, he fell on top of her, panting and wet with sweat.

She gave a long, breathless sigh of sated pleasure, wrapping her arms around his neck. "Mercy," she breathed. "You win the game."

Through the haze of exhaustion, he chuckled. "Are you conceding defeat?"

"For now," she said thoughtfully. "You may have won the battle, but you did not win the war, sir."

And then she yawned.

He yawned, too, feeling tired for the first time in a long time. Probably all the sex that did that to him. He rolled off her and moved to the bathroom, taking a few minutes to dispose of the condom and then toweling himself off. He grabbed a fresh towel for her and moved back out to the bed. "Did you want—"

She was fast asleep, hugging his pillow, her purple bangs stuck to her forehead.

Sleep was probably a good idea, he thought, eyeing the way she was hogging his bed already. He leaned over the bed and carefully moved her sprawled limbs over a few feet, giving himself enough room on the bed, and then pulled the covers over the two of them.

He turned off the light and curled around her body, satisfied.

For the first time in five years, there was a woman in his bed. For the first time in five years, he'd made love to a woman until they were both sweaty, exhausted, and utterly sated. It felt right. No, better yet, it felt like coming home.

Who would have thought that Brenna, of all people, would be the one to wake him from his emotional coma?

Grant brushed a lock of hair off of her shoulder in an affectionate gesture and pressed a kiss to one of the bluebirds on her shoulders.

FOUR

When Grant awoke, sunlight was streaming through the window onto his face. He squinted at the light and shielded his eyes, then turned to his alarm clock. 7:17 AM. *Damn*. This was early for him. What had woken him up? Normally he had trouble sleeping and worked out until late, then fell into bed, only to wake up sometime around ten in the morning, groggy and exhausted.

Last night, though, he supposed he'd been distracted. Flashes of last night with Brenna made his morning wood a little harder and he rolled over, reaching for her.

The bed was empty.

Grant wiped the sleep from his eyes and sat up, surveying his room. The bedcovers hung off the side of the mattress, as if Brenna had crawled from bed and not bothered to fix them. Her pillow was on the floor, next to a scatter of buttons from his shirt. Clothing was strewn everywhere.

His dresser drawer hung open, shirts spilling out onto the floor.

She was obviously awake. He wrapped the sheet around his nakedness and moved to the edge of the loft, standing near the ladder and peering down to the floor below. Brenna was seated on one of the barstools at his kitchen counter, dressed in one of his oversized T-shirts, her legs bare. She was flipping through a magazine and eating what looked like a piece of toast.

This was a picture he could wake up to for the rest of his life.

Grant grabbed his boxers from the floor and threw them on, then descended down the ladder and moved toward her. "Good morning."

She glanced up and nodded. "Hey."

He leaned in to kiss her cheek, arms going around her waist. Her hair was wet—she must have showered already.

Brenna stiffened in his arms. "What are you doing?"

He pulled away, surprised at her reaction. "I was just greeting you."

She looked confused. "Yes, but why are you kissing me?" She took another bite of her toast and gave him a puzzled look, as if he'd just done something ridiculous. "You feeling okay?"

"I'm trying to kiss you because I want to kiss you." He leaned in again, and when she took another bite of toast, her brow wrinkled in consternation, he sighed. "That's what couples do, Brenna."

She coughed, thumping her chest as if the food had gone down the wrong pipe. He waited for her to catch her breath and, after a moment, she choked out, "Couples?"

Now he was starting to get annoyed with her again. "Yes.

You know. People who date and have sex together. People in a relationship."

She put down her toast and slipped away on the other side of the stool, crossing the kitchen back to his refrigerator. "We're not in a relationship, Grant. At least, not a real one. That stuff was for show, remember?" She opened the door and studied the contents of his fridge. "You have any orange juice?"

He moved to the fridge and shut the door. *Could she not pay attention for five minutes?* "You and I had sex last night. We slept together."

"Yes, we did." She looked unconcerned.

"So what was that, then?"

"Fun?"

"Fun? That's all it was to you?" It was the first time he'd had sex with someone since Heather died. Not that there hadn't been offers—he just hadn't been interested. This was big for him. Momentous. A changing point in his life. And she thought it was just . . . fun?

She shrugged. "I mean, it was really good and all, but what do you want me to do, Grant? Move in or something?"

He was actually thinking of something like that. "If you wanted."

Brenna blanched, looking ill at the thought. "I'll pass."

"You'll . . . pass?"

"Yep, I'll pass." She patted his chest. "You're nice and all, Grant, but I'm not interested in something permanent. I thought we were just having fun."

He stared at her. "Fun," he repeated in a flat voice.

"Yes, fun. With a side benefit of being really, really convincing." She grinned and headed to the front door. "I'm going to grab some pants and then head in for work. Shower's all yours."

And she waved at him and slipped out the front door.

He stood in his kitchen, staring at the door and trying to register what had just happened. She'd turned him down. Flinched away from his casual affection. All she'd wanted was a nice bit of fun last night? Seriously? That was all it was to her?

Last night had been amazing. He'd never had such incredibly intense sex with anyone, not even his wife. And she'd seemed to be as in to him as he was to her. What the hell had changed? His eyes narrowed at the door, as if imagining her still standing there.

He felt . . . used. Which was stupid, but there it was.

Well now, that had been uncomfortable. Brenna trotted down the steps, heading across the grass to her own cabin a short distance away.

Stupid Grant. Why couldn't he just enjoy a night of sex and not think anything about it? Why'd he have to start attaching feelings and commitment to things like that? When had sex ever meant you must move in tomorrow? *What the fuck?* It made her angry—angry that she couldn't just enjoy him without him trying to turn it into something more.

Sex didn't have to mean a relationship. It didn't have to mean moving in together and for better or for worse. In her eyes, those sorts of things only brought more pain. Permanence was a cosmic joke. Nothing ever lasted, not really. You enjoyed what you had for the day and forgot about it the next. That was the best way to live life. Anything else and you were just setting yourself up for failure.

She slipped into her own stripped-down cabin, eyeing the bare walls and spartan furnishings with relief. No artsy clutter here. One lamp, one table, one chair, one twin-size bed. The necessities. In her kitchen, she had one plate, one set of utensils, and one glass. That was all she needed for a home. Just enough to get by. Grant's cabin had been clean, but there had been enough artful decor—a rug, a statue, a wall hanging, a shelf of books—to make her anxious, the pit of her stomach clenching at the sight. Things like that could easily turn into mountains of useless junk.

And she just couldn't live like that.

Brenna pulled out a pair of jeans from her small pile of clean laundry and slid them on, adding a pair of ballet flats and then pulling her hair back into a messy topknot with a rubber band. She was presentable now and feeling more like herself after seeing her own refreshingly spare cabin.

They still had to work together. Sex wouldn't change that. But she could act like nothing had changed between them, of course. Nothing really had, except that now she knew that he was fun in bed and had a nice, hard stomach that sucked in when she kissed it, and hair that was perfect for knotting her fingers in, and a tongue that knew just how to work her piercing . . .

She sighed. Why did he have to be so stupid about sex?

Elise rolled over on the leather couch and nuzzled deeper into her pillow, her eyes closed. She was in that lovely period of awake-but-not-ready-to-get-up-just-yet and no one had come to retrieve her, so she might as well sleep a little longer. She tugged the blanket closer and snuggled into the pillow, ready to get back to her dream.

A shadow fell over her face and, after a moment, it registered in her sleepy mind and she opened her eyes.

And gasped, sitting upright and scooting backward in surprise, clutching the blanket to her.

A man—a stranger—loomed over the couch. He was tall, but not ridiculously so. Brawny. Big, muscular shoulders and corded arms bulging with strength. Barrel chest. It was the kind of build a bruiser would have, and it seemed at odds with his face, which was almost model pretty. Angular, with a square, perfect jaw and strong, firm nose, his eyes were vivid blue and surrounded by thick black lashes. His hair was cropped in a close trim against his skull.

And he was pierced and tattooed everywhere. She saw a piercing through his nose. He had spacer rings in his ears, and a ring on the left side of his lower lip. His arms were covered in sleeves of tattoos. He was dressed in black, too. All of it combined to make him look menacing and unapproachable, if it weren't for those inhumanly beautiful eyes. He was gorgeous and utterly wicked-looking, and yet so appealing to her.

He was staring down at her, too, as if fascinated. Really staring, as if he saw her.

And she wanted to touch her cheek and turn her face away, ashamed. What if he saw . . . it? Her fingers twitched with the need to pull her long hair in front of her face and hide as much of her as she could, but she couldn't seem to move.

"Sorry," he said in a low, gruff voice. "I didn't mean to wake you. I was looking for the person who placed this ad." He raised the paper to show her. "I'm here to apply."

Elise stared at the paper, her gaze moving back to him. Her mouth worked wordlessly, the only thing coming out of her throat a soft squeak of distress. "I . . ."

His mouth curved into a smile, and she was stunned by how gorgeous he was. Dark, tanned skin, those piercings, all those tattoos, and those heavenly eyes. He was the most beautiful man she'd ever seen. And he was looking at her with interest, his gaze moving over her long, tangled hair and her face.

As if she were appealing and not gross-looking.

"I'm Rome," he told her, his smile widening, and he extended his hand toward her to shake.

She just stared at him.

Those blue eyes studied her for a moment longer and then hardened. He pulled his hand back. "I'm not going to hurt you. I'm just here to apply for the job."

Hurt her? Did he think she was scared? She should say something. Move. *Something.* Brenna would laugh about how ridiculous it all was, and then chatter at him in a friendly manner. Elise had only known her for a few hours, but she adored her already for being everything that Elise wasn't. She wasn't incredibly shy around men, wasn't terrified of her own shadow. She wasn't a hideous creature that everyone stared at or mocked. Elise swallowed and tried again. "I . . ."

But her voice trembled and the words wouldn't come out. *I'm not scared of you*, she wanted to say. But it was like her body refused to obey as long as he kept staring at her.

His mouth thinned into an unhappy line, and she watched that fascinating lip ring move with it.

The back door banged and Elise heard steps in the kitchen. "Hey, Elise," Brenna sing-songed out from the other room. "You want breakfast or something? I can whip up a mean Pop-Tart."

Elise stared at the man, then back at the kitchen door. She should call out to Brenna. But her throat wasn't working. It was knotted with tension, the presence of the beautiful stranger making her tongue-tied and stupid. She cleared her throat and tried again, her mouth working for a minute. And another garbled squeak came out, and she flushed.

Dear Lord. He would think she was so incredibly stupid. Her head hung forward and she let the hair cover her face, ashamed.

The man watched her, fascinated by her movements. She wanted to crawl under the blanket and hide until he left.

"Elise?" Brenna called, and then stepped through the swinging door that blocked the way to the kitchen. Brenna paused at the sight of Elise and Rome standing over the couch. She blinked at both of them in surprise, her purple bangs flat and hanging over her eyes, dressed in a pair of Grant's boxers and an old T-shirt. "Oh, hi. I didn't realize we had company."

He gave one last look at Elise and then moved toward Brenna, extending his hand for her to shake. "My name is Rome. I've come to apply for the wilderness survival instructor job."

"Oh!" Brenna looked pleased. "You're our first applicant, then. And my. Look at you. Just delicious." She glanced over at Elise and gave her a knowing wink. "I bet you tried to climb this one like a tree, huh?"

Oh God. Elise's cheeks burned with humiliation and she ducked her head, averting her eyes as Rome turned back around to look at her. Truth was, she did kind of want to climb him like a tree, but he'd never look twice at a girl like her. He was gorgeous enough to get anyone.

Rome cleared his throat. "Here's my résumé. I'd love to answer any questions you might have." He sounded amused, and Elise wondered if it was because of Brenna's vibrant personality or something else. She peeked up at him and was relieved to see his back turned to her. It allowed her to study him without embarrassment, admiring the wide spread of his shoulders and the tattoo across the back of his neck.

He was like no one she knew. Elise's circle of friends was very small and conservative. But she found him fascinating. Completely and utterly transfixing. She couldn't take her eyes off him.

Brenna moved to the far side of her desk, gesturing for Rome to sit down on the opposite side. He did, and Brenna cleared off a stack of papers, shoving them to one side and then wrinkling her nose at Rome's résumé. "Blah, blah, blah. I hate these things." She put it down and smiled at him. "So you know how to survive in the wilderness?"

Rome nodded. "I've taken several classes and read many books on the subject."

"Great! Sounds like you're qualified to me. Can I feel your muscles?"

"Can you . . . huh?" Rome's eyebrows furrowed. "My muscles?"

"Just to check them."

"I . . . guess?"

She leaned forward, and gave one arm a squeeze, then shivered as if with delight. "That's really firm. Come feel, Elise."

"I . . . I'm okay," Elise breathed, the words so quiet they were barely audible.

"Party pooper." Brenna sat back and put her chin on her hands, studying Rome. "So where are you from, Rome?"

He hesitated a moment before answering. "Nowhere in particular. I tend to wander. I'm not much one for putting down roots."

Brenna seemed unbothered by his hesitation. "Me, too. Are you good with people?"

"I like to think so. Please don't let my tattoos frighten you off. I'm a very hard worker and a quick learner."

She waved a hand idly at him, dismissing his concerns. "You're talking to a tattooed woman with purple bangs. I'm not holding anything against you."

From her viewpoint, Elise could see the edges of his smile, could see his shoulders relax. She felt a pang of jealousy. He liked Brenna and felt comfortable in front of her. She wished it was her.

Brenna continued, pulling out a Post-it note and a pencil and scribbling something down. "We work odd hours and there's a lot of overnight campouts. Sometimes the guys go into the woods for almost a week at a time. That going to be a problem for you?"

"No, ma'am. I don't have family here. It's just me, and I don't mind long hours. I just need work. It's hard to find a job in a small town when you look like I do."

"Well, it's a good thing you're qualified, right?"

He said nothing.

"I'm afraid we don't pay much starting out. We're a newer business and still getting our feet off the ground. In addition to training exercises, we're opening up a paintball course on a section of the land and you'll be responsible for helping Pop run that."

"Pop?"

"Pop is Colt's dad. Colt's one of the other guys who works here. Pop's kind of our handyman and fix-it guy. Which reminds me." She tapped her pencil on the corner of her mouth and leaned over to look at Elise. "Could you do me a favor?"

Elise sat straighter, clutching the blanket to her pajamas. But she managed a brief nod.

"Super. Could you go flush a tampon down the toilet?"

"Um," Elise said quietly, a bit confused.

"Pardon me," Rome said politely. "But I think that will clog the toilet."

"I know. That's my point. I figure we'll give it an hour and then we'll call Pop in to take a look at it."

Rome stared at Brenna.

She reached out and patted one of his tattooed hands. "We like for Pop to feel needed. Now, let me tell you about the job salary. Like I said, we're a startup so don't think we'll be showering you with crazy money. We do, however, have cabins on site that all employees live in, so room and board is considered to be part of the salary. It's a nice perk."

As Brenna continued to chatter on, Elise slowly got up and crossed the room, moving down the hall to the bathroom. It was an odd request, but she'd been asked, so she'd do it. She felt a prickle on the back of her neck, as if she were being watched, and wondered if Rome was looking at her. God, she was in her frumpy flannel pajamas and she was sure her hair was a mess.

Sure enough, when she got to the bathroom, she stifled a gasp of horror at the sight of drool tracks at the corner of her mouth and the rings under her eyes. She hurriedly washed her face and then began to brush her hair quickly, trying to look as presentable as possible. Dear Lord. It was so unfair that such a good-looking man had seen her looking her worst. After she looked decent enough, Elise dug through the boxes under the counter until she found a package of tampons, took one out of its plastic applicator, and flushed it, wincing the entire time at the thought of the damage it'd create.

Calming herself, she smoothed a hand down the front of her modest flannel pajamas and headed back out to the main room of the lodge.

Brenna and Rome stood by the door, and she was shaking his hand. He was smiling down at Brenna, and Elise felt another pang of jealousy. She wished he'd looked at her like he did Brenna, that pleased expression on his face, gaze slightly flirty.

"I guess we'll see you tomorrow," Brenna said cheerfully. "You can meet the guys then, and we'll figure out rooming arrangements."

"Thank you," he said. "I sincerely appreciate the opportunity. You won't be disappointed."

"I know," Brenna said. "Plus, you're a total stud with all that inkwork. You'll look amazing in Elise's photo shoot."

His brow wrinkled a little, the piercing there bobbing. "Photo shoot?"

"Oh! Yes." Brenna caught sight of Elise and crossed the room quickly, moving toward her and looping an arm over Elise's shoulders as if to show her off. "Elise here is in town for the next few weeks and is going to be doing a pictorial spread of our instructors for a women's magazine. We're going to doll up the instructors and make them look hot and it should bring in some serious business. Isn't that right, Elise?"

That blue-eyed, dark-lashed gaze focused back on Elise again, and she panicked, her heart thumping.

Behind him, Brenna made a lathering motion, as if dirtying up Rome's abs.

Elise froze. She wanted to fall through the floor. Her mouth opened and closed as she tried to think of something clever to say. Something casual and funny. Heck, just something boring.

Nothing came out. She settled for a quick, jerky nod.

His mouth curved into a sexy half smile. "I'll be on my best behavior for the photos, then." He nodded at the two of them. "It was nice to see you, ladies. Brenna, if you need any further information from me, please give me a call."

"Will do. See you soon, Rome." She wiggled her fingers at him as he closed the front door behind him and Elise stood there like a mute statue. As soon as the door was shut, she turned and gave Elise a speculative look. "That man was sex on a stick, wasn't he?"

The breath she'd been holding exploded out of her lungs. "I . . . yes." Her cheeks went red. "He was very unusual-looking."

And already, she was picturing how she'd photograph him, her face hot at the thought.

FIVE

Brenna surfed the Web on her computer and yawned, waiting for Grant's inevitable return to their small office. She was alone, since Pop had arrived a short time ago and volunteered to give Elise a few lessons on driving the four-wheeler ATVs so she could tour the land. Elise hadn't looked thrilled, but she hadn't wanted to disappoint Pop, either, and so she'd gone.

That left Brenna waiting on Grant. For some reason, she was slightly tense. Maybe it was because they'd had sex and their relationship was bound to change in some way. Maybe it was because he'd oh-so-awkwardly tried to get her to move in with him after a single night of sex. She was starting to guess that Grant didn't do casual anything. The man had a pike up his ass the size of a flagpole.

And then again, maybe she was nervous because she'd just hired him a new instructor without bothering to check with anyone. But hey, he'd told her to handle the employee thing and she did. And Rome was fit and seemed like a decent guy. She suspected he wasn't qualified in the slightest but she didn't care about that. A big tattooed distraction was what this place needed to get the focus off her and Grant, and Rome fit that to a tee.

Plus, Elise had been staring at him, mouth slightly agape, and Brenna couldn't resist seeing what would happen if they threw the two of them together.

All in all, there were plenty of good reasons to hire Rome in her eyes. Grant would hate all of them. She chewed on a pencil eraser, thinking hard. They had five cabins now and six employees. Colt and Beth Ann lived in theirs and probably wouldn't budge, and she wouldn't ask anyhow. No one would want Dane and Miranda's cabin, because Dane insisted on no electricity. He was a "true survivalist" he told them. Brenna mostly thought he was nuts.

Grant would never give up his cabin, either. It wasn't really a cabin, but more like a tricked-out lodge that just happened to look like a cabin. It had all the amenities and since he was the owner of the business, she really supposed that he wouldn't want to plant a new employee there.

That left her and Pop. She couldn't ask Pop to move. The elderly man's trailer had collapsed just a few weeks ago, trapping him inside it for days and scaring the hell out of Colt. He'd moved Pop to the Daughtry Ranch so they could all keep an eye on him, and so moving him wasn't the answer.

That left just her. She continued to chew on the eraser, thinking. Grant was going to suggest that she move in with him again. She just knew it. And that conversation was going to suck. She didn't mind giving up her cabin for Rome, though. What she did mind was Grant's assumption that she'd just move in with him and turn into his girlfriend.

Maybe she just wouldn't tell him about Rome until she had to, then. What he didn't know wouldn't hurt him.

When Grant came into the office a short time later, he was dressed impeccably in a gray Polo that showed off the muscles of his chest rather admirably and a belted pair of dark blue chinos. She paused in her web-surfing to appreciate the look of him and when he glared at her, she shrugged.

So much for worrying about how things would be awkward at work. Him glaring at her? That was normal.

"Where's Elise?"

Good morning to you, too. "Pop's showing her the ATVs so he can give her a tour of the ranch."

He frowned. "That's not safe. ATVs are dangerous vehicles."

Brenna gave him an odd look. "The guys use them all the time."

He considered that for a moment, and then his gaze moved over her. "Do you suppose Pop drives safely?"

"I guess?" This was a weird conversation. Why was it okay for the guys to ride the ATVs through the woods but not Elise? It didn't make sense.

He grunted and sat down at his desk to work. They ignored each other until he put down his phone and said, "My parents left me a voicemail. They want to go out to the boat today and want us to come. And they insist on you going."

Brenna perked up. "Boat? You guys have a boat? Do people even go out on the lake in November?"

He gave her a curt nod. "It's housed at the marina. Bring a jacket. We'll be doing some fishing."

"Sounds like fun." When he said nothing else, she added, "Are you going to pout the whole time?"

"Pout? You think I'm pouting?" He gave a harsh snort. "Get over yourself."

She shrugged. "I don't know. Sounds like pouting to me. It's not like the sex wasn't any good."

Grant looked over at her. He got up from his chair and slowly, casually, walked over to hers and leaned over her desk. His gaze moved from her messy hair down to her borrowed shirt, and she wondered if he could tell that she wasn't wearing a bra underneath. Or that her nipples had gone hard the moment he'd leaned over her desk. "The sex," he said in a low voice, "was spectacular. And if I misinterpreted your signals, that's on me. Rest assured that I'm not going to harass you to stay with me again, Brenna. You made it loud and clear that all you want from me is sex and pretending. So we'll pretend for the sake of my family and leave it at that. Understand?"

"Good," she said brightly, but for some reason it didn't feel so good. Had she hurt his feelings? Normally Grant was a pain in the ass, but he was never icy like this.

Dane wandered in, yawning, and paused at the sight of Grant leaning over Brenna's desk. "Something going on?"

Grant pushed off her desk, giving her one last searing look before moving back to his desk. "Nothing. I was just instructing Brenna on a new task."

"Oh," Dane said, and then searched Brenna's face. She smiled at him, hiding her emotions, and gave him a quick thumbs up to let him know everything was fine.

She didn't know what to think of Grant's response. It was what she'd wanted to hear, of course, but the tone had been so very . . . detached.

Whistling to himself, Dane wandered into the kitchen of the main lodge and returned a minute later with a water bottle. He leaned on the door jamb and glanced over at

Brenna's computer, where she was playing solitaire and distinctly avoiding talking to either of them. "Huh," he said after a minute.

"What?" Grant snapped.

Dane shrugged, not taking offense at Grant's tone. "I was just surprised that Brenna went to Tulane, too. You two didn't know each other back then, I thought?"

She had no clue what he was talking about. It took a moment for it to register, and then she glanced down at her chest. Sure enough, she'd picked up a Tulane University T-shirt from Grant's drawer. His alma mater. *Oops.*

"Different years," Grant said shortly, and picked up his phone to end the conversation.

"Huh," Dane said again.

When they got to the marina, Justine took one look at Brenna's short-sleeved T-shirt and tsked. "You're going to freeze to death out on the water."

Which made Grant feel slightly justified, since he'd told Brenna that at least three times in the car ride over and she'd ignored him each time. But all he said was, "Brenna didn't want to change into a jacket."

Brenna shrugged, ignoring his foul mood and moving forward to hug his mother affectionately, a move that surprised Grant and pleased his mother. "I don't have a jacket. And I'm sure I'll be fine! It's not that cold today."

"No jacket!" She turned back to Grant. "Take this girl shopping, won't you?"

"No shopping," Brenna said just as quickly. "I don't need one, really. I'm fine. So is this your boat?" She stepped past Justine and onto the boat where Reggie was fiddling with the controls. "What's it called?"

Grant hugged his mother in greeting and headed in after Brenna, just to make sure she didn't do something stupid like lean over the rails.

"It's called the Bass Belle."

"Oh. You like fishing?" Brenna asked, moving to his father's side and staring at the controls as if she could figure it out. "What's this button do?"

Resisting the urge to slap her hand away from the controls, Grant left that for his father to handle. He moved to the stern of the fifty-foot yacht and laid a hand on his sister's shoulder and leaned in. "Think there's a chance in hell that Dad'll skip the fishing today?"

Elise laughed and glanced back to the cabin, where their father was dutifully pointing out controls to a wide-eyed Brenna. "Not a chance. He'll want to show Brenna that he can catch dinner. I think he likes her." She nudged her brother and then added, "We *all* like her."

With a sigh, Grant glanced back at the two heads bent over the controls of the yacht, one in a sailing cap and the other with a thick fringe of purple bangs. "You do? Half the time I'm not even sure *I* like her."

"Very funny," Elise said sarcastically. "I saw how you couldn't take your eyes off her at dinner last night."

That was because I was afraid of what was going to come out of her mouth, he wanted to tell his sister. But he said nothing. Because Elise had seen Brenna with the condoms and today she was wearing his shirt. It would be obvious to anyone that they were together.

Anyone but Brenna, that is.

He supposed he could have told Elise the truth. *Actually, she's just pretending to be my girlfriend so Mom and Dad won't harass me about dating. Oh, and she likes to annoy me and this gives her the perfect opportunity to get under my skin for a time. The condoms? We slept together. No big deal. According to her it was nothing.*

Which didn't sit right in his gut, of course. It was the first time he'd even looked twice at a woman since Heather had died, and the first time he'd touched someone in longer than that. The sex had been good. Hell, the sex had been amazing. He'd thought his mind was going to fry the moment he saw that piercing, and yet it had been so typically Brenna that it seemed natural on her. They'd gotten along so well over dinner and even afterward. She'd slept in his bed, curled in his blankets next to his side, and something about it had felt so incredibly right that he'd felt an intense bolt of longing rush through him. He'd wanted this.

Wanted Brenna.

And she'd totally blown him off. Wasn't interested. Was she willing to go so far to harass him that she'd have hot, uninhibited sex just to fuck with him? It didn't make sense.

Then again, not much that Brenna did made sense to him. He glanced over at Elise and saw her watching him with a curious look. "She drives me crazy," he told her, only half lying.

"More like you're crazy for her," Elise said, elbowing him teasingly.

"No, seriously. She drives me crazy," he told her, edging as close to the truth as he could. "Did you know that she does stuff deliberately to get under my skin? Like deleting reports that she knows I'm looking for. Or sprinkling flour all over the interior of my car. Jamming the other side of the door when I'm in the storage room. Unplugging my computer when I leave the room. She *literally* drives me crazy."

Hell, just thinking about all the stupid stunts that she pulled time and time again was making him a little hot under the collar. And aroused. Who'd have thought he'd be the type to get an angry hard-on?

"I think it's cute," Elise said cheerfully, her eyes sparkling. She crossed her arms over her chest, hugging her windbreaker close to her body. "She's just trying to shake you up a little. Maybe it's a passive-aggressive way of getting your attention?"

"I think she's just doing it to crawl under my skin sometimes."

Elise shook her head, still smiling. "It's a wonder you two got together, then. Though I'm sure you give as good as you get and crawl under her skin, too."

And that gave him a brilliant idea. Maybe he could end up giving as good as he got. And wouldn't that drive Brenna mad?

But first, he had to get a life jacket on her.

Brenna hated to say it, but Grant had been right. Not that she'd admit such things aloud, of course.

It was cold on the water. Maybe it was the balmy November air that wasn't more than fifty-five degrees and pleasant in the sun. But combine that with the breeze from the boat and the wind over the water? She was chilled. Darn chilled. She rubbed her arms and moved back into the cabin, even though she hated to do so. The water looked so nice in the sunshine that she wanted to be out on deck, soaking in the atmosphere. At least on deck, she'd feel like there was a point to wearing the stupid life jacket that Grant had shoved her way as soon as they left the dock. She'd tried to protest wearing it, only to have him refuse to listen and jam the thing over her head.

The man had a safety fetish.

"Come on, Brenna," Reggie was saying to her with a smile. "Let's do some fishing."

Out on deck, Elise and Grant mock-groaned in unison, which made her laugh anew. The two siblings were close. She liked that. Elise was great, too. She had a mind to take her out on the town one night, get her to hang out with Miranda and Beth Ann. The four of them would have such fun. "I'm coming," she told Reggie, giving her arms one last rub and then bravely facing the wind again.

"Sweetie, your lips are blue," Justine told her as she came back out on deck. "Grant, don't we have another jacket somewhere?"

"I'll take care of her," Grant said, and moved to Brenna's side. Before she could even question what he was doing, he stuck his hands in his pockets and opened his jacket, then wrapped his arms around her. It cocooned her against his chest and under his clothes.

And it was heaven. She almost moaned in bliss at the warmth of cuddling up against him.

He leaned in from behind and pressed his cheek against hers. "Better?" he murmured.

"Much," she told him, oddly pleased at his impulsive move. It felt so good to be pressed up against his body, and she was reminded of last night. Last night had rocked. She'd had such a good time in bed with him. It was a shame he'd had to ruin it this morning by trying to get all possessive.

Of course, his grasp right now was possessive . . . yet she didn't feel the need to run away. Mostly because he felt like a furnace and she was appreciating that at the moment.

Reggie grinned at them. "Y'all wait here and I'll get the fishing poles from below."

"We won't move," Grant said, leaning in and nipping at her ear in a way that made her entire body rock with shivers.

"This is me, not moving," Brenna chimed in. She glanced over her shoulder at Grant's face, so close to her own. "I didn't bring a pole with me."

He shrugged and she could feel the ripple of his muscles. His voice was a low murmur in her ear. "I guess you could hold *my* pole."

Had he just made a joke? A joke filled with innuendo? Stiff, proper Grant? She couldn't resist a response. "Won't your mother be scandalized?"

"Only if you don't catch something."

"Huh?"

Reggie returned at that moment, holding four fishing rods. "I've only got four on the boat. Brenna, you can use Grant's."

Ah. His *pole*. Her brain must have been frozen.

"That's fine. My hands are full at the moment anyhow." Grant's voice sounded easier than she'd ever heard it. Relaxed, even. And she could have sworn that he'd lightly tickled her through the pockets of his jacket.

This was not normal for Grant. Not in the slightest. A bit weirded out, Brenna reached an arm out of the jacket and took the pole that Reggie offered her. "I don't know how to fish."

One of Grant's hands wrapped around hers over the pole. Brenna blinked as she realized how big his hands were, and how warm. Not that she hadn't noticed last night. But she was really, really noticing it right now.

"Here," he murmured in her ear, and that small sound shot her body full of hot, wet longings. "Let me show you how to grip that."

And just like that, her mind went to dirty, dirty places.

He was doing it on purpose; she knew that. It was obvious that Grant was determined to make her suffer since her scheme had gotten him into this, and since she'd declined to be his little woman. So he was clearly intending on showing her what she was missing.

Normally she'd just smirk and go right on with her life, enjoying perverse pleasure of thwarting his wishes more than anything else. Normally. Except right now? Right now she wanted to crawl back into his bed and play games with him.

If he wanted to fool around? She'd show him that two could play this game. Brenna leaned back against Grant, feeling his warm arms around her. She sighed and wiggled her bottom, circling her hips in a subtle motion that wouldn't be noticed by anyone but the man she was pressed up against, and then leaned forward to cast the line, making sure her ass pressed up along his best parts.

By the time they got off the boat he'd be just as hot and bothered as her.

The afternoon of family time? Sheer torture for Brenna. She didn't understand wanting to spend endless hours just hanging out with family. To her, family were people you tolerated because you had to, and you escaped at the first chance. But Grant seemed to love spending time with his parents and his sister, and no one seemed in a rush to leave the boat.

No one but Brenna, of course.

She was turned on. She couldn't help it. Grant was sitting there, so very Grant-ish in his dark sweater and glasses, his hair mussed by the wind on the lake. He'd given her attention, solicitous to the bone. Polite, attentive, and utterly different from the man she normally encountered. Oh sure, Grant was nice and pleasant to all the visitors they had at the survival school, but to her? He was a scowling, nasty-tempered beast who was never pleased with a thing she did. This whole "nice" Grant thing? It was throwing her. She kept waiting for him to nitpick how she held the fishing pole or the way she stood. But he didn't. He simply kept his arms wrapped around her to keep her warm, nuzzled her neck upon occasion (as if he couldn't help himself), and was generally pleasant.

And he watched her like a hawk, too. That was probably her fault, since she'd decided to even the odds between them and had begun to brush her body against his, pressing her breasts to his chest when she said she was cold, and making sure her bottom was nestled against his cock when she fished. Running her hands all over him as if she couldn't help herself, either . . . and she couldn't.

She just kept thinking of the hours when she'd be able to get him alone again.

When the sun began to set, they finally left the fishing behind and the boat pulled back up alongside the dock. Brenna breathed a sigh of relief. She was ready to go home and strip Grant naked. When he took her hand to help her out of the boat, she couldn't help but brush her thumb over his knuckles, and she enjoyed seeing his eyes darken with pleasure. *Good.* Now he was thinking along the same lines that she was.

The Markhams had rented a car after driving back from the airport in her tiny Sunfire. Which suited her just fine. It meant that she could have Grant all to herself by the time they shut the car doors. If she played her cards right, she could have her hands under that sweater of his in a matter of minutes, and then he wouldn't take much convincing after that.

"Shall we go out to dinner?" Reggie asked as they all departed from the boat. "I'm famished."

Brenna gave what she hoped was a convincing yawn. "I'm really tired. I didn't get much sleep last night."

To her surprise, Grant's wind-reddened cheeks turned bright pink. Was the man blushing? Over that innocent comment?

"But we were going to go out for a lovely dinner," Justine protested. "It won't be the same if you don't go."

"Brenna's exhausted, so I think I'll just take her home," Grant said, looping a casual hand around her waist and pulling her close. "We'll order a pizza."

The small movement made her body sing with anticipation. *Soon, my hormones. Very soon.* And she slid her hand into Grant's back pocket and lightly caressed his ass through the fabric of his slacks, enjoying the way he jerked in response to her touch.

But to her dismay, Elise gave them an expectant look, her hands stuffed into her jacket. "I'll just hitch a ride back with you guys, then. Pizza sounds fine to me."

Thwarted by the well-meaning sister. Damn it. They couldn't exactly turn her down since she was sleeping on the lodge couch.

Grant's smile was a bit tight at the edges as he nodded at his sister. "That's fine."

It was? Brenna's brows drew together and she studied his crotch. She was pretty sure he was about to break free with a tent in the front of his slacks, so why not tell his sister to buzz off and give them some alone time? She would have

90

done that and paired it with a smile to let Elise know that she didn't mean anything by it.

But not Grant. *Damn him.* Now he was just doing this shit on purpose. Did he not want to be alone with her because she didn't want a relationship? If that was the case, she'd have to be persuasive when she got him alone. Because right now? She was really, really turned on and she wanted him in a bad way. Not the relationship, just the sex.

And what kind of man didn't want some no-strings-attached sex?

They said their good-byes to Grant's parents, promising to give them a tour of the survival school in the morning. All the while, Brenna yawned and tried to look fatigued.

And then they got in Brenna's car. Grant had wanted to drive, but Pop was still stymied by the Audi's mysterious malfunction the other day and wanted to tinker with the engine a bit more. Grant had shot her a few exasperated looks, but no one had wanted to be the one to tell Pop that most of the items he'd been repairing had been deliberately broken . . . so the Audi remained unusable and they'd driven in her junker.

She jammed the keys in the ignition, irritable with arousal. Elise slid into the backseat, and then Grant got in the passenger side. They waved a polite good-bye to Grant's parents as Brenna pulled out of the parking lot and back onto the highway, speeding back to Bluebonnet.

The car was silent. No one spoke for long minutes, and the interior was dark and shadowed. Brenna glanced in the rearview mirror. Elise had her head back, eyes closed, and it looked as if she was napping. Brenna looked over at Grant.

He was watching her, his eyes dark behind his wire-rimmed glasses. His hair was still tousled from the lake. That was sexy. When she shifted gears again, instead of putting her hand back on the steering wheel, she moved it casually to his knee to see what he'd say.

He adjusted in his seat, his leg twitching under her grip, but he said nothing. Didn't push her hand away, didn't speak and wake up his sister. It was like he was watching and waiting to see what she'd do.

Oh, little did he know. She'd do plenty.

Her hand slid a bit higher up his thigh.

He shifted.

Brenna kept her eyes on the road, but her hand went to cup his cock. Through his trousers, she could feel the stiff length of him, and memories flooded back of just how well equipped he'd been. Grant was the perfect size for her, all thick, blunt-tipped cock and smooth length, just wide enough to rub her in all the right places. She stroked her hand over his length.

His fingers covered hers, and she heard the sharp inhale of his breath.

Was he trying to get her to remove her hand? She shot him another look, but he was watching her. Brenna's gaze flicked to the backseat, but Elise was still out of it, eyes closed, breathing even. Perfect.

She ignored the palm covering hers and wrapped her fingers around the length of him. She could feel the bulge of his cockhead through his pants and she squeezed it, then ran her hand over the length of him again. Then stroked once more.

The silence in the car was almost oppressive with tension. Brenna could feel her pussy getting slick with excitement, Grant's flesh hot and practically throbbing under her grip. She shifted in her seat, practically squirming with her own need. Her pulse pounded low in her hips, all her nerve endings lit up, and she had to bite back her own groan when she stroked him again. Grant's head fell back against the seat's headrest. His hand still rested over hers, but now it seemed more of a guide than an admonishment. He certainly wasn't protesting. He could have pulled her hand away at any time.

And just to test that theory, she wrapped her fingers around his length and then didn't move, waiting.

His response came a moment later, when he realized she wasn't going to lift her fingers. His hand curled around hers, and he roughly dragged her hand, forcing her up and down his length, the movement made awkward through the fabric. But damn if that wasn't sexy as hell. He wanted this. She practically purred with her own excitement and began to stroke him again, her hand moving harder and faster, her touch becoming bolder.

Too soon, she saw their turnoff. *Damn it.* Just when she was starting to have fun. Poor Grant was going to have blue balls, she thought, swallowing her wicked giggle as she carefully removed her hand from his lap and put it on the steering wheel.

His eyes opened then, and he gave her a hot, incredulous look as if to silently say *why the fuck did you stop*?

She turned on her blinker, the clicking sound overloud in the darkness. "Almost home," Brenna called out, her voice deliberately cheerful.

Elise started awake and rubbed her eyes. "I always forget how long the drive back to Bluebonnet is," she said sleepily.

Brenna smiled at her in the rearview mirror and looked over at Grant again. He was staring out the passenger side window, and she noticed he'd carefully adjusted his coat so it covered up his erection. Lucky for him he had that coat.

She pulled into the nearly empty gravel parking lot of the survival school and was surprised to see a motorcycle parked in her usual space.

"Who drives a bike?"

Brenna frowned at Grant's question. "Don't know. One of Dane's friends, maybe? Or Colt's brothers?"

"Colt's brothers drive trucks," Grant answered, his voice strained just a bit. "We might have company." And he sounded dismayed at the prospect, which pleased her all the more.

Was it weird that she found it arousing to torment him? Probably.

They got out of the car, and she noticed that Grant was careful to keep his hip-length coat buttoned in the front, despite it being a fairly mild night. Her mouth twitched with amusement when he scowled at her, as if somehow needing someone to blame for his problem.

It wasn't her fault that he'd gotten turned on, now was it?

Well, maybe just a *little* bit her fault.

Brenna led the way into the main lodge, Grant walking a fair distance behind them. The lights were on, which told her that someone was up and hanging out. The lodge tended to be a bit of a rec center for all of them, since the cabins were small and didn't have much room for stretching out. Her own cabin was small, so she could only imagine how Miranda and Dane or Beth Ann and Colt felt in their own tiny cabins. A lot of evenings, she'd slip into the main lodge to make a sandwich and find both couples cuddled up on the couches, watching TV or playing video games. The two women were best friends, and the two men were, too, so it was natural that they all hung out together.

Brenna was a little envious of their clique, but the girls never forgot her when they were having a girls' night. She'd been dragged to have her hair and nails done by Beth Ann and Miranda more times than she could even think about. It was nice to have girlfriends after years of just hanging out with guys. Shy Elise could do well with some girl time, she suspected, glancing at Grant's sister. Elise seemed awkward and out of place at all times, unless she was with family. If she wasn't, she just tried to quietly blend into the background. And that sort of thing was foreign to Brenna.

She opened the cabin door and headed inside, surprised to see Pop sitting on the couch, drinking a beer, their new employee Rome sitting nearby. Uh-oh. "Hey, Rome," she called out cheerfully, waving at him. She shot a glance at Grant. "I thought I told you to come by in the morning?"

"In the morning? Is he the carpenter?" Grant looked at Brenna curiously.

"He might be," she said quickly, giving Rome a meaningful look.

Rome stood up, all black T-shirt and arms covered in tattoos. Even his neck was covered in tattoos, and he had gauges in his ears. His face was pensive as he watched her and the others as they entered the cabin behind her. "I'm sorry. Am I intruding?"

Brenna shrugged. "Can't really intrude. This cabin isn't private." She headed over and gave Pop a kiss on his leathery cheek. "How's it hanging, Pop? You fix Grant's car yet?"

"Not yet," he told her mildly. "Been working on that toilet all day. You're bad luck, missy." But he patted her arm affectionately.

"I must be," she said, winking at Elise's red face. "Things always seem to break when I'm around. I must have walked under a ladder or something."

Grant was frowning at Rome as if something wasn't adding together, and Elise looked uncomfortable as hell. *Oops.*

There went her plan for not telling Grant that she'd already hired someone. Well, she'd fix that in the morning. She didn't feel like talking about it right now.

"Pop," Brenna said, heading toward Grant's sister. "You met Elise earlier, right?"

A noise came out of Elise's throat that might have been a whimper, or might have been a really, really quiet hello.

Brenna ignored it. "Everyone, that guy over there with the fierce tats is Rome."

Rome's gaze was darting back and forth, and he had stiffened, almost as if he expected to be tossed out. "Pop mentioned I could stay here overnight, but if it's going to be a problem—"

"Not a problem," Brenna said, waving a hand. "Help yourself."

"Elise is staying here," Grant cut in. "I'm not letting my sister sleep in the lodge with a stranger here."

"She's not," Brenna said quickly. "She can stay in Pop's cabin and Pop can sleep out here on the couch, and Rome can stay in my cabin."

"Your cabin?" Elise asked, brows furrowing.

"Before I moved in with Grant," she said quickly, covering the lie. "The empty one."

"There's no blankets or a bed," Elise interjected, her voice so small it was barely audible.

"I don't need them," Rome said. "No big deal."

"Empty cabin?" Pop scratched his head. "I'm not sure—"

Brenna decided it was time to end this conversation before things escalated. "Grant and I are going to bed." She moved to Grant's side and dug her hands into the front of his jacket, dragging his face down to hers. She kissed the frown off his face, ignoring how stiff he was. Surprised, most likely.

Pop chuckled. "Well now."

Brenna swiped her tongue across Grant's tightly pressed mouth and was pleased to feel him soften under her grasp. The desire she'd been fighting all night was turning quickly into an inferno, and she wrapped her arms around his neck. She broke the kiss and glanced at the others. "I've been dying to get my hands on this man all day, so you guys will have to excuse us. I need to strip him naked and do dirty things to him."

"Brenna," Grant began.

She placed a finger over his lips to quiet him and looked over at Pop. "Can you order pizza for everyone? Grant's business credit card is in my desk. Leave us a few slices and we'll sneak out to get them later." She winked at the two men and the awkward, terrified face of Elise. The girl was in good hands with Pop, and Rome was cute as could be. She'd be fine.

Hell, Brenna didn't care if she was fine or not. She just wanted to get Grant alone and sate the itch she'd been feeling for hours. She glanced up at him and he looked as if he was about to protest again, so she leaned in and kissed him, then bit down gently on his lower lip, tugging on it.

"Come on, Grant," she whispered when she let him go. "You know you want to."

His gaze was dark with desire when he focused back on her face, and when she pulled on his collar, he allowed her to lead him away.

He said nothing until they got outside and headed toward his cabin. "I can't believe you," he told her, the harsh words tempered by the sexy rasp in his voice. "Now Pop's going to think we're sleeping together."

"We are sleeping together," she pointed out. "Your sister has my blankets, remember?"

"And now someone else is sleeping over, and I have no

clue who he is," Grant began. "And how the hell did you get my business credit card? And—"

They got to the front door of his cabin and she pushed it open, dragging him inside even as he talked. And then Brenna leaned in and gave his mouth a full-on, lingering lick that silenced him. "You going to keep talking or are we going to have some raunchy sex?"

"Are you trying to distract me?" His brows knitted.

She shrugged and moved away a step or two. "I mostly wanted to get laid, but if you're not interested—"

He grabbed her arm before she could dance out of his reach, and he dragged her back toward him. "Oh no you don't, you little tease." Brenna felt a wicked thrill when he pulled her back up against him, and his hands cupped her ass. "You've been rubbing up against me all day, and that move in the car was just dirty."

"Delightfully dirty, wasn't it?" Brenna trailed a finger down his front. "You liked it. I could tell." She leaned in and nipped at his chin with her teeth. "You were so hard in my grip."

He groaned, his hands clenching her ass. "My sister was in the backseat, Brenna."

"She wasn't looking," Brenna said, skating her hand down his flat belly and back toward his cock. "She was napping. I could have jerked you off and she wouldn't have noticed."

His breath sucked in when her hand slid back around his cock. "I noticed."

"Mmm. Then I guess you saw how horny it made me?" She clenched her thighs together in memory. "I was so wet just from touching you."

Grant stared down at her face with dark, tortured eyes. "So you want more meaningless sex with me? Is that what you're looking for?"

She sighed, dropping her hands. "Why does it have to be more? Why can't it just be sex because I want to fuck you and you want to fuck me?"

"Because that's not how I'm made, Brenna."

"Really?" She reached between his legs and grasped him again, caressing his rock-hard cock. "Sure feels like you're made that way to me."

"You want me to just use you?" he rasped, and dragged his wire-rimmed glasses off his face in a move that made her get wet with need all over again. "No emotions, just sex?"

"Exactly," she said enthusiastically. "One hundred percent just sex."

"Like we're strangers?"

She shrugged. "Whatever floats your boat."

Brenna was surprised when, in the next moment, he grasped the back of her neck and hauled her toward him in a fierce kiss. She melted when his tongue plunged into her mouth in a hard, dominating stroke. When the man gave in, he really, really gave in. Responding to his kiss, Brenna clung to the front of his shirt as he slowly stroked against her tongue, working her simmering desire to a fever pitch.

She barely noticed when he dragged their twined bodies over a few steps, until the backs of her thighs hit his couch. And then, to her surprise, he broke the kiss, staring down at her. "Just sex, right?"

She nodded, not trusting her voice to not wobble. Her legs were doing enough wobbling as it was.

With his hand still on the back of her neck, he pulled away and turned her around toward the couch, facing away from him.

Curious, Brenna let him lead her, not protesting. But her breath sucked in when he pressed down on her neck, indicating that she should bend over the couch.

She did so, and her ass went up into the air. And it made her wet all over again. This was so not like Grant. Or maybe it was. He loved control in the office, and in this, he was definitely in control.

Behind her, she felt him looming, and his hips pressed against her ass. She gave a small shimmy, bucking back against him, even as his hand continued to pin her to the couch. She could see nothing but fluffy, dark green pillows in front of her, and her imagination was making her wild, imagining what he was doing behind her.

His hand went to the front of her jeans and he pushed at the button of her fly, trying to open them. She helped him out, undoing the fastenings and then dragging the zipper down. As soon as she did, his hand went to the waistband of her pants, ripping them down her legs and letting them pool at her knees. And then he cursed. "Where the hell are your panties?"

"Didn't wear any," she told him breathlessly. "I'm out."

Grant ran a hand along her ass, then groaned again as he slid his fingers between her legs, testing her. "God, you're so wet. Wet and open."

She moaned into the pillows at his touch. "Told you I'd been thinking about this all day. You didn't believe me?"

His fingers slicked into her wetness, plunging into her pussy. "And this is from touching me in the car?"

Brenna cried out at the sensation, shifting her stance so she could spread wider for him. "You don't think . . . I can get like this . . . from touching you?" Her voice came out in little gasps.

"So is it touching me that makes you wet? Or just harassing me?" His fingers slicked in and out, and she was so wet that she could hear the movements of his fingers just as much as she felt them, and it turned her on all over again.

"Little from column A, little from column B," she told him breathlessly. Her hips ground against his fingers when he thrust again, pushing him a bit deeper.

The hand on her neck lifted for a moment, and when he pulled his fingers from her pussy with a wet sound, she cried out in protest.

"Stay there," he told her.

"So bossy." Her voice sounded ragged with lust. "That's sexy." And she did as she was told, because damn, a bossy Grant was kind of turning her crank.

She heard the sound of a condom package ripping and some shuffling clothing, and then in the next minute, that hand was pressing back down on her neck again, even as she felt his hips brush against hers once more. She tensed in anticipation.

Grant slammed into her from behind, seating himself to the hilt deep inside her.

Brenna cried out, the sensation nearly overwhelming her. "Oh Grant," she moaned. "Oh yeah. Do that again."

"Goddamn you, Brenna," he bit out, and slammed into her again. "You're supposed to fucking hate being used," he told her, and thrust hard again. "Not fucking eat it up." Thrust again. And then he began to hammer into her from behind, as if all control had gone out the wayside.

And oh God, Grant losing control? Made her wild. She felt her body ripple in a shudder of excitement, and then her pussy followed. To her surprise, she was coming hard and fast. She tightened around him and whimpered when he bit out another curse, plunging into her harder and faster, her body pinned under him as she quaked in a violent orgasm.

And then he growled out her name, and she felt him clenching up against her, the impossibly rough pounding slowing down until he was gradually moving in and out of her with leisurely strokes. He'd come, but for some reason he hadn't stopped moving. His hand moved under her T-shirt to stroke her lower back. And he breathed her name. "Brenna."

"Mmmm," she said softly, acknowledging him but too blissed out to do more than that.

"I didn't hurt you, did I?"

"You didn't hear 'ouch' did you? I didn't fling you off me." She snuggled into the pillows of the couch, eyes closed, not caring that her bare ass was in the air and Grant was still on top of her. "Now be quiet. You're harshing my post-coital buzz."

"Oh, were you finished?" He slid away for a moment, and she lifted her head to see him heading to a nearby garbage can and stripping off his condom. His pants were still on, though they were undone and he had to hitch them at his hips to keep them from pooling around his knees like hers were currently doing. Then he returned to where she was sprawled and helped her sit up. "I kind of thought the evening had just gotten started."

"Did you, now?" Okay, so she sounded more breathless than she thought she'd be. But to be fair, she'd just been fucked within an inch of her life. So if she was staring at the guy with a bit of a glazed expression on her face, she had the right. "What else did you have in mind?"

There was a wicked little smile curving Grant's mouth, and her entire body quivered at the sight. "Let's play a game."

Naughty man. "All right. Let's play. What kind of game?"

He gave her a little push backward, until she was heading over the side of the couch and landing on her back, her legs in the air. She giggled at the awkward position. Legs over her head, pants still around her knees, and now she was on the couch, nestled amidst the sofa cushions.

Grant leaned over her from the other side of the couch and said, "I want to play Make Brenna Scream."

She tilted her head, staring up at him. "I'm not sure if this is a good game or a bad game."

"Oh, it's a good game," he assured her, then tugged her jeans off her legs. "I promise you."

Brenna was intrigued. More than that, she was fascinated by this side of Grant. He'd been good in bed last night, but right now? With his assertive, domineering sexual personality? She was kind of digging this other side of him. Who knew that she'd be one of those girls who liked to be told what to do in bed? "What do I need to do for this game?"

He gave her an arch smile that set her pulse to racing. "Why, I want you to scream, of course."

She looked at him warily. "You're not going to pull out a giant paddle and start spanking me, are you?"

"Nope. Unless you're into that."

"Not all that much."

He nodded, and his hands went to her hips. To her surprise, he hauled her forward, until her hips were resting on the low back of the couch and thrust into the air above her. And Grant ran a hand along the back of her thigh, then pressed her leg forward. "Hold this for me, please, would you?"

She shivered and did as she was told, but she noticed how very open it left her. His ravenous gaze fell on her slick sex, and then he extended her other leg backward. She put both of her hands behind her knees and held her legs back. This . . . was an odd position. Kinda like a yoga something or other. Her weight was on her shoulders, and her ass was in the air, her legs spread wide. With the way she was positioned, she kind of had a bird's-eye view of her own pussy. Which was great, she supposed, if she were into that sort of thing, but she kind of preferred looking at guy parts. "So how does this game work?"

Grant leaned forward, and his hands went to the backs of her thighs, pressing her down a bit more. "It's simple. I'm going to lick you and play with this piercing until you scream."

And he gave her a wicked, wicked smile.

She might have trembled a little at the sight of it. He leaned in and did no more than breathe close to her skin, and she shivered madly. "I think I like this game."

"I think you will," Grant agreed, and his mouth moved to the mound of her sex. As she watched in fascination, his tongue dipped between the lips of her pussy and slicked over her piercing and her clit.

She moaned. Oh God, that was erotic. Both the touch and the fact that she was watching all of this from her vantage point was really, really hot. She wanted to put her hands on his head and direct him, but she had to hold her legs back.

Grant nuzzled in, moving deeper, and his tongue circled her piercing and her clit. He experimented a little, pinching her flesh in a way that caused her piercing to rub perfectly against her clit, and then began to lick again, flicking and caressing at that sensitive bud of flesh.

Her body, still twitching from the last orgasm, began to quake with need. And the more she trembled, the faster he seemed to lick, clearly relishing her response. Brenna cried out as the intensity of his attentions grew more fierce, and she began to give small jerks of her hips in response, whimpering each time. She wanted to pull away; she wanted to push against his mouth. He was making low sounds of pleasure in his throat as well, as if he loved the taste of her.

One finger slid deep into her pussy, and he curled it, stroking her from inside.

"Grant, oh damn. I love it when you touch me like that," Brenna moaned, unable to take her eyes off his mouth devouring her, fascinated by the occasional flash of her piercing, the constant slicking of his tongue. "It's almost too much."

"I'll stop when you scream," he murmured, and she felt every movement of his lips against her flesh, which caused her to be wracked with an entirely new set of shudders.

"I'm a lot of things, baby, but I'm not a screamer," Brenna told him breathlessly.

"That remains to be seen," Grant said, and he was so smug with purpose that she was fascinated. "But I think you're trying to distract me, aren't you?"

"Never."

"Mmm." He pinched the flesh around her piercing again, making it push against her clit once more. When she moaned and wriggled in response, he began to flick his tongue over her again, the curled finger working inside her pussy.

She came a moment later, shattering, her leg muscles tightening so hard that she thought her entire body would snap. But the only sound she made was a soft gurgle in the back of her throat that was more of a choked cry than a real, honest-to-goodness scream.

"Not quite," Grant said, seemingly pleased at her response. "Guess we'll have to try again."

And she moaned as he bent over her flesh again.

The Make Brenna Scream game lasted for about fifteen minutes longer. By that time, she was insensible with desire, had orgasmed twice more, and was twitching every time he touched her. The last time she came, she came so hard that a rush of liquid flooded out of her, and Grant seemed even more pleased at eliciting that response from her. She'd screamed with that last orgasm, though, and screamed his name to boot, which seemed to satisfy Grant immensely.

After that? She'd been too tired and sleepy to protest when he'd dragged her into the shower and supported her as she cleaned off. He'd tenderly toweled her dry and then hauled her to bed, and she could have sworn that he'd kissed her temple before drifting off to sleep.

That was entirely too possessive of him, she'd decided. And she'd tell him so. Tomorrow, when she had the energy. Brenna rolled over and propped her head against Grant's chest and fell asleep.

When Brenna woke up, she was alone in Grant's bed. She yawned and stretched and glanced around for him, but he was nowhere to be seen. *Huh.* Wasn't like him. She shrugged it off. He was probably giving her the space she wanted, and she liked that. Rifling through his drawers, she found a pair of boxers and a sports T-shirt and pulled them on. Then, still yawning, she left his cabin and headed for the main lodge, since it was a work day.

After all, just because she was having casual sex with the boss didn't mean that she didn't have to work.

Brenna padded into the main lodge and went straight for the kitchen, skirting the living room. She was starving, and she was pretty sure there was some cereal somewhere in one of the cabinets, since Beth Ann insisted on having normal breakfasts and thought Brenna should, too. Sure enough, there was a box of whole grain something or other. Brenna opened the box and took a handful of cereal directly from it and popped it into her mouth. Then she went to the fridge, drank some milk directly from the carton, and paused.

It sure was quiet for a work day. She glanced at the clock. Seven fifty-eight. That meant the guys should have been coming by, but it was too quiet. Carton of milk still in hand, Brenna took another drink and headed out into the living area of the lodge that also functioned as the main office.

Three sets of eyes stared back at her.

Colt. Dane. And the new guy, who sat on the couch with his arms crossed. Grant and his sister were nowhere to be seen. And Colt and Dane were frowning at her in a major way.

Brenna took another swig of milk. "Morning."

Dane made a face and leapt up from his seat to rescue the carton of milk from her. "Don't drink straight out of the carton, Brenna. That's nasty. We all drink that milk."

"Why is it nasty?" she protested.

Dane yanked the milk carton from her hand and headed to the kitchen with it. "We don't know where your mouth has been," he called behind him.

"Or do we?" Colt said in a dry voice, giving her a look of reproach.

She rolled her eyes and headed to her desk. "I take it Pop's been here already? That man gossips more than a school girl."

"Well," Colt drawled. "It's not every day that two people who profess to hate each other start shacking up."

"We're not shacking up," she told him, exasperated. Brenna moved to the end of the couch, near where Colt sat, and thumped down. "Elise needed to borrow my blankets, so I slept over at Grant's."

"And he requires kissing before letting you use one of his pillows?"

She scowled at him. "Exactly how much did Pop tell you?" She'd known that they'd be talking about it this morning. "And where's Grant, anyhow?"

"Grant took Elise to get breakfast, since someone still hasn't done grocery shopping," Dane said cheerfully, wiping his hands as he returned to the living room. "And that milk was expired, so I tossed it. You're welcome."

She made a face. "I'll go grocery shopping soon enough. Get off my jock."

"You don't have a jock. You're a chick," Dane said, bouncing down on the couch next to her. "And I'm glad someone went and got breakfast. I'm starving."

"Doesn't Miranda feed you before she turns you loose?" Colt asked.

"My cabin isn't wired for electricity, remember? So unless I wanted beef jerky for breakfast, Miranda told me I was on my own." He grinned.

"I don't blame her. I wouldn't want to light a fire just to feed your ass Pop-Tarts," Brenna said, elbowing him. Everyone thought it was weird that Dane preferred to go off the grid for his small cabin, but it made him happy, so whatever.

He elbowed her back and looped a thick arm around her neck, dragging her against him in a headlock. "So, you gonna tell me and Colt how come you decided to mindfuck Grant and sleep with him?"

She twisted the hairs on his arm to try and make him let go of her, squirming out of his grasp when he eased up. *Boys. Sheesh.* "I'm not mindfucking him!" After a moment, she added, "At least, it's not his mind I'm fucking."

"I knew it. They're sleeping together." Colt shot Dane a triumphant look.

"Damn it." Dane reached into his pocket and slapped a five down into Colt's outstretched hand. "I lost that bet."

"So fess up, Brenna. How long has this been going on?"

"About two days."

Colt grunted. "Thought it'd been longer, honestly."

Her brows drew together. Longer? "I'm just pretending to be his girlfriend while his parents visit."

"Dang. You really get into character, don't you?" Dane whistled.

She elbowed him again, because he was getting on her nerves. "What's the big deal? I can't fuck a guy without everyone thinking we're married? The eighteenth century called and they want their morals back."

"Again," Colt drawled, "you don't normally fuck someone you can't stand."

Since when did everyone think she couldn't stand Grant? Brenna glanced over at Colt, curious. She liked Grant. She liked all three men who she worked with. It was just that Grant nitpicked so very much that she felt like she had to give him a hard time. Did that mean they thought she hated him?

Did Grant think that, too? That couldn't be the case, because why would he start proclaiming her his girlfriend if he hated her?

So, you gonna tell me and Colt how come you decided to mindfuck Grant and sleep with him?

It wasn't a mindfuck . . . was it? Suddenly irritated at both men, Brenna leapt up from the sofa . . . and realized Rome was still sitting in a chair across the room, watching them, his arms crossed over his chest. The situation probably seemed odd to him—Brenna and Dane horsing around on the couch and Colt giving her a pop quiz about her sleeping arrangements. She rather hoped that Grant hadn't had time to quiz him yet. She smiled brightly at Rome. "Been here long?"

"Not long," he said quietly.

"Did the boys say hello?"

Dane frowned, his handsome face a bit confused. "I thought he was the plumber and that Grant had called him. Some idiot flushed something down the toilet again, you know."

"A tampon," Brenna said. At Dane's look of horrified disgust, she explained, "For Pop. And Rome's our new employee, not the plumber."

"He got good credentials?" Colt turned his narrow-eyed gaze on Rome, sizing him up. The dark skullcap of hair, the tattoos, the guarded expression on his face.

"I don't know, but he's sure pretty, isn't he?" Brenna beamed at Rome approvingly. "He'll be perfect for the shoot Elise wants to do. Girls love a bad boy spattered with mud."

"Shoot?" Colt asked.

"Mud?" Dane inquired.

Brenna waved a hand. "Long story. I'll tell you some other time."

Rome strode forward and offered his hand to Colt and Dane. "Pleased to meet you. I won't let you down."

Colt grunted again. It might have been a sign of approval. You could never tell with Colt. "We'll have to sit down and jaw sometime. For now, though, I need to head out. I'm speaking at a local elementary school."

Dane groaned and got to his feet. "And since we don't have classes today, Miranda's dragging me to go taste cakes."

"That doesn't sound so bad," Rome said.

"It's at a tea parlor." Dane grimaced. "I'm picturing gray-haired old ladies sipping from china with their pinkies out. I told her she should have taken Brenna, but then her feelings got hurt, so here I am." He shrugged. "So I'd better get going. See you guys later." He headed out the front door, whistling.

Colt rolled his eyes. "For all the bellyaching Dane does, you'd think he's the most henpecked man in the world. What he doesn't tell you is that if Miranda has so much as a tear in her eye, he loses his shit and bends over backward to make her happy." Colt shook his head and headed toward the door.

Brenna bit back her own smirk because Colt had more or less described, not just Dane, but Colt's relationship with Beth Ann to a tee. She turned to Rome as the two men exited and gave him a cheerful smile. "Guess you're stuck with me for your first day."

His blue eyes focused on her, and he blinked slowly. She noticed he had the longest lashes she'd ever seen on a man. Elise had to get that on camera. "Miss, can I ask you a question?" he said, his voice low and smooth.

"Shoot."

"Is this job for real?"

She tilted her head, studying him. "Why wouldn't it be?"

He glanced down at her clothing. "You're not dressed, your boss doesn't know anything about me, and neither do those two guys. You barely looked at my résumé, and you haven't asked me anything about my work experience. Just seems a bit strange to me."

"I'm a strange girl," she said lightly. "And listen, we run a survival school. Dane and Colt run the classes, Grant rides everyone's asses, and I basically file paperwork and take

111

pictures. They're opening a paintball course, so we can put you in charge of that. I don't see what the big deal is. You want to work here, right?"

"I do," he said solemnly. "I need the job."

"Well, we need another employee," she told him.

He nodded, but the suspicious look was still on his face.

"Would you feel better if I put on some pants?"

"Marginally, yes."

"All right then, I'll have to find some. Come on. I'm sure I have some in my cabin." She paused, then added, "I think."

They headed toward the row of cabins and Brenna waved a hand at them. "One of these will be yours, as soon as we figure out sleeping arrangements."

"The cabin I slept in last night. It's not empty?"

"No, that's mine."

He looked surprised. "You don't have much stuff."

"I don't, do I?" she said, feeling more cheerful by the minute. That was nice to hear from someone. Relieving. She constantly worried that she'd somehow turned a blind eye to her possessions and she'd wake up surrounded by piles of overwhelming junk.

"You a minimalist?"

"Something like that," Brenna said. "Though only with my own stuff." She had no problem borrowing from other people, because other people tended to want their stuff back. As long as it was going home with someone else? She didn't much care. "But once we reshuffle the cabins, you'll have one for yourself. Do you need to make relocation arrangements?"

His fathomless blue eyes fixed on her face. "I'm relocated."

"I don't see a box of stuff?"

"I'm relocated," he repeated.

"Well then," she said, pushing the door to her cabin open. "I guess I'm not the only one who packs light."

Once inside her cabin, she found her last pair of jeans and a T-shirt she'd borrowed from Beth Ann. She changed and grabbed her few possessions—toiletries, a paperback, and her spare bra—and headed back out to where Rome was patiently waiting.

"She's move-in ready," Brenna declared, and waved the handful of possessions. "Just let me dump this at Grant's and we can start the grand tour."

"Move-in ready?" He gestured at her cabin. "You mean this will be mine?"

She nodded. "I'm staying with Grant until his family leaves. After that, I'll just sleep in the main lodge. I don't really need a cabin."

He gave her a dubious look. "I don't want to push you out of your home."

"Actually, I'd prefer not to have one." It was one of her weird hang-ups, but she didn't try to explain it. No one ever understood.

A smile slowly blossomed over Rome's handsome face and, for a moment, he looked pretty enough to be a model. "Thanks." He gave the cabin another proud look, and she recognized that expression instantly. It was the expression of a man who didn't have much and appreciated what he got.

It made her like him all the more.

"Come on," she told him. "Once I drop these off, we'll get the ATVs and I'll show you around."

Only one of the ATVs was working that morning. Hoisted by her own petard, more or less. She dug out two helmets and had Rome ride behind her, and she drove around the wilderness camp for more than an hour. There were no classes, so she felt comfortable gunning through the woods at high speed, Rome's hands clinging to her waist. She drove him past the creeks, pointed out Dane and Colt's favorite camping spots, showed him the storage cabin that they kept emergency supplies in, and circled the area that the guys had designated to be the paintball course. It was toward the front of the property, so any paintball enthusiasts wouldn't have to go traipsing into the deep woods just to get to the course.

Rome was quiet, absorbing it all in with quick nods.

By the time they circled back to the main lodge, Grant's car was in the parking lot, and he and Elise were heading out the front door to greet them, likely drawn by the loud purr of the ATV. Brenna waved enthusiastically as they ripped past, and she could have sworn that Grant frowned at the two of them. With her luck, she was probably just in time for a lecture about keeping both hands on the handlebars while driving. She drove up to the ATV shed and let Rome get off before driving in to park, and then tossed the helmets into the shed instead of restoring them to their proper spot.

"Shouldn't we put those away?" Rome asked.

"Probably." But she didn't turn around to fix it. She was curious what Grant was going to say and that was spurring her forward. She shoved her hands into her pockets and began to head back to the front of the main lodge. "So what do you think, Rome?"

He thought for a moment, and then answered. "Too much acreage, if you ask me."

"What do you mean?" Brenna asked as Grant and Elise

met them halfway. Grant had a definite scowl on his face, so she moved in and put her hand on his cheek, bringing him close for a kiss in greeting (that would also serve as a distraction). It worked rather well, too—Grant definitely had a distracted look on his face.

"You have too many acres set aside for the paintball," Rome said slowly, as if unsure that he should be offering advice. "There's no natural landmarks or coverage, just trees. To be really successful, you'd be best with setting up some sort of buildings for cover, like a fort or fake walls. You want people to set up as teams and strategize."

"Won't it be unsafe if we set up a lot of obstacles?" Grant rubbed his chin, thinking. "I want safety to be a consideration for our guests above all else."

"Safety is one thing, but you'll need to give them some sort of cover or scenario to work through. You could even set up different tracks—one for beginners, one for advanced players, and one for experts, and scale the courses accordingly."

"So the new guys won't be slaughtered by the experts," Grant mused. "Not a bad idea."

"Rome's brilliant," Brenna enthused. "That's why we hired him." And Grant was still frowning down at her, so she nibbled on his ear a little.

He shivered and jerked away when her tongue traced the shell of his ear. "Are you trying to distract me?"

"Yes," she murmured, but then glanced back at Rome. "You want to change things, you need to talk to this man, here." She patted Grant's chest, and then copped a bit of a feel of his pectorals while she was at it. It was kind of fun to manhandle him.

Grant laid a hand over hers, stopping her exploration, but

she noticed he didn't pull her hand away. He considered Rome for a long moment. "We actually discussed hiring a carpenter to come in and build some obstacles for the paintball course."

"No need," Rome said, and his stance relaxed a little. "I can do that for you. I know a little carpentry."

"That's great," Grant said, enthusiasm in his voice.

"You ever thought about running a paintball gear shop, too? Might be a good idea. People come in for paintball and buy stuff while they're there."

Grant seemed impressed by Rome's business acumen. "That's a good idea, too. And it'd give Pop something to do so Brenna doesn't have to keep breaking things for him." His hand slid around her waist and he gave her a light squeeze. "I'm getting tired of my Audi constantly being on the fritz. Sounds like you have a lot of paintball experience."

For some reason, that made Rome a bit more guarded. As Brenna watched, he seemed to visibly withdraw. "I've got a little bit of everything under my belt."

"And he'll look hot for Elise's photo shoot," Brenna pointed out.

Grant's brows drew together and he frowned down at her.

"I don't recall agreeing to a photo shoot."

"I'm pretty sure we discussed it at dinner with your parents."

"Yeah, but discussing isn't agreeing to."

"Isn't it?" Brenna said in a light voice. To distract him, she slid her hand into his back pocket and squeezed his ass. She looked over at Elise to fill in the picture. But for some reason, Grant's sister had totally withdrawn into her shell again. She was staring at the ground, one shoe scuffing in the dirt. Her long, smooth hair had swung in front of her face, obscuring it from view, and she wasn't saying anything or participating in the conversation. She looked as if she wanted to hide.

Well heck. Clearly she couldn't count on Elise to step into the argument, so Brenna took the reins again. "Come on. It'll help your sister out to get the spread. And think of the business you'll get with some pictures of hot guys all muddy and woodsy." She fluttered her lashes at him in an obvious way. "It's great promo."

"From a woman's magazine?"

"Uh, yeah," Brenna said. "If I want to take a survival class, I'm going where the trainers are ripped and studly. No-brainer." She glanced over at Elise, but the shy woman's face was bright red and she still wasn't speaking up. "Anyhow, it's decided. Right, boo?"

"Don't call me 'boo,'" Grant said. "But it's not a bad idea. We'll discuss it later with the guys."

She gave his butt a pat. "Don't think you're getting out of the picture day. Four studs sells more magazines than three."

He gave her a startled look. "I'm not a trainer."

"So?" She scratched his stomach, pretending to draw lines across his washboard abs. "You've still got a hot body. Women everywhere will be wanting to sink their teeth into you, right, Elise?"

"He's my brother," Elise said, her whisper just barely audible.

"We'll discuss it later," Grant said again. "For now, we need to pick up my parents from the bed and breakfast so they can get the grand tour."

We? She stifled a groan. She'd signed up to be his fake girlfriend, though. She supposed she'd have to deal with this sort of thing. "So what am I supposed to do with Rome? I can't leave him unsupervised on his first day."

"Where's Pop?"

"I don't know. I'm not his owner." Brenna brightened, a devious idea coming to her mind. "I know. He can take Elise around and show her some of the nearby areas so she can get an idea for the photo shoot."

Rome's gaze went to Grant's quiet sister, and she could have sworn that he'd warmed up a bit. Elise, however, looked utterly stricken, her eyes wide.

"I don't think that's wise," Grant began.

As he spoke, Brenna watched Rome grow shuttered again, the cold look coming over his face. *Wrong thing to say.* She sighed. "Maybe some of us need to talk privately," she told him, "and can't do it with your family in the car. Or, you know, do other private things." She fluttered her eyelashes up at him.

He turned bright red.

Just then, Colt pulled up in his jeep.

"Problem solved. We'll send Colt with them," Grant said, and then tugged at her waist. "Come on."

Brenna frowned at Grant, and then gave Rome and Elise a helpless look. "We'll be back soon."

Rome nodded crisply, and Elise gave her a mutely pleading look that Brenna ignored. Rome was hotness personified—it'd do Elise well to spend some time with him, since it was clear that Rome was interested in her . . . if she'd ever make eye contact with him.

When she got into the Audi with Grant, she continued to wave cheerfully at the others until they pulled out of the parking lot. Then she reached over and thumped Grant on the arm.

"Ow! What the hell was that for?"

"You were mean to our new employee!"

Grant shook his head, staring out the windshield. "I hope to

God that he had some incredible qualifications for you to hire a guy who looks like him that fast. I didn't even see his résumé."

"I'm sure his qualifications are fine," Brenna told him. "And what do you mean, a guy who looks like him?"

"You're sure his qualifications are fine? Jesus, Brenna! Did you even look at them?"

"Does it matter? So Colt will show him how to rub some sticks together and make some fire. So what."

He stared at her as if she'd grown another head. "Are you kidding me? There are certifications and trainings that someone needs to have to qualify to teach classes. We were hiring someone who had those."

She shrugged. "I liked Rome, and he needed the work."

"He's covered in tattoos. He looks like a hoodlum!"

"I'm covered in tattoos, too! You didn't seem to have a problem with mine."

"They're not covering you up to your neck."

"They can. Maybe I'll go get a few more tomorrow."

He shot her a dark look. "Very funny."

She stared at him, astounded. "I can't believe you don't like him because of his tattoos."

"I can't say I don't like him. I don't know who he is. I don't know anything about him, actually," Grant bit out. His face was drawn into angry, grim lines. "That could be why I don't want to leave my incredibly shy sister with a stranger. I can't believe you went off into the woods alone with him."

She rolled her eyes. "What was he going to do, feel me up while I was driving the four-wheeler?"

"Maybe. You never know."

"Well, he's moving into my cabin, so I'm sure there will be plenty of opportunities for him to continue his orgy of molestations."

Grant screeched on the brakes. "You're kidding, right?"

Brenna held on to the dashboard. "It's not like I'm going to be in there."

His face softened as he looked over at her, and there was a hint of a smile on his mouth. "Because you're going to move in with me?"

Whoops. Someone honked at them, distracting her, and she glanced at the car behind them, since it was easier to focus on than Grant's hopeful face. "Actually, I thought I'd just sleep on the couch in the lodge."

His mouth hardened again. He started the car forward once more, glaring out the front windshield. Great, now he was all pissy again.

And she had a realization. "You're jealous."

"How can I be jealous? We're just having crazy, no-strings-attached sex, remember?"

"Exactly! So why are you jealous?"

"I'm not. I just don't understand why you'd rather have no home than to stay with me."

Like she was going to admit the whys and hows of her hang-up to him? Brenna crossed her arms over her chest and slouched in the passenger seat. "Maybe because you're being a dick?"

"It's a good thing there's no emotion involved in this relationship then, isn't there?" His voice was caustic with anger. "Or else you'd probably be mad."

She was mad, actually. She was furious at him and his high-handed ways. But she didn't say anything, because if she did, she'd just prove him right. Irritated, Brenna glared out the window at the passing scenery, and neither of them spoke until they arrived in Bluebonnet.

Reggie and Justine were waiting for them in front of the

Peppermint House. They seemed a little stymied by the foul moods of both Brenna and Grant.

"Don't worry," Brenna told them in an innocent voice. "This will just make the make-up sex all the sweeter."

And she relished the withering look that Grant sent in her direction.

SIX

He couldn't believe her.

Brenna would rather sleep on a couch than move in with him. It was ridiculous.

Seated at his work station in the main lodge, Grant clenched his teeth and stared at his computer screen. While his family was out getting a tour of the grounds, he figured he could get some work in. That was, if he could concentrate. Grant rubbed his jaw, determined not to look over at Brenna's desk. If he did, then she'd know he was thinking about her. He could hear her humming an off-key little tune, as if nothing in the world was bothering her.

And that drove him even crazier.

It was like she honestly didn't care about *anything*. She'd hired Rome with no qualifications other than the fact that he would look good with dirt rubbed on him. She slept with

Grant—mindblowing, soul-destroying sex—and then was surprised that he wanted more than just a quick fuck.

The thing was, when she was 'pretending' to be his girlfriend, it felt so natural and easy that he immediately wanted that in his life on a permanent basis. Her playfulness, her sexuality, her inability to take things too seriously? It attracted him like food attracted a starving man. She reached for him so casually, her affection so seemingly sincere that he had a hard time adjusting when she pushed him away and demanded that things be casual. He wasn't a casual kind of guy. He just wasn't.

And ever since Brenna had climbed into his bed? He hadn't thought about Heather once, not until he sat down at his desk, still fuming from his fight with Brenna, and opened his drawer to find the hidden picture of his dead ex-wife staring up at him.

It was weird. Normally he thought about Heather daily, the ache of her loss still ripping through him, the guilt a constant companion. But Brenna had him so distracted with her actions that he hadn't had time to dwell on the past. Instead, he was anticipating her next move, trying to figure out ways to get a step ahead of her. Trying to figure out how to make her want to be with him as much as he wanted to be with her.

Grant took off his glasses and rubbed his eyes, a headache starting when Brenna's humming paused and then went up a too-screechy note. "You can't sing worth a damn, Brenna."

"I'm also a lousy dancer," she said in a cheerful voice, typing away on her computer. "Your point?"

"You're making my head hurt."

"Oh." She paused for a minute, and then began to hum louder.

Instead of pissing him off, though, he had to bite back a

smile. He should have guessed that she'd do that. She constantly sought to get under his skin. And somewhere along the way, he'd grown addicted to their constant needling of each other. When had he started to look forward to her challenges?

Probably the day that she'd grabbed him at the airport and planted a kiss on his mouth. That was when all the challenges and small harassing moves became less like aggravation and more like—as Elise had commented—foreplay.

But he was still pissed at her. Still pissed that she'd jaunted off into the woods with dangerous-looking Rome and thought nothing of it. Pissed that she'd hired the guy for his looks. What if she decided she wanted casual sex with him, too? Where would that leave Grant? He fought the swell of rage in his chest, his mouth tightening as he stared at a monthly budget spreadsheet.

The lodge was too quiet. Too goddamn quiet, too still, and he was simmering with way too much emotion at the moment. Colt had taken Grant's parents, Elise, and Rome out on a tour of the grounds, since he could do a much better job of it than Grant could. Grant had cited pressing work, but the truth was, he'd simply wanted to be where Brenna was, so he could wait for her explanation. Ideally, her apology.

But it seemed like he'd be waiting a long, long time.

The humming stopped. She looked over at him. "Are you going to keep doing that?"

Grant finally looked over at Brenna's desk. It was covered in wadded paper, stacks of folders hanging messily off one corner. Her monitor was shoved off to one side, and a mug—his favorite, mind you—hung half-off the edge of the desk, a lipstick ring on the lip. Her feet were planted on the desk and she had the keyboard in her lap, typing. She wore no shoes, her bare feet wiggling, and he caught a glimpse of bright blue toenail polish. Her jeans were tight and show-cased her sexy legs, her shirt ill-fitting and probably bor-rowed from someone. Her messy, dark curls were pulled into an equally messy ponytail, her purple fringe of bangs flirting with her brow. And her full mouth was frowning over at him.

Damn, she was sexy as hell. He was getting aroused just looking at her. "Am I going to keep doing what?"

"Sighing." Annoyance flashed in her eyes.

"I'm not sighing."

In response, she gave a big, gusty sigh, mimicking him. And then sighed again a moment later, just to drive the knife in a bit further. "Look, if you're going to be a sad panda all day, I'll just leave."

"Where are you going to go?" he couldn't help but ask. "You gave up your cabin, remember?"

"Are we still fighting about that?"

"We might be. I'm still mad at you."

"Well, I'm getting mad at you, too, because you're being annoying. I like you much better when your mouth is occupied."

The sexual comment made his dick immediately hard as a rock. "I could tell," Grant murmured, his voice going low and husky. It took everything he had to continue to sit casu-ally at his desk, hands flat on the surface. "You kept scream-ing my name and getting wetter every time you came."

Her eyes grew soft, and he watched her suck in a breath, as if remembering last night. Her nipples grew visible through her T-shirt, and he wanted to drag her across his desk and lay her out so he could play with them.

"I'm tired of fighting," she declared. "Can we kiss and make up, already?"

"I'm fine with that," he said hoarsely, and every nerve in his body jumped when she got up from her desk and crossed the room toward him, that purple fringe of bangs framing a pair of very interested eyes. Grant didn't get up, and when she came to his side of the desk, she slid a leg over his and then hopped onto his desk, straddling him.

Then she leaned in, and he met her halfway to kiss her.

Her tongue was sweet and soft as she brushed it against his, her lips tasting faintly of cherry lipgloss. And she made a small noise of pleasure when their tongues caressed, which got him even harder. He put everything he had into the kiss, his hand going to the back of her neck and pulling her closer. She moaned softly, apparently enjoying his hand at her nape, tangled in her ponytail. And he stroked deep into her mouth, his other hand moving to brush across her small breast as she leaned in, her hands supported on the arms of his chair.

She pulled away moments later, breathless and sexy as hell. "We all better now?" she murmured.

"You're forgiven," he breathed against her cherry lips.

She grinned. "I wasn't apologizing, just distracting." And before he could protest, she slicked her tongue over his lips again, and he didn't care who was apologizing to who any longer.

He just wanted to keep kissing Brenna.

"Let's play a game," she breathed against his mouth, and gave his chair a little push backward.

"Oh?" If he got any harder, he was going to bust some seams in his pants. But he couldn't stop staring up at her, at her gorgeous, sensual face, that wicked look in her eyes.

"Let's play Make Grant Yell Brenna's Name," she said with an evil grin on her face, and slid down under his desk.

His eyes widened, his hands clenching on the armrests she'd just released. This was the worst possible timing to do something like this, he told himself as he watched her purple and brown head disappear under his desk. He wanted this, more than anything, but Colt and his family would be back at any minute, and they couldn't—

Grant's train of thoughts died when he felt her hands on his zipper, her elbows digging into his thighs. "Brenna," he groaned.

"You can't start yet," she teased. "You have to wait for me to get my mouth on you before you start screaming my name."

And her hands undid his zipper, then opened the clasp of his belt. He heard the jangle and whisk of his belt as she pulled it aside, and then he felt warm hands tugging down his boxers, until the hard ache of his cock was released. Her hands immediately went around it, and she made a small noise of approval, as if pleased that he was already so hard for her.

A hot, wet mouth closed over the head of his cock. Grant groaned and tilted his head back, his eyes closed. All thoughts of stopping Brenna had gone out the window as soon as she'd put her lips on him. Her tongue flicked and rubbed against the slit of his cockhead, and pleasure rippled through him. He wanted to tangle a hand into her hair again, and drive her face down on his cock until she was moaning with pleasure, too. Would she let him fuck her face? He groaned again when her tongue swirled around the head of his dick in a circular, teasing motion.

The front door of the main lodge opened.

Grant stiffened, his eyes flying open. His hands clenched on the arms of his chair as Dane came into view. Brenna had to get out from under his desk now, and they'd have to explain—

Except she didn't seem to be stopping. She'd gone silent at the sound of the front door opening, but her mouth was still on his cock, and she was expertly licking the underside, rubbing it with her tongue. She clearly had no plans of stopping.

"Hey, man," Dane said, letting the front door slam shut behind him. He went to his desk across the room and flopped down, looking weary. "You would not believe how many types of wedding cakes there are out there."

Fuck, Brenna's tongue was rubbing hard against the crown of his cock, and her fist was squeezed around the base. Grant's eyes threatened to glaze over, but he forced himself to concentrate, act as if nothing was going on. Dane couldn't see Brenna because the lodge desks were massive and made entirely of oak. The cube of space left for someone to stretch their legs was enclosed on the other side, so no one would see Brenna kneeling before him and servicing him.

And damn if she wasn't servicing the hell out of him.

He made a small noise in his throat, and then cleared it when Dane gave him an odd look. "There are a lot of cakes," Grant said in a strangled voice. "Did Miranda find one she liked?"

Ah, God, now Brenna was pumping him with her fist and taking him deeper into her mouth. The suction around his cock increased.

"You okay, bro? You look like you're sweating." Dane raised an eyebrow, then leaned back in his chair. "You're not coming down with something, are you? Next week's going to be busy and we're going to need all hands on deck."

"No, I'm fine." He forced himself to reach up and wipe a hand across his brow. "Just didn't sleep well is all."

"Uh-huh. Sounds like you got something in your throat."

And with that, Brenna took him deep, and he felt the head of his cock butt against the back of *her* throat. His legs clenched, and it took everything he had not to buck into her mouth.

"Uh . . . yeah." *Christ, what was he talking about?* He had no idea. All he could think of was Brenna sucking on him while Dane sat there and tried to have a conversation with him. Was she wet? Did this turn her on? Were her little nipples poking through her T-shirt, still? God, he wanted to see her, watch her head going up and down on his cock. Just the thought of that made him shift involuntarily.

Dane gave him another weird look. "Anyway. It's good that I caught you. Colt and I wanted to talk to you about the new guy. That was fast."

"Brenna moves fast," he wheezed out as she took him deep again. God, did she move fast. "I have no complaints."

He nodded. "Seems like a nice enough guy. I don't know if he has the experience we're looking for, but he looks athletic enough to keep up, and that's all that really matters. Colt and I can teach him the rest."

"Good." Fuck, he should have said more, but his mind was a blank. It was like she was sucking away his thoughts as she deep throated him.

Light fingers tickled his balls, and then Grant had to clench the arms of the chair all over again as she began to roll his testicles in one hand, still working him with her mouth.

"I wanted to talk to you about Brenna, too—"

"Now is not the time," Grant barked out. Ah, fuck, she was going to make him come if she kept that up, but her fingers were driving him wild.

Dane put both of his hands up. "Whoa. I was just asking. Didn't realize it was so sensitive."

Sensitive was not the word to use right now. More like delicious torture. He couldn't think past Brenna's mouth, and how badly he wanted to push deeper into it. Her motions picked up a rhythm, and she wrapped both hands around the base of his cock, pumping again as she began to work him. He leaned forward on his desk, and he felt beads of sweat break out on his forehead with the strain of keeping his cool. God, he was going to come . . .

Dane was still talking, and Grant had to force himself to concentrate on what his friend was saying. ". . . should probably take Rome out for a beer. Get to hang with the guys and get to know us if he's going to be working with us."

"Sounds good," Grant gritted between clenched teeth. *Fuck.* He could feel his need rising in his cock, felt his balls getting tight. He was about to burst.

"Cool." Dane sat there for a moment longer, just giving him an odd look, as if trying to figure out exactly what was wrong with Grant. When he couldn't, he pulled out his phone and began to text. "I think I'll see if Miranda needs me to bring her lunch or something."

Dane disappeared out of the lodge.

Grant's hands clenched into fists, trying to control himself while Brenna worked his cock. And when that didn't work, he reached under the desk, fisted his hands into her hair, and began to thrust into her mouth, desperate with need. Her soft murmur of surprise made him so fucking horny he could hardly stand it, and he began to pound into her wet mouth, slicking between her lips, pushing into her. Harsh, panting breaths escaped him, and he was nearly insensible with need.

And then she tightened the suction.

He came, biting out a curse even as he drove into her mouth, his entire body wracked with release. The ferocity of his orgasm made his legs cramp and his toes curl, and hot cum shot into her mouth. He felt her pull back a little, felt her throat working as she tried to swallow, and goddamn if that didn't feel incredible, too. But he pulled out, collapsing backward in his chair, and tried to catch his breath. "Fuck me."

Brenna pushed forward a little, shoving his chair backward and emerging out from under the desk. She delicately ran a finger along her lips, as if determined to catch every drop. "We might have to," she said in a light voice. "You never called out my name."

"That means you lost," he told her, panting, and hastily shoved his cock back into his boxers and pants before anyone came in and saw him with his dick hanging out.

"Mmm." She ran a hand down the front of her shirt and then caressed her breasts. Her nipples were hard and erect. "I did lose. And now I'm really, really turned on." Her voice had gone breathless. "I don't suppose you want to—"

"Yes, I do." Grant grabbed her hand and they raced to his cabin.

If anyone wondered where he was that afternoon, they didn't say. Grant emerged from his cabin several hours later, freshly showered, completely spent, and in a fantastic mood. Brenna was curled up in his sheets, sleeping. He felt a bit guilty for abandoning his visiting parents, but he could cite a work emergency. Or something. He suspected they'd just be happy that he was dating again.

Or so they thought.

He found Dane and Colt sitting in the main lodge with Rome. Pizzas had been ordered and the smell of hot pepperoni and cheese filled the air. Dane sat on one of the couches, beer and pizza in hand, while Rome and Colt played one of the shooting games that Colt loved. A case of Dane's favorite Canadian import sat on the floor nearby.

Grant headed over to the couches and sat down across from Dane, grabbing a beer and popping the lid off. "I thought we were going out for beers."

"We were," Dane said around a mouthful of pizza.

"But someone went into hiding and left us with his parents. I had to drive them back to the Peppermint House and they decided not to wait on you for dinner. So we did the same. Hope you like pizza, cause you bought it."

He reached for a slice, his mood mellow. "Pizza's fine." He dropped a piece onto a paper plate and then took a swig of the beer, grimacing at the strong taste. Dane loved Canadian beer—a leftover from his NHL days, Grant supposed. Shit would put hair on your chest.

"So," Dane said slowly. "You seen Brenna?"

Two sets of eyes were suddenly focused on him, though Rome kept playing the video game.

Grant took another gulp of beer, thinking about what to say. He went with the truth. "She's up sleeping in my bed."

Colt raised a hand for a high five.

He hit him back, then took a bite of pizza. "It's not like that," he said after a moment. "We're just having casual sex."

"Hell yeah," Dane said, and then he leaned forward for a high five as well. "That's my man."

Grant scowled at Dane, but smacked his hand anyhow.

"You don't strike me as the casual-sex type," Colt observed.

"That's because I'm not." Grant shook his head, still unable to wrap his brain around the concept. "Brenna insists. She doesn't want to be in a relationship. I told her she could move in with me, and you'd have thought I'd stabbed her or something. She freaked out."

Dane grimaced at him, popping a cap off his beer and chugging it before saying, "You mean to tell me you nailed her and then asked her to move in with you? No wonder she freaked. She's going to go down on you and you'll be showering her with engagement rings or something."

"No, I wouldn't," Grant said in a surly voice. He was getting irritated. Sure, Dane had been a player before Miranda had whipped him into shape, but Grant wasn't like that and his friends knew it. "I'm still, I don't know. Adjusting. With Heather's death, I just . . ." He sighed, picturing Heather's bright blond hair and radiant smile. Then he pictured miles and miles of mountain and rock and snow, and then her crumpled body half-buried. He shuddered. "I don't know."

Colt leaned to Rome. "Grant's first wife died about five years ago," he told him, catching him up. "Brenna's his first hookup since she passed." He gave Grant a disapproving look. "And she's our coworker and friend, so if you hurt her, it's going to get ugly. She's like a sister to me."

"And by sister, you mean all redneck and crazy?" Dane teased. Colt threw a bottle cap in Dane's direction, and Dane deflected it with a big hand, grinning. "Brenna's a free spirit. You don't chain those down."

"What do you know?" Grant asked.

"I know a lot about women," Dane proclaimed. "Had my fill of puck bunnies back in the day."

Rome just took another slice of pizza from one of the boxes and ate in silence, watching the others as they talked. Grant got the impression that he was absorbing every bit of the conversation as well as the exchange between the men. Not intruding, just watching and listening and analyzing.

Colt rolled his eyes. "You're so expert, how come you nearly fucked it up with Miranda?"

"Because my baby's complicated," Dane said proudly. "But Grant here sucks with women." This time, he ducked when Grant tossed a bottle cap in his direction. "It's true. You're rusty and out of practice. You need some advice or she's going to run over you rough-shod."

Grant stilled. "What do you mean?"

"I mean, if you let her call the shots, she's going to call *all* the shots. You need to take control of the situation."

"Gee, you mean like letting her drag you to go taste cakes? Or dragging you to pick out wedding colors?" Colt said in a dry voice.

Dane shot him the bird.

Rome smiled into his pizza.

"Fuck you, man," Dane said, but his grin belied the hard words. "This isn't about me. I already know she's got me whipped."

"True enough."

"Thing is, Grant here's a control freak."

"Hey, now—"

"True enough," Colt said again, smirking.

"And Brenna's the same, but she's just controlling in a different way."

Now that was an interesting way to look at it. Grant considered Dane. "How so?"

"She's deliberate in everything she does. Didn't you notice?" Dane gestured at her desk. "All the crap she has piled on there? It's other people's stuff. She borrows and snatches what she can, which makes you think that she's broke, right? Except she gives away all her own money, too. And her clothes."

"And her cabin," Rome murmured. When all three men turned to him, he continued. "When she gave me the tour earlier, she told me I could have her cabin. I thought it was empty. Other than a few pieces of clothing, there were no personal items in there." He gave them a curious look. "She new here, too?"

"No," Grant said in a sour voice. *What the hell?* How did everyone know more about Brenna than he did? Even Rome had been inside her cabin and deduced that Brenna was different. Grant had never been in there. He'd never bothered.

And now it bugged him that he'd never looked beyond Brenna's flighty surface.

"I'm telling you, man. There's some sort of freaky-deaky control thing going on in Brenna's mind. You just gotta figure out what makes her tick, and you'll understand her." Beer in hand, Dane extended a finger and pointed at his temple. "It's about control for her, too. She wants control of the situation with you. You want control of the situation with her. One of you's going to have to yield."

"Or compromise," Colt drawled, his accent thick on the word. "There's a concept."

Dane snorted. "You ever tried to compromise with Brenna?"

The man had a point. Grant was thoughtful, pondering Dane's words as he devoured his slice of pizza. He knew he was a controlling sort. He liked things done his way, and he liked organization and neatness. That was why Brenna usually got under his skin. She was the antithesis of neat and orderly.

But what if that was another kind of control, and Dane had been the only one to see it? Grant vowed that he was going to pay more attention to Brenna from this point forward. Watch what she said, what she did, everything. He needed to find out what made her tick.

Because then he could figure out how to make her want to be with him, instead of pushing him away. On a hunch, he got up and walked over to Brenna's desk, examining it. He rescued his coffee mug from where it was dangerously close to tipping over the side. He glanced at the stack of folders on her desk—all of them had Dane's handwriting.

He opened a drawer and found two chewed pencils—those were Colt's, since he tended to chew on both pens and pencils. A pack of Altoids—those were Grant's, Grant's business credit card, Grant's monogrammed letter opener, and his business card wallet. Frowning, he shut the desk.

Taking a swig from his beer, he headed to the back of the main lodge and flipped on the porch light. The spotlight was glaringly bright, and three cabins came into immediate view—Pop's, Brenna's old cabin, and his. He headed for Brenna's and opened the door.

It was empty inside. There was a small coffee table that was so beat up that it had either been picked up at a yard sale or gifted from Miranda's mother, who ran a junk-slash-antique store in downtown Bluebonnet. There was a narrow twin bed, which was currently stripped of all linens.

And that was it. No television, no phone, no nothing.

Brenna was a hurricane of a mess when it came to the office, but when it came to her own personal space, she lived like a Spartan.

It didn't make sense.

SEVEN

Inspiration struck at unusual times, but whenever it hit, Brenna always gave in to it.

It had been days since she'd pranked Grant. Absolutely days and days. He probably thought he was in the clear now that they were having sex.

How very wrong he was, she thought with a grin as she headed into the lodge, yawning at the early hour. It was barely six in the morning, and she'd be the first one in. Which was perfect, really. It'd give her enough time for her newest prank, and she couldn't wait to see Grant's reaction.

There was nothing better than shocking the hell out of that man. Well, other than having sex with him. Shocking him was a very close second, she amended.

When she went into the lodge kitchen, however, she was surprised to see that Rome was already there, a big bowl of cereal in front of him. He wore a plain black shirt, the collar slightly ragged with wear, the sleeves tight enough to show off his rather impressive tattoos.

He stiffened at the sight of her, the look on his face flashing guilty for a moment, then defensive. "The guys told me I could eat here," he said. "The food was for the employees."

"It is," Brenna said. "Calm down. I'm not here to steal your Cheerios." She headed past him to the pantry and opened it, searching the shelves. She'd seen that look on Rome's face one too many times—heck, she'd lived it. It was the look of someone who was scrounging a meal and had been caught. From her drifter days, Brenna knew that when money was lean, you sometimes took food and apologized later. And it told her a lot about Rome.

Mainly, that he was flat-ass broke and desperate.

She found the item she was looking for—a roll of foil— and grabbed it, then headed to the breakfast bar and sat down across from Rome as he ate. As he did, she opened the foil roll and began to tug the long sheet open, studying it.

Rome scarfed another bite of cereal, then asked, "Are you baking?"

"Nope. Don't get your hopes up. I'm about the opposite of domestic." She scrutinized the sheet of foil and asked, "Do you think this will cover a telephone?"

Rome stared at her. "A telephone?"

"Yeah, Grant's phone. I've been letting him have it easy for a few days, so it's time to wake him up again. I figure that a nice, festive desk covered in foil will do the trick, but I'm not sure I have enough."

"Foil?" The corner of Rome's hard mouth tugged up in a reluctant smile. "Will you get in trouble?"

"He'll probably want to kill me for about five minutes," she told him. "And then he'll be so turned on that he'll want to sex me a million times during the day. I figure it'll even out."

Rome's face was carefully neutral and he picked up his cup of coffee. "So, uh. Not sure if there's a polite way to ask this, but I saw you and Grant kissing the other day. You're sleeping with your boss?"

"I'm sleeping with *our* boss," she corrected.

"That . . . doesn't make it better."

"We do things a little differently around here," Brenna said in a light voice, tearing off the sheet of foil. "Like, for example, we hire the newest instructor and don't ever bother to check his credentials."

He froze.

Brenna waved her sheet of foil at him. "Don't worry. I'm not going to tell on you. I hired you because you looked like you need the money."

After a long, long moment of consideration, Rome told her, "I do."

She nodded. "I thought I recognized it in your face. You have any survival experience at all?"

"I'm a fast learner."

Yeah, that wasn't what she asked. But she only said, "I figured. That's why I hired you. We take care of our people here."

He said nothing.

Brenna guessed she'd made him uncomfortable. That wasn't a surprise. He seemed intensely private. Time for a distraction. "I do need to ask you a favor, though."

His jaw flexed, and his features looked hard and unyielding, his expression guarded. "What's that?"

"If you're working with the paintball equipment—which I suspect you will be—I need you to break some of it on a regular basis. For Pop."

The look on his face told her that hadn't been what he'd expected her to ask. It also seemed like he thought she was more than slightly crazy. She didn't care.

"Excuse me?" Rome asked politely, his manners at odds with all those piercings and tats. "I'm not certain I heard you correctly."

"You did," Brenna told him. "It just sounds weird. Basically, Pop is Colt's dad. He needs a job but won't take charity, so we hired him to be the handyman around here. Except that we're a small business, so he runs out of stuff to fix pretty fast." She leaned forward conspiratorially. "So I break lots of things around here to keep him busy."

"I can't decide if that's crazy or sweet."

"Story of my life," Brenna told him with a grin, sliding off the stool. She tucked the roll of foil under her arm and fluttered the sheet at him. "Now I'm off to go cover a man's stapler, phone, and desk in foil."

"Don't forget his chair," Rome called back at her.

He was going to fit in just fine, she decided. Brenna set to work and five minutes later returned to the kitchen, shaking the empty roll of aluminum foil at Rome. "I barely covered his phone before I ran out. I need more foil, stat. If I give you the keys, can you run to the grocery store and grab me all the foil they have?"

"You trust me with your car?" He looked surprised.

"Dude, you haven't seen my car. I'd be shocked if you actually wanted to keep it." Brenna grinned at him. "But you're welcome to take the keys any time you need it. I don't mind."

He gave her a skeptical look, as if he didn't quite believe that her motives were pure. "I'll take my bike to the store. You said you have a corporate card?"

"Did I say that? It's Grant's visa. Just wear sunglasses when you use it and no one will suspect anything."

"You do realize this is a small town and I'm an outsider? That's a surefire way to get arrested."

Jeez, it seemed Grant wasn't the only paranoid one around here. "I have tattoos and no one's stopped me."

"Yeah, but you're a cute girl. I'm a big scary man on a bike."

"Fine, fine." Brenna pointed at him. "You drive, I'll shop. We'll just consider it team building or something."

His mouth twitched. "Fine."

A half hour later, they returned to the main lodge with twelve rolls of foil. Brenna was pleased to see that no one was up yet, so she bounded to the desk and began to dump her foil out on Grant's desk. "Thanks for driving me into town."

"Sure." Rome sat down across from Grant's desk and watched her as she began to move stuff off the top of Grant's desk.

"Your bike's pretty sweet," Brenna commented, trying to make him feel at ease. He wasn't the most chatty sort. "You ever been in a biker gang?"

"Motorcycle club," he corrected. Then added, "Why would you ask that?"

She shrugged. "You ride a bike."

"I can't just own a bike? What kind of car do you drive?"

"A Sunfire."

"You ever been in a Sunfire club?"

"All right. Good point." Brenna unrolled a long sheet of foil and began to smooth it over the surface of the desk. "I suppose that was kinda dumb for me to ask, right?"

"Nah." Rome's tone was guarded. "I get asked that a lot. And I didn't say that it wasn't true, just wanted to know why you'd ask."

Oh. Okay, now she didn't know what to think. But clearly

Rome was reluctant to talk about it, so she decided to let it die. People were allowed their secrets. She certainly wasn't going to be the one to press him for details. "So what do you think of our business so far?"

"It's different."

That wasn't a ringing endorsement, and it bothered Brenna. They'd worked hard to make their small niche business a success. Well, more like Grant, Dane, and Colt had worked hard and she'd kept them company. She glanced up at Rome's face and reached for more foil. "Different like how?"

"Well, far as I can tell, you have an ex-hockey player, an ex-marine, a handyman who you don't need, and a secretary who's sleeping with her boss. None of that exactly screams normal."

"Normal is overrated," Brenna said between noisy crinkles of foil as she unrolled another sheet.

"It is." He seemed to relax in his chair a bit. "That's why I applied here. I figured if anyone around here'd accept me, it'd be you guys."

She smiled at him. "That's sweet."

He rolled his eyes at her.

That was the sort of thing Brenna was used to, though, so she didn't mind. It *was* sweet. She went back to covering Grant's desk with foil.

"So do you harass all the guys with foil?" Rome asked, curious.

"Nope. Just Grant."

"To show him that you care for him?"

Brenna stopped mid-foil, then frowned in Rome's direction. "No one said I cared for him. I just said we were sleeping together. We actually really don't get along all that well."

"Uh-huh."

She pulled Grant's monitor closer and began to cover it. "Now what does that 'uh-huh' mean?"

"It means that I don't believe you."

"You don't believe that I don't get along with Grant?" She snorted. "Did you not see me buy all the foil in Bluebonnet a half hour ago?"

"Yeah, but I don't think that you're foiling his desk because you want to annoy him. You say that, but I can't imagine that you sleep with all the people who bother you." He leaned back in the chair and went to kick a foot up . . . and then paused, clearly rethinking placing his foot on all that shining foil. "I think you do this stuff because you want his attention."

She paused again. Looked over at him. Snorted in derision once more. Then she went back to wrapping. Want Grant's attention? Please. She did this sort of thing because she liked to get under his skin. There was nothing better than seeing that expression on his face go from incredulous to exasperated in the blink of an eye. Then he'd scowl and turn his gaze on her and—

Oh shit. Rome was right. She loved getting Grant's attention. *Well, that was an obnoxious self-discovery,* she thought to herself. "Let's not talk about me anymore. Are you going to sit there and distract me or are you going to help me?"

"I'm not helping," Rome said. "The last thing I want is to be an accomplice."

"Chicken," she told him.

He bent his arms and flapped them like wings.

By the time Grant arrived into the lodge for the morning, the sun was shining, birds were singing in the crisp morning air, and every inch of Grant's desk was covered with gleaming silver tinfoil, right down to his stapler and the three pens he kept on his desk in a Wilderness Survival Expeditions branded coffee cup (also covered).

He stopped as he entered the room and stared at the desk. Really *stared* at it for a long, long time. It was difficult for Brenna to keep working as if nothing was wrong, knowing that he was standing ten feet away and staring dumbstruck at his desk. But she kept typing. It was quite a work of art, if she admitted it to herself. She'd already taken a few pictures with her phone and posted them to a few social media websites so her friends could appreciate her artistry before Grant woke up and tore it all down.

A moment later, the skin on the back of her neck prickled and she knew he was staring at her. And she couldn't stop the silly smile that started to curve her mouth, no matter how much she tried to bite it back.

Grant laughed. He laughed hard and loud, and that made Brenna look over in utter fascination.

She'd done prankish things to his stuff before. There was the time she'd put pink glitter all over his keyboard and phone. The time she'd put flour all over his car just before it rained. The time she'd forwarded his calls to an erectile dysfunction support group. There were a half dozen other, smaller pranks she'd played, too. He'd been furious at all of them, no matter how big or how small the annoyance. Completely and utterly furious each and every time, and each prank had ended up with her being yelled at or Grant vowing to get rid of her. Which never happened, of course.

But he'd never laughed before.

And she had to admit, Grant in an open, laughing mood? Was a gorgeous thing to look at. His normally somewhat stern features were drawn into a pleasant, almost rueful grin as he carefully picked up his stapler in one hand and examined it.

And the entire time, he kept chuckling to himself, as if the fact that she'd foiled his desk was the cutest thing in the world and it gave him great joy.

When he looked over at her, still laughing as he picked up a foil-wrapped pen, she found herself beaming back at him. Maybe Rome was right and she did do all this crazy stuff just to get his attention. Being the focus of Grant Markham's full attention? Not the worst place in the world to be, she decided.

"Did you . . ." he began.

"Now why would you assume it's me?" She fluttered her eyelashes at him innocently.

"Because you're the devil incarnate," Grant said, but the words had no sting in them. Rather, they had a husky note of affection.

She'd clearly have to prank him more often. The look on his face? Total turn-on. Brenna licked her lips. "Takes a bad boy to know a bad girl."

Brenna could see the look on his face and knew exactly the moment that his amusement changed to total lust. It was like a wave rolling over him. His stance changed, stiffening slightly. Then she saw his jaw clench, the smile going tight, his eyes growing dark. His hand tightened around the coffee mug and his focus went entirely on her.

Which naturally made her nipples harden.

She might have made a sound in the back of her throat. Maybe. Just maybe.

Grant set down his coffee mug. Both of them ignored the crinkle of the foil. "Brenna," he said in a low voice. "Come here."

Oh God, why did that authoritative sound in his voice make her so incredibly wet? She stood up, pushing her chair backward, and then stepped out from behind her desk. She moved toward him one step, and then stopped. Why make this so easy for him? "Is there a problem?"

"My desk is covered in foil." He said it like the words were foreplay all on their own. And she shivered with excitement.

"Does this mean I've been naughty?" Her voice was so incredibly husky that she was surprised she didn't fall to the floor and throw her legs open in blatant invitation. "You going to punish me?"

"You might like that too much," he told her, moving toward her. And he came to stand before her, just inches away, and gazed down at her.

She practically vibrated with need. "You should totally fire me," she whispered.

"I should. At the very least, I should spank you." His voice was caressing. "Teach you a lesson."

Brenna bit her lip at the mental image, her eyes nearly rolling back in her head out of sheer desire. Why wasn't he touching her? She needed it so badly. Her hands fluttered at her side, and she wasn't sure what to do with them. Touch him? Touch herself? Slap the man for torturing her with all this *conversation* and not giving her the sex she needed? So she asked, "What kind of lesson?"

"The kind where I take you back to my place," he said in a low, husky voice, looming over her. He was so close that she could feel the heat of his breath, dancing along sensitive flesh. He smelled sweet and clean, like toothpaste. Who knew that minty fresh would be such an aphrodisiac? "And I throw you down on the couch . . ."

"Yes?"

"And make you find a use for all of this foil you've wasted."

Spoilsport. "Guess I'll have to wrap your desk in condoms next time," she murmured. She could smell his aftershave if she leaned in, and he smelled so spicy and clean that it was driving her crazy.

He studied her face. "Is this your way of telling me that you want to have sex, Brenna?"

Was the man totally oblivious or just messing with her? "We don't have to have *sex* sex," she told him. "We could just get a little oral in before the day starts."

He grabbed her hand and dragged her to the back of the lodge, not that he needed to do much dragging. She was sprinting with him, incredibly turned on.

They ran back to Grant's cabin and were tearing each other's clothes off before the door was shut. Grant's mouth covered hers even as his hands snagged her shirt and began to drag it over her head. That was fine with Brenna, since she was tugging at his belt.

Then his hand was on her breast, and she moaned against his mouth. "Condom, Grant. Get a condom."

He groaned and squeezed her breast, then tore himself away from her, racing across the cabin to his bathroom.

She watched him go for a moment, then clawed at her clothing. It needed to come off, stat. Her shirt went over her head and to the ground, and her pants quickly followed. By the time Grant returned, his slacks flapping loosely at his hips, she was naked and practically jumping with need.

Grant returned to her side and pulled her against him. "Your bouncing is making me crazy. I hope you're in the mood for hard and fast."

Oh God, when was she not? She nodded.

"Good." He dragged them both to the floor, Brenna under him. His hands slid to her hips, adjusting her even as she parted her legs for him. He groaned at her movements, his face contorting as if barely holding his control. Grabbing the condom packet between his teeth, he quickly ripped it open even as Brenna ran her hands all over him, raking her nails on his skin.

Her gaze went to his hands as he rolled the condom onto his thick length. Anticipation made her bite her lip, and she gave a small sigh as he finished and poised himself at her entrance.

Then he paused, and his hand went to his mouth. He licked his fingers with a long, slow drag of his tongue that gave her shivers to watch. "Need to make you wet, Brenna. Want this to be good for you, too." His hand slid between them and moved to her sex.

His eyes widened, and he groaned. "God, you're so wet already."

"Totally," she agreed, shifting her hips so she rubbed up against his fingers. "But feel free to touch me as you like."

Grant gave a small groan and pushed two fingers inside her, sliding deep. Then he scissored them, which made her arch with pleasure. "How do you get so turned on so fast?"

"All that foil," she breathed, closing her eyes and savoring the sensation. "I kept thinking of your reaction as I did it. I guess that turned me on."

The fingers slid away and he shifted. She felt the head of his cock probe her and held her breath, waiting for that delicious moment.

"So the thought of aggravating me turns you on?"

Maybe it did. She gave a small shrug. "Are we going to talk all day or are we going to have sex? I—"

Her words broke as he plunged forward, shoving into her. She felt that familiar, delicious stretch as her body adjusted to him, and a small moan escaped her.

"You feel so good," he murmured, leaning in to kiss her throat. Then he pumped slowly into her again and began a languid rhythm, moving in and out of her.

He felt incredible, too, the sensations moving through her body in a pleasant ripple. Her mouth curved into a dreamy smile. "Whatever happened to hard and fast? Not that this is bad, mind you. It's really the opposite of bad."

"Mmm. Disappointed? I do hate to disappoint." Grant thrust again, this time hard enough to make her breasts bounce.

She gasped in response, holding on to him. "Never disappointing."

"Still, I did make a promise," he told her, strain in his voice, and rocked hard again, causing the pleasantness of his thrusts to slide up a notch, exciting her.

"You did," she told him, breathing a little harder with anticipation. She lifted her legs and wrapped them around his hips, locking them against him.

His thrusts began to pick up speed and strength, until she was gasping with each hard slam into her, her nails digging into his back. She lifted her hips to match him, aroused by the power he was driving into her. She knew Grant was strong, but he'd never used it against her . . . until she'd asked for more. And oh, he was giving her more. She moaned and writhed against him with each thrust, loving the power he was unleashing on her. She'd be walking bowlegged when they were done, but she'd be the happiest bowlegged woman ever.

Desire continued to build as he rocked into her, their bodies shoving across the rug with the power of each drive into her body. Grant grunted with every thrust, close to losing control. "Almost there," she told him with a whimper. "So close . . ."

"Need a little more to drive you over?" Grant asked her, grit in his voice. She felt him shift again, and then his fingers were down at her pussy. "I might know just the thing."

And then he began to play with her clit, rubbing her piercing against it.

Her entire body stiffened and an orgasm blasted through her, making her emit a small choking sound. Words escaped her as pleasure poured through her, rocking her even as Grant thrust again with wild, frenzied motions. Then he groaned her name and stiffened against her, one last hard push pounding through her before he collapsed on top of her.

They both remained where they'd fallen against each other, saying nothing and struggling to regain their breath. Brenna ran a light hand over his shoulders, feeling the dampness there. He'd worked up a sweat fucking her brains out. *Good man*, she thought with a chuckle.

He lifted his head and looked down at her through smudged, slightly askew glasses. "What's making you laugh?"

"Just thinking that you won't need to work out today, since we just burnt quite a few calories." She traced a finger along his muscles.

He grinned down at her. "I blame you. You knew how worked up I'd get with all that foil. Where on earth did you find so much?"

She shrugged idly. "I had Rome drive me into town."

Grant stiffened against her, all easiness escaping him. "Rome? The new guy? You trusted him to go into town with you?"

"Why wouldn't I?" She patted his chest consolingly. "I mostly wanted to get a ride on that cool-looking motorcycle of his."

This time, Grant lifted off her and stared down at her in shock. "You rode on the back of his bike?"

"Uh, yeah?"

Anger pinched his handsome features. "Did you wear a helmet?"

Weird. "Who are you, my mother?"

"Damn it, Brenna! Those things are incredibly unsafe.

Not only do you go off gallivanting with a stranger, you do it on the back of a motorcycle and don't even wear a helmet? What the hell are you thinking?"

She stared up at him in surprise as he lifted off her and stormed out of the room, heading to the bathroom. It would have been a funny sight—him with his pants around his knees—if she wasn't so mystified by his reaction. What the heck was that all about?

He was actually pissed off . . . about safety?

She remained where she was, naked and on the floor, watching for him to return. He did a few minutes later, his clothes straightened, a furious look on his face. He glanced at her, scowled, and went to a nearby closet and pulled out his gym bag.

"What are you doing?"

"I need to go work out."

"We just built up a sweat. You can't tell me you want to work out again?" Hadn't the man heard of cuddling or something after sex?

"You should probably go back to work," he told her coldly.

"O-kaaaay." Sometimes Grant confused the hell out of her.

Brenna watched Grant curiously as he typed into his computer, seemingly all business. Ever since their fight—well, she didn't know if it was really a fight since only one of them had been mad and it wasn't her—he'd been ignoring her. That meant no possessiveness, no demands to have her move in, no nothing.

It was refreshing, but it was also a bit mystifying. Troubling, if she was honest with herself. Nah, she settled back on mystifying. Grant wasn't acting like Grant. He'd been perfectly happy to have sex but the moment he'd found out she'd ridden into town with Rome, he'd freaked out. Jealousy, she wondered? How could he be jealous of Rome, when she was sleeping with Grant?

"Are your parents coming over today?" she asked, because she couldn't stand the silence any longer.

It took a few minutes for him to look up from his computer screen, his expression intense. Then he focused on her through his glasses and shook his head. "They're visiting friends in Houston."

"Oh. I suppose that means we don't have to play pretend today," she said brightly.

"Nope."

Her brows furrowed together. No response to that, either? It was almost like things were back to normal between them. And for some reason, it was sitting oddly on her. "Your sister went with them?"

He glanced over at her again. "No. She said that she'd just stay in her hotel room."

"That's no fun. Someone should take her out on the town."

"You volunteering?"

"I am," Brenna said with determination. "I should take her to meet Beth Ann and Miranda. I need to get my bangs retouched anyhow." When he said nothing to that, she sighed and picked up her office phone, then cradled it against her shoulder while she looked up the phone number to the Peppermint House.

Emily Allard-Smith answered it on the first ring. "Peppermint House."

"Hey, Emily, it's Brenna from the survival school. Is Elise Markham there?"

"I believe she is," Emily said, a softly rolling drawl in

her sweet voice. "I made some cookies earlier and she came down and had a few. Hang on and I'll ring her."

Brenna's stomach growled at the thought of Emily's cookies. The entire town considered Emily the best baker in the county, and people tended to show up at her house just to see what she'd baked that day, including the entirety of the local sheriff's department.

"Hello?" Elise's voice was soft and breathy as she answered.

"Hey, Elise. It's Brenna. I was wondering what you were up to."

"Hi, Brenna." Was it just her imagination, or did Elise sound a little disappointed? "I'm just . . . hanging out today, I think. I don't have any plans."

"Want to meet me and a few girlfriends for lunch? I can pick you up."

"Oh, actually, that would be good." Enthusiasm crept into Elise's voice. "When we got the tour of the ranch from Colt, the sun was setting and so I wasn't able to get a good feel for the lighting. The weather's perfect today, though, so I wouldn't mind circling back to a few spots if you don't mind."

"I don't mind at all," Brenna told her. "I'll make sure one of the ATVs is prepped and ready to go."

That got Grant's attention. She watched his head jerk up from the computer screen, and he stared at her.

"Perfect," Elise said, brimming with enthusiasm.

"I'll pick you up in a half hour, then?"

"I'll be here."

Brenna hung up the phone and was surprised to see Grant scowling at her, his expression black. "What?"

"Why do you need to prep an ATV?"

"Oh." She waved a hand idly. "Elise wants to look at the

lighting at a few spots for her photo shoot. I told her I'd drive her around."

"No."

"What do you mean, no?"

"I mean no. Those ATVs are dangerous."

Uh, okay. "Well, they're not cuddle-mobiles but I'm licensed to drive one, and we'll wear helmets."

"Elise is fragile." He shook his head. "I forbid it. You shouldn't drive them, either. Something might happen to you. There are hundreds of accidents on those things every year. Even a helmet isn't enough to save you if it flips over and pins you underneath."

Where was this safety lesson coming from? She'd ridden the ATVs dozens of times in the past few months and Grant had never had a problem with it. As far as Elise being fragile—the girl was tall and healthy-looking from what she could tell. Weirded out, Brenna stared at him a moment longer. "Okay," she said after a long moment. "We won't." It was a total lie, but what he didn't know wouldn't hurt him.

He watched her for a few, then nodded. "Good. Thank you."

She picked up her car keys and slipped out of the front door of the main lodge, a little troubled by Grant's over-protectiveness. What did he mean that Elise was fragile? She seemed perfectly fine to Brenna. *Strange.* Maybe this was just more of Grant's controlling. She rolled her eyes at the thought as she slid into the front seat of her car.

Weird situation, all around.

Brenna honked her horn outside of the Peppermint House, and Elise bounded down the steps a few moments later, her long, smooth hair fluttering in the breeze like honey-colored silk. She gave Brenna a shy smile and got into the passenger side of her car, a large Ziploc bag of cookies in hand. She passed it to Brenna. "Hi. Emily says hi and sends these along."

"Are these lemon drops? Sweet. I'll tear into these later." Brenna grinned. "You ready to go?"

"Ready. Where are we going?"

Brenna gave her an evil grin. "I'm going to introduce you to my partners in crime, and then we're going to sneak away into the woods."

Elise gave her a puzzled look. "We are?"

"Your brother's being weird."

"Ah," she said, understanding dawning on her face.

Brenna glanced over at Elise as she drove. "What do you mean, 'ah'? What does that mean?"

Elise was quiet for a moment. Then, she said, "Nothing I can talk about, really. I'm sorry. If Grant hasn't said it to you, I probably shouldn't."

Brenna frowned to herself. Grant had secrets? Secrets that he wasn't telling her? That didn't seem fair. She turned down Main Street and parked in front of Beth Ann's adorable salon. Miranda's beat-up truck was already there. Perfect. She hadn't even had to call them.

The cowbell clanged on the door of Beth Ann's small salon. A blond head poked around the corner of the decorative wall, and Beth Ann's lovely face lit up in a smile. "Brenna! Hi! Come on in. Miranda was just getting her nails done and showing me some bridesmaids' gowns." She glanced at Elise and gave her a curious look, then looked back to Brenna.

Huh. Beth Ann had grown up in this town and she didn't recognize Grant's sister? "This is Elise Markham."

Recognition dawned on Beth Ann's face. "Of course! The missing Markham!" She gestured for the two of them to come sit down in the salon area. "I didn't recognize you."

"I thought you grew up in Bluebonnet," Brenna told Elise.

The woman shook her head, looking acutely uncomfortable. "I went away to a private school."

"Oh." Well, maybe that was why she was so shy. Brenna put a hand on Elise's shoulder, leading her forward. "Come say hello to Miranda."

Miranda sat at the manicure table, her hands under the ultraviolet light and a large bridal magazine open in front of her. Her dark hair was beautifully smooth and falling around her shoulders, and her bangs looked as if they'd been freshly clipped. "Hey, Brenna! Come and see the dresses I'm looking at. I'm trying to decide between three."

"No, she needs her bangs done first," Beth Ann decreed. "Honey, your roots are showing something awful."

"That's why we're here," Brenna said, dropping into the salon chair with a grin. "That, and I figured Elise might need some girl conversations after being cooped up all day with her parents."

"Dane said that Grant's family was in town," Miranda commented, carefully turning a page in the magazine. "Are you guys enjoying yourselves?"

"It's just like I remember it," Elise said quietly, and Brenna caught a glimpse of her in the mirror as Beth Ann spun her around in the salon chair and settled a cape over her. Elise had sat down at the back of the small room, in the hair dryer chair. Her long, silky hair had fallen in front of her face again. Grant's sister was pretty and sweet. Why did she look so terrified of people?

But then Beth Ann was in her face with foils and a mixing

bowl, and Brenna lost sight of everything except Beth Ann's breasts as she began to fix Brenna's bangs.

"You want to go purple again, honey?"

"How about white? Like a skunk?"

Miranda snorted.

"How about no?" Beth Ann gave her a disapproving look. "It's your head but everyone will know I've done it, and I'm not about to have you go around looking like a lost polecat."

"What about clown red?"

"You're too pale. It'll look awful."

"Green?"

"Fades to gray too fast. You want pink or purple. Blue if you must."

"Purple it is, then."

Beth Ann nodded approvingly and began to paint her bangs with highlighting chemicals. "So tell me what's new," she said in a sweet voice. "You seeing anyone, honey?"

Brenna groaned. "Can no one around here keep their mouth shut?"

"Nope," Miranda said triumphantly. She turned around from her seat and waved her hands in the air to dry them. "So spill the beans. How long have you and Grant been doing the deed?"

She watched in the mirror as Elise glanced at Miranda, confusion on her face.

"We've been together a while," Brenna lied, keeping the story going. "We just haven't told anyone. It seemed best."

"Lordy," Beth Ann said, wrapping Brenna's bangs in a foil and then patting it. "We can't leave you two alone for a minute, can we?"

"We hired someone new," Brenna said, changing the conversation. "He's a smoking hot, tatted-up guy. You seen him yet?"

Beth Ann's eyes widened. "No, but I want to hear more."

"Elise has seen him," Brenna said innocently. "What did you think of him, Elise?"

Elise colored bright red. "He seems nice."

"Nice and well muscled," Brenna teased, pretending to squeeze imaginary buttocks. Of course, Grant was hiding an amazing body under those yawn-inducing sweaters and tailored shirts he wore, so it wasn't like she was missing out.

"So are you going to go after him once you've finished breaking Grant's heart?" Miranda asked.

"No hearts are involved. Just sex and animal lust when it comes to me and Grant. Nothing more."

Miranda and Beth Ann exchanged a look in the mirror. "Mmmhmmm," Beth Ann said. "And this is *Grant* you say you're sleeping with?"

Brenna was getting a little tired of everyone assuming that she had to marry Grant if she was fucking him. "It is, though I might go after Rome. He seems more my type."

To her surprise, Elise flinched slightly.

Well now, that was interesting. She got up from the chair, her bangs fully foiled. "Trade places with me, Elise. I have to sit under the dryer for a bit."

"I can trim your hair," Beth Ann offered. "It's gorgeous the way it is, but a trim is always good for the ends."

Elise shook her head, her hair falling in front of her face again. *Even more curious*, Brenna thought as she sat under the dryer. There was a lot going on behind the scenes that it seemed she wasn't all that aware of. It made her feel uneasy. Things had been simpler when it had been just her and the boys, and Grant had been there to harass them. Now the boys were paired off and she was sleeping with Grant and getting upset when he wasn't harassing her.

Even more, it bothered her that she was bothered.

Miranda fluttered her nails once more, then stood up. "I'm heading across the street to the coffee house. You guys want anything?"

"My usual," Beth Ann said, and turned to Elise. "You want something, honey?"

"Nothing for me," Elise murmured politely. "But thank you."

Brenna raised her hand. "I do. Hot chocolate. Pay you later?"

Elise pulled out her purse. "If you need a few dollars, I have some."

Miranda shook her head at Elise. "Brenna always does this. She doesn't have money."

Elise looked puzzled. "She doesn't?"

"She's always broke," Beth Ann said with a faint smile, dropping her combs into the sterilizer as Miranda disappeared out the door. "But on payday, dinner and drinks are on her. We just get her the rest of the time."

But Elise still looked concerned. "Does my brother not pay you enough?"

"Never," Brenna said solemnly.

"Oh please," Beth Ann said. "Honey, don't let that sweet face fool you," she told Elise. "Brenna gets paid just fine. She's just bad at holding on to it. What did you buy this week, Bren?"

"Nothing." At Beth Ann's skeptical look, she amended, "The last time I went to Maya Loco, there was a nice man playing a guitar for tips."

Beth Ann groaned. "You didn't."

Brenna shrugged. "It's just money." And if it wasn't in her hands? She couldn't buy anything. "He was really good, too."

Beth Ann just snorted and pulled out her broom, beginning to sweep. Elise just stared at her with wide eyes. "You gave that man your entire paycheck?"

"Not the entire thing," Brenna amended. "I filled up my gas tank first. And bought drinks for the house!" She grinned.

But Elise wasn't smiling back at her. She looked troubled.

Time to circle the conversation once more. "So I was thinking about getting more tattoos," Brenna said blithely. "I haven't been able to take my eyes off those big guns of Rome's. Why do you think he's so covered? Prison tats? Needle fetish?"

Elise blushed and ducked her head again. "I don't know."

"Prison tats?" Beth Ann sounded horrified. "Does he look like a prisoner?"

"Not at all," Elise protested.

Distraction taken care of, Brenna thought smugly.

EIGHT

G rant's parents insisted on having another big family dinner that evening. The local Mexican food place, Maya Loco, was a favorite growing up, and was still the only restaurant in Bluebonnet that served alcohol, so it was the place of choice. Brenna was her usual effervescent and irreverent self, chatting happily with Elise and his parents about one of their first classes and how Miranda had insinuated herself into Dane's group, unbeknownst to Dane until it was too late. Her voice was animated, and she squeezed Grant's knee while they sat outside the restaurant on benches, waiting to be seated.

Watching her, you would think that she'd been his girlfriend for years. She was so easy with him, her posture relaxed and happy, and she had charmed his parents despite her offbeat airs. She was dressed in a cute black dress, the fabric dotted with cherries, and a matching red cardigan tossed over it. He was pretty sure he'd seen Beth Ann in the same ensemble. But while the cool Southern blonde had looked merely pretty and put together in it, there was something about Brenna that made the outfit perfect for her vivacious personality. Her bangs were bright purple and curled into the Bettie Page hairstyle she loved, and with the dress and hair, she looked like a wickedly sexy, sensual rockabilly sort. Totally wrong for him. But then she'd put her hand in the crook of his arm and lean in, and it felt . . . perfect.

Even if it was a lie.

His thoughts kept him occupied even when they were seated in the restaurant. As soon as they were, the waiter rushed off again. He stood. "I'll get drinks from the bar. The usual for everyone?" When his parents nodded, he looked to Brenna. "What would you like?"

"Get me something fruity with an umbrella," she told him, grinning. "I feel fancy tonight."

"I'll join you, Grant," Elise said quickly, and got up as well.

They made their way through the crowd—Maya Loco was always packed to the gills—and headed to the counter. He flagged down the bartender to let him know they needed to be served, but the man was at the far end of the bar.

"Please don't take this the wrong way," Elise said under her breath. "But I have some concerns about Brenna."

Grant frowned and glanced over at his sister. "Oh? Why is that?"

She smiled at him. "Please keep smiling, Grant. They're looking over here and I don't want them to know we're talking about Brenna."

He forced a smile to his face, though it felt false. His

stomach had clenched up hard at Elise's words. "What's going on with Brenna?"

His sister tilted her head and then said, after a long pause, "Are you sure she's not with you for your money?"

He couldn't help but laugh. "I'm pretty sure she's not. Why do you ask?"

Elise dragged a finger on the scarred wooden bar, digging a fingernail into an old scratch. "She just seems . . . careless with her finances. I worry that she latched onto you because you're grieving and you're wealthy. That's all."

Grant stared at Elise. He moved closer to his sister, turning his shoulders so the others couldn't see their discussion. "Brenna's careless with everything. What did she do to make you worry?"

Elise chewed on her lip, thinking. "I know you like her a lot, Grant, and I'm so happy that you're dating again . . ."

"But?"

"But she gave away her entire paycheck to a street musician. And her friends say she never has any money on her, no matter when she's paid." Her brows knit together. "Is it possible she has a drug habit?"

"I don't think she does." But he wondered. Brenna was so open with almost every aspect of her life. It was possible that she was hiding things simply because of omission. He'd had no idea that she lived in such an empty cabin. He'd had no idea that all the items on her desk belonged to other people. She drove an old beat-up car and seemed enthusiastic about her job, but did he truly know her? He made a mental note to ask Dane and Colt more about her when he got back to the lodge. The others had known her since their days in Alaska. Grant hadn't.

Was it possible that he was missing a big piece of the puzzle?

"I'm pretty sure that she's not using me for my money, Elise." Grant patted his sister on the shoulder to reassure her. It was almost comical. He would have loved it if Brenna were using him for his money, because that meant she was interested in something long-term. If anything, Brenna was the opposite of a gold-digger. She didn't want *anything* from him. But he couldn't tell Elise that. "I'll be careful. If it'll make you feel better to know it, I've never bought her anything."

Elise relaxed a little. "I'm glad to hear that. I just don't want someone taking advantage of you while you're still vulnerable."

Vulnerable? It was on the tip of his tongue to ask what she meant by the puzzling comment, and then he realized she was talking about his widowhood. Except for the first time in five years, he felt like a regular guy, not someone who'd been ripped in half and left bleeding. For the first time, he could safely say he'd truly moved on from Heather. He still loved her and always would, but it was time to move forward, and he was more than ready.

"I'm doing just fine, I promise."

A hint of a dimple shone in Elise's face. "You do seem happier than I've seen you in a long time. Is it because of Brenna?"

"She infuriates the hell out of me," he admitted. "Half the time I want to strangle her for her hare-brained ideas. And she seems to thrive on antagonism."

"You seem to be thriving on it, too."

Maybe he was. But now he was curious if there was something ugly about Brenna that he needed to know about before losing his heart to her entirely. Because the sex was incredible. When they were together? It felt right. She was smart and funny and quirky, and she constantly kept him guessing. She never bored him. She was sexy and wild in bed.

And every time he saw her, he could see himself with her for the long term.

Just as soon as he found out what her secrets were. The next time he got into a relationship? He didn't want any surprises.

The next day, despite his confident words to his sister, Grant found himself wondering about Brenna.

Not that he thought she was after him for his money. She'd never mentioned it and money seemed to be the last thing on her mind. But she had this weird hang-up about stealing things. He'd woken up that morning after a night of wild lovemaking to find out she'd borrowed another T-shirt from him and was drinking out of his favorite coffee mug when he'd gone into the main lodge.

He'd almost think she was a klepto, except she never seemed to notice when he took things back. That, and she didn't seem to own anything of her own. Was that normal kleptomaniac behavior?

So he'd decided to test a few theories. She liked his coffee mug so much? He'd buy her one. He'd driven his family into Houston that day to meet up with friends, and had gone shopping. By the end of the day, he had a personalized purple mug with her name on it, a multi-colored bead bracelet that had been so garishly ugly that he knew she'd like it, and a few pairs of sexy panties that would cling to her cute little ass and drive him crazy.

When he'd driven back to Bluebonnet that night, she'd been the only one still working in the office, a pencil stuck through her messy bun of hair and pretending to type, even though he knew she was just watching videos on YouTube. He'd given her the bags of presents and watched her reaction.

He was pretty sure most women liked presents. His first wife, Heather, had loved to get gifts. She'd laughingly insisted on being "surprised" with presents for every holiday she could think of, and back then, he was wild enough about her to do so, not caring about how much money it cost them. Money had never mattered to him.

But Brenna? She'd acted like he'd dropped a snake on her desk. She recoiled visibly, then looked up at him in horror. "What's this?"

"A couple of presents," he'd told her.

She reached for the bag with a look of revulsion on her face. She'd softened for a moment at the mug and the bracelet, as if she'd been somehow pleased—despite herself—in the gifts. The lingerie had brought a knowing smirk to her face. "Presents for me, huh?"

"Mostly for you."

And then she'd dragged him back to his cabin and showed him her thanks—predominantly by straddling him and riding him like a cowgirl for most of the night. She'd said such filthy, wild things that he was pretty sure he'd been blushing at some point . . . and had never been more aroused. She'd seemed happy about the gifts.

But the next day? He'd found Colt drinking coffee out of the purple Brenna mug and Miranda had shown up wearing that godawful ugly bracelet.

He'd asked about the mug. Turned out that Colt had rescued it just as Brenna was about to throw it away. The bracelet? Miranda said Brenna had seen her this morning and offered it to her first thing, because she was "going to toss it out."

There was no sign of the panties he'd bought her. She'd gone commando that day, too.

Which was downright weird.

So he'd gone through the duffel bag of clothing she'd brought with her . . . and had been surprised.

One bra.

One pair of panties.

One pair of jeans.

One sweater.

One T-shirt.

One towel.

That was it. Necessities, but no more than that.

And Grant was pretty much flummoxed. Brenna wore different bizarre outfits every time he saw her. Then again, most of them did seem to be from castoffs and piecemeal junk that most people would only wear on laundry day.

He wondered how much of it was borrowed. And then he wondered where the rest of Brenna's stuff was. Something about all of this just wasn't right. What kind of person went around with no possessions, no clothing, and gave away her home?

That night, when she came to bed, yawning and stripping her clothes off, he didn't pull her to him and begin to kiss her. Instead, he watched her, waiting for her to say something. But when her hands went to the waistband of her pants and she pushed them down, he wasn't surprised to see that she was naked underneath.

And instead of turning him on, it infuriated him. "Not wearing the panties I got you?"

She snorted, as if the idea was ridiculous. "I can pick out my own clothes, thank you very much."

"So you'd rather go around with no panties than wear something I bought you?"

"You called it. I didn't ask you to buy me anything." She kept her voice a silky, playful purr and moved forward to trace a finger along his jaw. "Besides, don't you prefer me all naked and quivering?"

Grant sighed. "Fine. I give up. Just give them back to me and I'll take them back to the store."

That made her pause. "Well, now, I can't really do that."

"You wore them?"

"Not exactly. I threw them away."

He grabbed her hand before she could run her thumb along his lower lip, seemingly unconcerned that she'd just tossed aside his gifts. "You what?"

"Threw them out? I didn't want them."

He eyed her suspiciously. "I saw Miranda wearing the bracelet I gave you."

"Didn't want that, either." But she had a wistful look in her eyes for a flash, as if she regretted it.

And now he really, really didn't understand her.

"What the fuck, Brenna?" He pushed off the edge of the bed, having sex the last thing on his mind at the moment. "Are you doing this just to mess with my head? Is this your newest game?"

She gave him a puzzled look, as if she couldn't figure out why he was angry. "Doing what?"

"Throwing away the things I give you. Acting like none of this matters."

Brenna's eyes narrowed and she put her hands on her hips, unconcerned that she stood in front of him in her bra and nothing else. "What exactly about this 'matters', Grant? I volunteered to be your pretend girlfriend to get your parents off your back, because I didn't like how they were harassing you. We just happen to be having some really great sex on the side. I didn't ask you to buy me gifts, and I'm not moving in with you. I thought I'd made that pretty clear. If you want to have just sex, I'm fine with that. What I'm not fine with is all this weird possessive crap you're pulling."

"Possessive?" He sputtered, shocked. "You don't have any place to live so I offered to let you live with me. You don't have any goddamn panties so I bought you some. What about that is possessive?"

"You're trying to control me." Her mouth thinned with irritation.

"I'm trying to clothe you and give you a roof!"

"A roof is not necessary. I've been homeless before. It's preferable, really."

She'd what? He stared at her as if seeing her for the first time. "When were you homeless?"

"In Alaska, when I met the boys." She shrugged. "I was living out of my car."

"In Alaska? Are you kidding me? It's freezing there."

"Only in the winter."

"Are you crazy?"

She looked wounded at his words, as if she'd trusted him and he'd betrayed her. "Not everyone needs a ton of shit to be happy, Grant. It's not like I stole someone's identity and cleaned out their bank account."

"Hell, how do I know you didn't? It's not logical, but neither is living out of your car in *Alaska*."

"You really think the worst of me, don't you?"

"Brenna, I . . ." His words trailed off. He honestly didn't know what to say. Her thought process was so completely foreign to him that he didn't even know where to begin. He couldn't process it. And the fact that she didn't see anything wrong with her behavior was even more baffling to him.

"Forget it." She pushed away from him. "I'm not in the mood for sex tonight if you're going to be like this. I can play with my own clit and it won't be bugging me for commitment and stuff. I'll go sleep on the couch in the lodge."

Grant grabbed her arm, halting her. "Wait."

She turned, looking toward him, and he thought she seemed almost . . . hopeful.

"You can't go out there. The others will think we're fighting and it'll get back to my parents."

That hopeful spark on her face died and she rolled her eyes. "Fine. I'll sleep on your couch."

"I'll sleep there," he told her, getting out of bed. "You can sleep in my bed. I'll take the couch."

She rolled her eyes again and thumped down on the side of his bed. "This is not some misplaced sort of chivalry, is it? Because that shit gets tiresome."

"No. I just need to think. Not going to bed yet, which means you can have the bed." He needed to walk around. Exercise. Something. Anything to get his mind off the dark places it was going. Brenna being homeless. Brenna being alone and without a penny to her name in Alaska. Brenna sleeping in a car while it snowed around her.

It was risky. God, he hated risk. He wasn't going to be able to function if he thought about that. Hell, as it was, he wasn't going to be able to sleep. Grant pushed away from the bed, ignoring her small harrumph of irritation, and skidded down the ladder. Time to go work out and take his mind off things.

It was either that, or go and shake her until she started

talking sense. And he suspected that if he did, he'd be shaking her for a long, long time.

She was flying through life without a safety net, and it bothered him. He needed to somehow fix that for her. Protect her from the worst life had to offer. But how?

NINE

Brenna couldn't sleep. It irritated her that she couldn't, that she needed Grant curled up beside her in this lush bed. She was still smarting over his words last night, his shock at the fact that she'd thrown away his unwanted gifts. And she was hurt that he'd somehow taken "living in her car" and turned it into "one step above thievery."

But most of all? She was aroused and incredibly frustrated.

She'd been fantasizing about Grant all day. That was her own fault, really. But when he was working and he'd look up and give her one of those focused looks from behind his glasses? She'd imagine what was going through his mind. Her straddling him while he sat in his desk chair? Throwing her over his desk and pounding into her from behind like he'd done on the couch? Him tossing her onto her back and licking her piercing until she was sobbing his name?

She'd been wet with need all day. And then he'd had to go and ruin it. And now she was sleeping alone in his big, ridiculous cabin filled with ridiculous cluttery decor that wasn't even necessary to survival. Paintings of landscapes and expensive knickknacks and so many dishes that the man could run a kitchen.

And despite all that? She still wanted him.

She'd told him she'd just use her hand, but the fact of the matter was that her hand? Not nearly as fulfilling as Grant. She'd had boyfriends where it had been the opposite—after an unfulfilling round of sex? She'd just work herself over with her fingers and get the orgasm she'd needed and he hadn't provided. But with Grant, she'd had orgasm after orgasm, and she hadn't even had to work that hard for them. It was like he delighted in arousing her beyond capable thought, and then driving her over the edge.

A girl could get addicted to something like that.

If only they weren't fighting over stupid stuff.

Brenna rolled over in the bed, staring out into the darkness, her nipples aching and her thighs slick with her own need. She supposed she could go down to him and apologize. After all, it wasn't a real apology if she didn't believe it, right? Or she could just go downstairs and come onto him and see how things worked out. She wouldn't even have to fake-apologize if her mouth was full of his cock. Then he could apologize to *her* for making this all difficult, and they could get back down to their regular, sex-filled, angst-free relationship.

She liked the thought of that.

Tiptoeing naked out of bed, Brenna winced with every creak of the floorboards and the ladder as she stole into the living room. He was normally a pretty sound sleeper, so she was confident he'd still be crashed.

Except when she leaned over the couch to see his sleeping form, he looked back up at her in surprise, his eyes hollow. "Brenna? What are you doing here? Is something wrong?"

"A little something," she agreed.

He reached for the blankets, alarm on his face. "What is it? Are you hurt? Do you need the hospital?"

What? How had he jumped so quickly to that conclusion? Strange man. She shook her head and sat down on the edge of the couch and then slid over the side, onto her back, landing on him. Her legs were up in the air and she wiggled her toes even as she glanced over at him. Her back was on his hips—not the most comfortable of positions, but she didn't plan on being there long. She slid her hand between her legs and sighed dramatically. "My pussy is *so* wet and there's no one to lick it for me."

His eyes widened and he groaned as if in pain. "God, you don't play fair."

"Is this not fair?" She gave a tiny sigh. "All right. I guess I'll just have to do it myself."

And her hand slipped between her legs and she began to rub. She was so turned on that she couldn't stop the whimper of tormented pleasure that escaped her the moment her fingers brushed up against her clit. Man, she was aroused. She began to slowly, torturously rub, making small noises with every circle of her fingers.

"Goddamn it, Brenna," Grant rasped. He reached for her, then hesitated.

That was agony, too. She arched her back, letting her nipples point into the air. She could feel the heat of him, the erection that was now stabbing against her back. And he wasn't touching her? What more did she need to do? Brenna spread her legs wide and then used her other hand to spread her pussy lips. She licked the fingers of her other hand and then slid them back down to her clit and began to rub some more. Not that she needed the moisture, but it was a showy, delicious gesture, just as much as spreading herself wide was. And as she began to rub herself again, she closed her eyes. "Grant," she moaned deliberately.

She felt him stiffen underneath her, felt the low groan that he was biting back. One warm hand closed over her breast and she gasped when he pinched her nipple, rolling it between his fingers. She began to rub herself harder, her fingers working faster as the shockwaves of pleasure tore through her. Even that small touch was enough to make her crazy with lust. "Grant," she breathed again. "God, I wish you were touching me between my legs. Rubbing me hard so I could come—"

His fingers pinched her breast hard, and when she gave a little gasp of shock, it was followed by a squeal of pleasure when his hand covered hers over her pussy and he began to rub in tandem with her. *Oh yes, that was lovely.* She whimpered when his fingers laced with hers, and then it was two sets of fingers rubbing along her clit, two sets of fingers sliding into the well of her pussy and stroking deep. Two sets of fingers slick with her own juices. Her hips rolled in response to the touch, the mindless orgasm building to a frenzy deep inside her.

She looked over at him and was entranced at the fascination etched on his features. He watched her as she rubbed, the wet, slick noises the only sounds mingling with their breathing. His hand kneaded and rubbed her breast, teasing her nipple even as his other slicked in and out of her pussy. And suddenly, she really, really wanted him deep inside her. Fucking her, on top of her with that same intense look of concentration on his face.

So she stopped rubbing, her hand trapping his. And she met his gaze. "Finish me off the right way?"

His response was to drag himself off the couch, nearly tumbling her to the ground. Then he was back a moment later, a condom in hand. He ripped it open with his teeth and slid it over his cock before she could do more than pick herself up off the ground.

A quiver of excitement rushed through her and she tensed, waiting with anticipation to be tossed back down to the couch and plowed into, her legs trapped between them and knees at her ears.

But to her surprise, he moved close and instead of tossing her down on the couch? He pulled her in and gave her a long, wet, seeking kiss, full of tongue and promise. Brenna nearly melted against the heat of his mouth, the intensity with which he made love to her lips.

He pulled her arm to his neck, and she greedily twined her fingers in the hair at the nape of his neck, loving the feel of him against her. One big hand went to her thigh and hauled her leg up around his hips, and her other arm went to his neck. She clung to him to keep her balance and gasped when he dragged her other leg up around his waist.

They were standing, her hips cradled against his cock, her legs wrapped around him. Her eyes widened as she realized he intended on making love like this. He had to be strong as hell for something like this . . . and the thought was even more arousing.

He kissed her again, then murmured, "Guide me inside you, Brenna. I'll hold you in place."

She whimpered, working her hips against him again, then slid a hand away from his neck. His hands were tight on her thighs, cradling her in place without the slightest hint of her weight slipping. She reached between them, her fingers finding his latex-sheathed cock, and she flexed her own hips. He lifted her, steering a bit as she guided him to her entrance.

And then Grant pushed forward, his cockhead sinking into her warmth. And she was unable to stop the moan that escaped her as her muscles clenched with joy around him. God, this was definitely what she needed. Her hand went back to his neck and she flexed her hips even as he jerked his own, and she felt every inch of him dragging inside her, sliding into her wet, slick pussy.

"Fuck, right there, Brenna. I've got you, sweetheart." His hands dug into her hips, clenching her against him. His feet braced apart as he widened his stance, and then he lifted her hips, dragging her back down against his cock, and she could feel every inch of him.

"Ooh, that's more like it." She clenched her pussy around him as he rocked into her again, her eyes closing with bliss. "If you could just keep doing that all night—"

His rough, choked laugh made her smile. "I'm going to come long before that, Brenna."

"As long as you take me with you," she told him breathlessly.

"Then ride me," he said in a husky voice, and his hands drove her hips down on him again. And again. His movements became rougher and faster, and she whimpered with excitement as his thrusts worked her harder and harder. Every tiny movement rushed through her system in glorious, exquisite sensation. He stroked into her, and then paused. "Look at me, Brenna."

She groaned, digging her nails into his skin in protest. "Why are you stopping?"

"Look at me," he told her. "I want you to see me when you come."

For some reason, just his command to stare at him while he pounded into her felt incredibly intimate. It was like peeling off a layer of privacy, and she kept her eyes squeezed shut for a moment longer, hoping he'd lose his control and start fucking her all over again.

But he didn't. He just waited, his hands dug into her ass, his cock deep inside of her. And she was *squirming* for release.

So she opened her eyes.

He drove into her again, his eyes holding her gaze. The moment was incredibly intense, and she could feel a spark run all the way down to her toes. A gasp escaped her, and she lost herself in his gaze as he continued to thrust into her, a look of such intense concentration on his face that she was aroused all over again.

It was as if Grant existed just to pleasure her. The thought rippled through her a moment before the orgasm did, and she felt her sheath spasm and clench tight, even as he continued to drive into her, that magnetic gaze pinning her. She clung to him, her mouth working silently as the orgasm ripped through her and she lost control.

And as she watched, his jaw clenched tight, and he ground out her name. His fingers dug into her ass and he gave her one last long, rough stroke, staring deep into her eyes—

They both fell to the floor, Grant landing on top of her.

"Ow!" Brenna winced, rubbing her ass and glad for the plush rug covering Grant's floor. "You okay?"

He braced himself on his elbows, and his face was bright red. "I, uh, forgot about muscle control when I came." His cheeks were flushed with embarrassment. "You're not hurt, are you?"

She giggled, the moment so absurd and full of relief after

that intense, locked-eyes orgasm. "Next time, remember to keep your knees locked when you come."

"I'll keep that in mind," he murmured, a sheepish grin on his face.

And suddenly everything was right again in their world. Nothing like a good round of sex to relieve tension. She draped her arms around his neck again and pulled him down for a quick kiss. "Come back to bed with me?"

His gaze searched hers. Whatever he found there, it seemed to please him. He nodded.

Brenna was humming the next day when she went into the main lodge. The sun was shining, birds were singing, and she'd had some pretty awesome sex last night. Life didn't get much better than that.

As if the universe was full of post-coital happiness, Brenna walked in on Dane and Miranda making out at Dane's desk. She was cradled sideways in his lap, her legs crossed and dangling over one side of the chair. His hand was in her shirt and their mouths were glued together. They were so cute when they were horny.

"Morning," Brenna sang out cheerfully. "I see some of us are working up an appetite."

Miranda gasped and tugged her shirt back down, slapping Dane's big paw away. She grinned with relief when she saw it was just Brenna, but she still struggled out of Dane's grasp and sidled away from him. "I just thought I'd come by and see my fiancé before heading off to work for the day. He's going to be gone overnight, so I need to let him know what he's missing."

"Just make sure that his mind is on his class and not your

ass," Brenna quipped. She couldn't help but notice that Miranda was wearing the pretty purple bracelet again. That little tingle of wistfulness touched Brenna, and she forced it away. Give it a few weeks, she told herself, and she wouldn't miss it. It was just stuff.

She hated stuff. Stuff had no use. Stuff just piled up and made a mess. Stuff wasn't real.

Frowning at herself, Brenna thumped into the chair at her own desk . . . and whimpered at the flare of pain that shot up from her backside. She rubbed it with a scowl. It seemed Grant had dropped her harder than she thought. Glancing up, she saw both Miranda and Dane were watching her, Miranda with a look of curious amusement, and Dane with a look of abject horror.

"What?" Brenna said crossly. "Haven't you ever seen a girl rub her ass before?"

"Rough night?" Miranda asked in a silky voice, unable to stop her teasing.

"Ugh, I don't want to hear this," Dane said, grabbing his coffee mug and racing to the kitchen.

So funny. She couldn't help but milk it a bit. "I told Grant he needed to use more lube," Brenna called out in a loud voice as Dane exited the room.

"La la la la can't hear you," he shouted back.

Brenna giggled, and at Miranda's even-more-curious look, she added, "I got dropped on my ass last night."

"Should I guess how?"

"You can guess, but it's pretty obvious," Brenna told her.

"For someone who's been dropped on her butt, you sure seem happy," Miranda told her, smiling. "This little thing you have with Grant seems to be working out well."

"Oh, it's not a thing," Brenna told her. "We're just having some no-strings-attached sex. It's not like we're serious."

"Sure you're not." Miranda didn't look like she bought it for a second. "Can I point out that I'm the genius who tried to have revenge sex with Dane and have it not mean anything? And it totally backfired and I fell for him?"

"Trust me, I have no intention of falling for Grant," Brenna said, her voice cheerfully light as she flipped on her computer. Even as she said it, though, the words were sour in her mouth and she couldn't help but glance around the main lodge. She didn't want Grant hearing those words. Why, she had no idea. So his feelings wouldn't get hurt? She made a face at herself. Like she cared if he started having feelings.

Mental note, she told herself, *do something to annoy Grant today*. It had been a few days since she'd done something like that. Time to remind him that complacency was for wimps.

"Well, I'd love to hear more but I have to run." Miranda grinned at her and headed for the kitchen. "I'm going to want a full recap via email, though."

Brenna gave her a cheerful mock-salute as her friend disappeared into the kitchen to kiss Dane good-bye one last time. Then she got up and approached Grant's desk. Nothing was out of place, his office supplies neatly lined up and organized. His calendar datebook was laid open to the current date, and on impulse, she pulled the page out just because that would irritate him.

Then, guilt nagged her and she put it back. She settled for changing the settings on his ergonomic chair and adjusting the lighting on his monitor. Small, harmless irritations instead of her normal insouciant destruction. Why couldn't she pull off the big ones anymore?

Was she getting soft toward him? Just because he was good in bed? Was she dickmatized? Hell.

Brenna grabbed the ripped-out page, crumpled it into a ball, and tossed it into a nearby wastebasket. *Screw that*.

She worked—okay, emailed some friends in between updating the expenses spreadsheet, but whatever—for about an hour before Grant came in to the main lodge. "You slept late," she commented in a flirty voice. "All worn out?"

"Just thinking."

Uh-oh. She watched him sit down at his desk and didn't even experience a twinge of pleasure when he frowned and adjusted his chair. He was thinking. That was never a good sign. Grant already thought too much as it was. The fact that he'd actually put time aside to think meant that she was not going to be pleased with whatever it was.

When she said nothing, he got up from his desk and moved over to hers. "I'm almost done with the expenses spreadsheet," she told him. "I know it should have been done yesterday, but I was busy."

He shrugged and her hackles went up.

Grant *never* shrugged about expenses. Never.

Brenna watched him with wary eyes as he came and sat on the edge of her desk, next to where she was seated. He sat so close, she could have reached over and jiggled his junk. Heck, maybe she would just to distract him.

"Brenna," he said in a soft voice. "We need to talk."

Oh no. "You're talking right now," she told him casually. "Newsflash."

"I'm being serious."

"You're always serious."

"And you're never serious, which is what brings me back to what I wanted to talk to you about." He adjusted his glasses on his face. "The future."

She groaned. "Again? Do we have to? I thought we were on the same page for once."

"I'm concerned that you don't have a solid life plan.

When you told me you were homeless, I . . ." He shook his head, seemingly unable to continue. "It's unfathomable. You can't coast along in life for the next fifty years."

Actually, she'd kind of planned on doing just that. "I don't see why this is coming up now."

"It's coming up because . . ." He sighed heavily. "I like you and me. Together. In my bed."

"I like it, too. So what's the problem?"

Grant reached out and brushed a lock of purple hair off her forehead. "The problem is that I worry about your safety. And I think of what you did for me—protecting me when you knew I needed it. I want to do the same for you. You're exciting and sexy and just what I need to make me get my head out of the sand. And that's why I think we should get married. So we can continue like this, and even if we decide to go our separate ways later, you'll have safety. Financially, anyway."

She recoiled from his touch, her chair skidding backward a foot. "Did you just propose to me?"

"I did." When she simply stared at him, he continued. "We can look at it as insurance, of a kind. I care for you and don't want you to worry about your financial future. Think of it like . . . a 401(k)."

"A 401(k)," she repeated blankly.

"Yes. You put away money in a 401(k) to save for your future. You could marry me and it'll be an investment in your future. You'd never have to worry about being home-less again. It's a sound decision, if you think about it."

Sound decision? 401(k)? Investment in her future? Was this a marriage proposal or a banking inquiry? Brenna studied him, then forced a pleasant smile to her face. "No, thank you. I'm not interested."

"What do you mean, you're not interested?"

She kept the smile on her face, though it was getting difficult in the face of his disapproval. "I mean just what I said. I don't want to be tied down, and marriage is the ultimate in being tied down."

"It's about security—"

"I'm not interested in that."

"How can you not be?" He didn't seem to grasp it.

"The same way I'm not interested in a relationship with emotions and all that crap," Brenna snapped. "Quit pressuring me."

"I'm not pressuring you. I just want this thing—"

"There is no 'thing' between us," Brenna said. "Unless you mean a sexual free-for-all."

"That's not true—"

She stood up. "Look, Grant. Clearly you're getting confused about the nature of our relationship. I like having sex with you. That's it. No more, no less. I don't want anything from you other than sex. That means no coffee mugs, no bracelets, no panties, and no emotions, all right? Just sex. This thing started out between us because I didn't want anyone harassing you but me, all right? That hasn't changed."

"Just sex," he said flatly. "That's all?"

"That's all," she told him. "And if you want more than that, you've got the wrong girl. I can move out of your cabin if it's making things too difficult."

"No," he said harshly, getting to his feet. "Wouldn't want you to be homeless again."

And he stormed out of the room.

Well, that went well. Brenna sat back down at her desk and stared at her computer screen. She felt . . . weird. Numb. Hollow. Kind of like crying, which was stupid. There were no emotions involved in this, she reminded herself. Just sex.

No one got hurt when it was just sex, right?

Grant ignored her for the rest of the day. She told herself that it was what she wanted, anyhow. She needed a break from him, so she'd snagged Rome on his way into the main lodge and decided to train him on how to drive an ATV. They spent the day riding up and down the trails, and delivering paintball equipment to Dane's crew out in the woods so they could get their game in. The paintball team games were popular with all of the visitors, so they made sure every group had at least one run. Rome was helpful passing out guns and paint ammo and listening to her instructions as if she were spouting gold. He already seemed to be friendly with Dane. Then again, everyone got along with Dane.

When she couldn't stand waiting any longer, she eventually headed back to the main lodge and parked her ATV in the garage. She didn't even have the heart to tinker with it to give Pop something to do. She was too distracted. She might have said she was depressed, but she wasn't letting emotion get to her.

Why did Grant have to go and ruin a perfectly fun relationship? Count on him to take something that was so enjoyable and turn it. She should have known better than to get involved with him.

But you're not involved, that little voice in her head said. That was the problem, according to Grant.

When she got back to the main lodge, the lights were off and the room was dark. She frowned, glancing at the clock. It was just a hair past five. Normally everyone hung out and worked late. Grant sure did. But tonight he was nowhere to be seen. Had he gone home without her?

"It's *not* home," she muttered to herself as she sat down at her desk. Great. Now he had her saying that stuff, too.

Her message light was flickering, and she picked up the phone and hit the voicemail button.

"Brenna, this is Justine," a sweet voice said. "I just talked to Grant, and he sounded so sad. He told me you two had been fighting and, well, I just wanted to call and ask if you were okay."

Brenna softened at that. She should have been annoyed at Grant's mom interfering with their relationship—*it's not a relationship*, she reminded herself—but it was nice that Justine was checking in on her and seeing if *she* was okay.

"Grant can be a little difficult at times," Justine continued. "And a little pigheaded when he gets his heart set on something. But his heart's in the right place, you know. Ever since Heather died . . . well. I don't want to talk about her to you. But I wanted to tell you that he seems happier and more alive with you than he has been since he was with her. Since before that, actually. Not that Heather was a bad girl. She just wasn't right for him. But you're good for him, you know. And I don't want you to give up on him too soon. Both Reggie and I like you enormously, and Elise does, too. We'd love for you to be a permanent fixture in Grant's life."

And just like that, her emotional pleasure at Justine's kindness popped like a bubble. Permanent fixture in Grant's life, eh?

She deleted the rest of the message without listening to it. Brenna wanted to be no one's permanent fixture. She grabbed a decorative woven throw blanket off the back of the couch and curled up with it, turning on the TV. She'd be sleeping here tonight, if only to prove a point.

TEN

Two days later, Brenna was feeling . . . unhappy.

It wasn't something she liked to admit to herself. She liked having no worries, no cares, no ties to anything. The reason why she liked this job so much? No responsibility and being surrounded by friends. She could pack up her car and leave the next day and it wouldn't matter much to anyone but Dane and Colt, who treated her like their wacky kid sister. Rome pretty much kept to himself or stuck to Pop's side, since the elderly man was showing him how to do maintenance and get familiar with the area.

Since Grant was ignoring her and the others were out? That meant the days were long. And it made her restless and miserable. Before, she and Grant had a strange kind of friendly rivalry. Coworkers who didn't necessarily like each other but had to get along. Now? They got along just fine because he didn't talk to her except to answer pointed questions. If she asked what the weather was going to be like, he'd say "cloudy." If she asked if he had work for her, he'd say "no." If she asked him if he wanted to go grab dinner, he'd given her a look that told her just what he thought of that suggestion.

Brenna had never really bought into the theory that sex ruined everything. Sex was awesome, unless it sucked, so how could it possibly ruin a friendship?

Except now she knew better.

She hadn't realized until now that she had feelings for him. Not love and smoochiness—she refused to feel that way about anyone—but real affection and friendship. Tied in with the sex? It was almost like a real relationship.

And that freaked her out.

More so considering that she didn't have any of that affection or friendship anymore.

She had slept on the couch in the lodge the last two days. At first she'd been fine with it, since she'd slept on more couches in her life than real beds. But sleeping on a couch after sleeping next to a big warm body? Not fun. And the couch here in the lodge had been chosen for looks instead of comfort. It was a rustic-looking couch, with leather seats and wooden arms and legs. It also gave her the worst crick in the neck. She was getting soft.

And if she was honest with herself? She missed the sex. A lot.

Grant was the best she'd ever had, and she'd had more than her fair share (though she hadn't mentioned that to Grant, and he hadn't asked). She'd loved his attentiveness in bed and the way that he acted as if she was constantly blowing his mind. She had to admit, she was a fan of that, too. She even liked his possessive hovering before and after, the way he liked to touch her constantly, the way he picked out clothes for her or made her a snack, or held her in the shower so she could rinse off when she was too boneless from multiple orgasms to stand up on her own.

But those weren't things that fit into the Brenna lifestyle. Things like relationships fell into the same category as stuff. It was good for other people, but had no value in her life. The fact that she'd somehow gotten dragged into a quasi-relationship bothered her. She was the one who would be free-spirited and independent forever.

So yeah, sex had ruined everything.

Which stank because she really, really wanted more sex. Why couldn't Grant humor her in such a small request?

As if her turbulent thoughts had brought him into the office, Grant came through the front door of the lodge, dropping his keys into a nearby bowl and shaking off his raincoat. It was a drizzly day and Colt and Dane were running Rome through his paces before taking his first class out in two days. The weather was nasty but they thought it was perfect, since part of the survival school package was that you didn't get to pick your weather. It was just Brenna in the lodge.

And she hadn't realized how lonely it had been until Grant walked in and she felt herself light up. She straightened in her chair. "Hey, how's the weather?"

He glanced at her. "Wet."

"You want some coffee? I just made some."

"No." He moved past her, shaking out the dampness from his dark hair and heading to his desk.

"You going to work for a few hours?"

"Depends."

"On?"

"Nothing important." He flipped through his mail and then tossed it down on his desk. He sat down in his chair and stared at his desk drawer for a moment, and her heart thudded. Was he thinking about the picture of Heather that he had hidden away in there? But to her relief, he pulled out a letter opener and began to slit open an envelope.

Relief escaped her in a sigh.

Grant glanced up. "What?"

"Nothing." She bit her lip. This was not working. Even watching his hands as he went through the mail was making her ache. Stupid man, depriving them both of sex because there weren't any feelings attached. So she had to offer. "You know what would be good right now?"

He looked up from his desk. "What?"

"A nice, steamy orgasm." Brenna put her chin on her fists and had a dreamy look on her face. "I sure could go for a deep dicking right about now."

He stared at her for so long and was so quiet that she couldn't tell what he was thinking.

"Well?" she asked him.

"You're serious?" he said slowly, gaze on her.

"I am."

"You moved out."

"So? That shouldn't have anything to do with whether or not we have sex. You're good at sex. Why can't we have some nice, passionate, vulgar sex without involving anything else?"

He was going to turn her down. She just knew it. She'd given him a challenge—to be no strings attached—and she knew he'd pass on it.

"Fine."

Brenna blinked in surprise. "Really?"

"Really," he said, getting up from his desk. "You want no strings attached? That's fine with me."

"Great," she said enthusiastically, bounding over to his desk. She slid her arms around his neck and reached up for a kiss.

He gently pushed her away. "No kissing. Too much attachment there."

"Oh." For some reason, that hurt. But she pulled away and nodded. "That's fine." Her hand slid to his groin and she cupped him. "Want to be naughty and fuck on the couch? No one's around today."

"Fine with me."

She grabbed his hand and led him to the sofa. When she got there, she pushed at his shoulders, moving him down to the couch so she could straddle him. Excitement was pulsing through her, and she slid onto his lap, her legs spread wide over him and her face inches from his.

He wouldn't look her in the eyes. His hands grabbed ahold of her hips and he pushed her down into his lap, grinding his cock against the vee of her sex. But he wouldn't look at her.

That was fine, she'd make him look. Brenna dragged off her top and tossed it onto the couch. She wasn't wearing a bra underneath, since it was a loose top and there was no one around today. Her breasts bounced and jiggled an inch from his face.

And that got his attention. Dark eyes gazed on the flesh she was practically shoving in his face, and he leaned in and lightly bit at the curve of one breast.

Brenna moaned, her hips bucking against him. This was what she needed.

"Take the rest of your clothes off," he told her, his lips moving against her flesh.

She nodded and slid off his lap, quickly shucking her pants. She was now naked of everything except her socks, but she didn't want to bother with those. She just wanted to crawl back into his lap and feel his skin against hers. So she did, straddling him again.

His hand slid between them and his fingers brushed between her legs, heading for her piercing, and began to toy with it.

She moaned in response, arching against his hand. Oh God, that felt so good. Her fingers dug into his shirt and she clung to him, riding against his fingers.

"Get undressed, Grant," she murmured as he continued to finger her. "Want to feel you against me."

"Shhh," he said, and rubbed hard against her clit.

She cried out at the sensation, arching against him, and forgot about everything but his fingers against her flesh. He stroked her slippery folds, rubbing her, and then slid two fingers deep into her sheath. Brenna gave a startled gasp at the sensation. It felt incredible. His thumb slid to her clit even as his fingers stroked inside her, and then he began to work her, stroking deep and brushing against her clit with his thumb. She moved her hips in time with his strokes, lost to the feel of him. She buried her head against his neck, clinging to him, lifting her hips with violence and slamming onto his hand. She needed more, needed him, needed so much that she ached. "Grant," she moaned. "Grant, please fuck me."

"Shh," he told her again.

He continued to work her with his hand until she could stand it no longer. A choked moan escaped her again, and then she was coming, shivers all over her body as she clenched and clenched around his pumping fingers. "Grant," she panted. "Oh God, Grant. Yes."

Then his hand slipped from her thighs, and she was left clenching at nothing, her arms wrapped tight around his shoulders. The only sound in the lodge was the soft patter of rain and her own heavy breathing. Grant was utterly silent.

She sat up, studying him. His expression was shuttered, impossible to read. Brenna ran a hand along the front of his button-up shirt. "Let's get you out of these clothes—"

His hand closed over hers before she could undo the first button. "No."

"No?" She blinked at him, surprised. "I thought we were having sex?"

"You said you wanted no strings attached, right?" He shrugged his shoulders, a careless move so at odds with the Grant she knew. "Are you satisfied?"

By a little heavy petting? Yes, and no. Yes, because it quenched the itch, but it also left her wanting more. Wanting him. She frowned at him. "That wasn't really sex."

"That's the only 'no strings' I know how to do," he said in a cold voice. "Sorry. And if we're done, I'm going to go change my clothes."

She reeled as if stung. *If we're done?* "What about you?"

"I'm fine."

"Oh." She moved off him—she couldn't move off him fast enough. Brenna found her shirt and dragged it back on, then began to slide on her jeans. She didn't look at him. Couldn't. A weird sense of humiliation was sweeping over her. He'd basically diddled her just to shut her up. How cold was that?

She zipped her jeans and turned around . . . but he was gone. She was the only one in the lodge.

Oh good. That meant she could cry now. Brenna burst into tears without really understanding why she was so upset, then grabbed her car keys.

She needed to talk to someone. Maybe Miranda wasn't busy at the library.

Grant shut the door to his cabin and leaned against it, groaning with pain.

He felt like the world's biggest asshole. The biggest asshole with the world's biggest hard-on. What he'd done to

Brenna was cold. He'd known it was cold, but he couldn't help himself. She wanted no-strings sex? He'd do his best to make sure she was satisfied and nothing more. Maybe then she'd see how much it hurt him that she didn't want anything with him—even a casual relationship. Even sleeping in the same damn bed. They didn't have to get married, but she also didn't have to throw everything in his face.

Just like the way he'd done to her.

He leaned back, knocking his head against the door. Stupid. Stupid. Whatever he'd had with Brenna? He'd pretty much trashed it just now, and he was the only one suffering for it. His hand was still slick from her warmth, still smelled like her warm, wet pussy. The front of his pants was tight from his own erection and damp from her arousal. What exactly had he been trying to prove to anyone except that he was a jackass when his feelings were hurt?

He tore at the waistband of his pants, suddenly desperate to free his erection. Jerking himself off after he'd had a sexy, willing woman in his lap seemed like a fitting punishment. He shoved his pants down, then his boxers, and his cock sprung free. He grasped it in his hand, and then paused.

He lifted his fingers to his face and dragged them across his lips. Brenna's salty, delicious taste filled his mouth and nostrils, and he groaned hard, stroking his cock. Within three beats, he climaxed, cum splattering on the hardwood floors.

Fuck this whole "sex without entanglements" thing. Why was it when he tried to give a woman issue-free sex, he ended up feeling more mixed up than before?

Brenna wandered into the Bluebonnet library a short time later, pushing her wet hair out of her eyes and shivering, her shirt plastered to her skin.

"Oh my God," Miranda said, hurrying out from behind the checkout counter. "Brenna! Are you okay?"

"Just fine," Brenna said, but there was a glum note in her voice. "It's raining outside. Kinda cold."

"Well, you're dripping water!" Miranda exclaimed. She fluttered closer, wearing a tight pencil skirt and a filmy white blouse and that damned purple bracelet. "Where's your jacket?"

"I don't have one."

Miranda gave her an odd look, and then gestured at her. "Wait right there and don't drip on any periodicals." She disappeared into her office and then returned a moment later with a fluffy gray cable-knit cardigan. "Here. I keep this at work in case the air-conditioning's too cold, but you need it more than I do."

"Thanks." Brenna took it and dragged her arms through the sweater and wrapped it tight around her. "I think I'm having a bad day." And to her horror, tears began to streak down her face again.

"Oh, oh no. Please don't cry. I'm not good at comforting." Miranda wrung her hands. "Do you want me to call Beth Ann? She's better at this sort of thing than I am."

"No, I'm fine." Brenna sniffed loudly. "Honest."

Miranda's big brown eyes stared at her, frozen. Then, she glanced around the small, narrow library and then gestured at Brenna. "No one's here. Come in my office and we can talk. I'll make you a hot tea."

Brenna shuffled behind Miranda, her canvas shoes squishing and wet. She sank down into the chair across from Miranda's desk, which was stacked high with books. Miranda turned and pushed a coffee mug under the percolator and hit a few buttons. A long moment passed and neither woman said anything, the only sound that of brewing tea.

"So," Miranda said, finally handing her the steaming mug. "You want to talk about it?"

Brenna wrapped her hands around the cup and sighed. Part of her didn't want to talk about it, and part of her wanted to weep out her troubles. "Have you ever had a friends-with-benefits scenario?"

"Friends with benefits?" Her eyes widened and Miranda twisted the pretty purple bracelet on her wrist absently. "I . . . well, not really? When I first started sleeping with Dane, I didn't even really consider him a friend. Just a lay, you know?" Her cheeks pinked at the thought.

"Yes, exactly!" Brenna set the mug down. "How did that work out for you? Just having sex?"

"Not so well," Miranda said with a laugh, grabbing a stack of books and flipping open the cover of the first one. She began to press stickers inside it and wrote something on the cover, clearly readying it for circulation. "I got all attached and mad at myself because I didn't want to be attached."

Brenna frowned. That wasn't the answer she'd been hoping to hear. The opposite, actually. "So what did you do?"

"Do?" Miranda giggled and looked all lovesick for a moment. "We moved in together. Turned out I wasn't the only one that couldn't have sex without getting attached."

Brenna made a face. "But what if you don't want to get attached? Aren't men supposed to like not being tied down?"

"Most men would," Miranda agreed. "But we're talking about Grant here, right? The man's more loyal than a Doberman. He hasn't dated since his wife died, remember? Why would you think he'd be a good choice for some no-strings-attached sex?"

Gritting her teeth in frustration, Brenna did admit that Miranda had a point. When it came to choices for a quick shag, Grant wouldn't have been high on anyone's list. So why was she so determined to sleep with him? It couldn't have been because she had feelings for him, could it? *Ugh*. She was so confused. "He asked me to marry him," Brenna said sourly.

Miranda gasped. "Oh my God. He did?" Her face lit up, and then she narrowed her eyes at Brenna. "You don't seem excited about it."

"That's because I'm not. It was the most unromantic proposal ever!" Brenna sipped the hot tea. "He came to my desk and went on and on about responsibility and safety and how he'd take care of me since it was clear that I couldn't even take care of myself. So to do me a favor, he was going to marry me and make me his little woman." She rolled her eyes at the thought and took another sip of tea. "He didn't even bother to propose with a ring."

Silence. She peeked at Miranda over the rim of her mug. The librarian was watching her with a curious look, squinting as if she was trying to make out Brenna. Her long, straight brown hair slid over the shoulder of her cream blouse.

"What?" Brenna mumbled.

"I'm confused," Miranda said, flipping the book shut and placing it atop a pile, and then moving to the next one. She opened it and then began to sticker it. "I thought you wanted no-commitment sex?"

"I do."

"So why are you mad that he gave you an unromantic proposal and no ring?"

"Because that's not how you do it! If you're going to crap things up with a proposal, you might as well make it a good one."

Miranda's lips twitched. "But maybe the no ring, no emotions proposal is Grant's way of being no strings attached. You never know."

Brenna considered this. "Or maybe the man just wants to be married again."

Miranda began to say something, then changed her mind, shaking her head. "I just wonder that this isn't a conversation you should have had with Grant."

"I'm not talking to him right now. I'm actually pretty mad at him."

"Dare I ask?"

Brenna considered, wondering how much to share. Beth Ann and Miranda were close friends and had been since grade school. Brenna felt a bit like an outsider when the two of them were together, but they were also her closest girlfriends since moving to Bluebonnet. How much did Miranda want to know? "You sure you want details?"

Miranda gave a firm nod. "I can't help if I don't know what's going on. And you've been crying, which makes me want to go and kick Grant in the nuts on your behalf."

"Okay, but you can't tell Dane."

That made Miranda pause and she gave a heavy sigh. "Fine. I won't tell Dane."

Brenna fiddled with one of the sleeves of the sweater, adjusting it so she wouldn't have to meet Miranda's knowing gaze. "Grant proposed to me a few days ago and when I said no, I started sleeping apart from him. Today, I told Grant I wanted no-strings sex, right? So I approached him for sex and he said it was fine. Except all he did was finger me until I came, and then asked me to get off him."

Miranda's jaw dropped.

Brenna felt a little better about things at seeing her reaction. Okay, so maybe she *wasn't* crazy for feeling all hurt and emotional. "He wouldn't even kiss me. Didn't come, either. Just told me that if I wanted unemotional sex, he was more than willing to lend me a hand, but that was the only involvement he wanted." She frowned in memory. "I wanted sex, not a human vibrator."

Miranda was quiet for a moment, and then said thoughtfully, "Unless he was shaking all over, he'd be more like a human dildo."

"Har de har. You know what I mean."

"I do, and wow. That was kind of cold of Grant. I'm honestly surprised. He seems like the least likely type to pull a douche move like that."

"I know," Brenna said, and her tone was miserable. "And now I feel like shit. He's ruined everything. Even orgasms."

Miranda thought for a long moment, toying with the ends of her long hair. Then she glanced over at Brenna again. "You want my opinion? Honest, no holds barred?"

"I think I do? Unless you plan on making me cry, too."

She chuckled. "Not my game plan."

"Then go for it."

"I think he probably doesn't realize how much he hurt you." Miranda's voice was soft, as if she were reluctant to deliver bad news. "You have to remember that Grant's been wallowing in five years of self-torment and misery because of how Heather died. He's always going to think that he's the problem in a relationship—any kind of relationship," she added quickly when it seemed as if Brenna would protest the state of their "friendship." "And here's the thing. You're so happy and nonchalant most of the time that you probably come across as not caring about anything. And I don't think that's true. I think you care, but I think you try to hide it. Maybe you don't want to care, but it's clear to me that you do. You need to show Grant how much he hurt you and I think you'll see him falling all over himself to apologize."

"So basically, go to him and start the waterworks?"

Miranda laughed. "That's one way of putting it. But you

could always try to just have a sensible conversation about how you do have feelings and he trampled all over them because you turned down his proposal. His rather impromptu proposal, I might add. I mean, you said that you two have been sleeping together for a while, but still . . . that's kind of moving fast."

"Really fast," Brenna muttered. So she might have told a little white lie about the timeframe. Miranda would definitely not understand Grant if Brenna confessed the truth and that they'd only started sleeping together when his parents had come into town. She felt weird about defending him, though. He kept messing things up for them. And yet . . . what if he honestly thought he was giving her what she asked for?

It was a mess no matter how she looked at it. Brenna rubbed her forehead. "Jeez, all I wanted was to pretend to be a guy's girlfriend and have some kinky sex. Is that too much to ask for?"

"Apparently." Miranda's mouth twitched with amusement. "Did you want to check out the library's copy of the *Kama Sutra*?"

She thought about it for a moment. "Actually, yes. I think I would."

ELEVEN

Grant's car wasn't in the parking lot when she pulled up to the lodge. He must have been visiting his family. That suited her just fine. She avoided the main lodge and headed straight to his cabin, letting herself in. She found a fluffy stack of towels and a bathrobe, so she took a shower and then wrapped herself in his bathrobe and toweled her hair dry. Then she sat down on his couch to wait for his return, idly flipping through the pages of the *Kama Sutra*. Who knew that a picture book would have so many words in it?

Her hair was almost dry when she heard the sound of steps on the gravel path, and she opened to a specific page, then glanced over at the door.

When Grant walked in and saw her in his bathrobe, reading a book, he looked momentarily dumbfounded. Then he frowned. "What are you doing?"

She held up the book. "Reading."

"No, I mean . . . what are you doing here? I thought you moved out." He set his keys down on a nearby table and approached her.

She shrugged. "My grand plan of living in the main lodge didn't involve a shower. Hope you don't mind."

"Of course I don't mind. You know my home is open to you." That husky, affectionate note had returned to his voice, and just hearing it made her skin prickle with awareness. He moved forward, and then paused. "What are you reading?"

"Oh, this old thing?" Brenna waved the book idly. "Just brushing up. Did you know there's a position in which a man windmills around while the woman bounces on his dick? I can't say I'd ever want to try that one, but I'm open to a few of these others. I've bookmarked a few pages." She held it up and showed him several dog-eared pages, and then added in a silky voice, "Not that you care about that."

"Brenna." He sat down on the edge of the couch, near where her feet were. "I'm sorry about earlier."

"You should be. You hurt my feelings." To her horror, tears started to form and she blinked rapidly, trying to quell the onslaught. "If I wanted a mount, I'd just buy a dildo. Understand?"

He sighed and moved closer. "Don't cry, Brenna. I never meant to hurt you. I was just . . . frustrated. And I took it out on you. I'm sorry."

"I just . . ." She sniffed, then swiped at her nose with one hand. "I just don't understand why we can't do things simple. Why we can't just enjoy each other without having to make it about more. I just like being with you. Why do you have to change that?"

"We don't," Grant murmured, pulling her close. "I like

having you around. I don't want that to change. It's just my nature to try and protect you."

"Can you be a little less protective and a little more open to less commitment?"

"If that means we have to have wild, meaningless sex, then that's what we'll do."

She sniffed against his chest. "Good."

He stroked her hair. "Does this mean you're coming back to bed with me?"

"Is it a no-strings-attached bed?"

"It can be."

"Then yes."

Grant grinned, brushing the backs of his fingers along her jaw. "Do you want to go to that no-strings-attached bed right now?"

"I don't see why not." She tilted her head, as if pretending to consider things. "I'm already dressed for it."

"It looks like you're dressed for a bath."

"I can fix that." She stood up and shrugged the robe to the floor, then delicately stepped out of it. "You coming?"

"Hell yes," he said, following her behind the ladder.

Brenna shimmied up the ladder to the loft, trying not to be distracted by how he reached out and caressed her ass repeatedly while she did so. By the time she made it to the bed, she was turned on, but wary. Was Grant really going to give her what she wanted, or was he going to hurt her feelings again?

She turned to face him and noticed that Grant was still dressed, though he'd taken off his glasses and had tossed them onto a nearby bureau. "You going to get naked with me this time?"

"Absolutely."

He began to unbutton his shirt, and she sat on the edge

of the bed and watched him, waiting. She wanted to help him undress, but she needed to see that he was going to give her this much, at least. Their last sexual encounter still weighed heavily on her mind, when he hadn't given her anything.

Grant finished undressing and instead of folding his clothes like he normally did, he kicked them aside. Then he was naked in front of her, and she reached out to touch him, unable to help herself. Her fingers smoothed over his chest hair and rubbed down the light line of hair that led to his groin.

"I'm glad you and I are better," she told him with a soft, pleased sigh, her fingers cupping his balls.

"Me too," he murmured, and he wrapped an arm around her waist, dragging her close. One hand went to cup her breast, and he thumbed her nipple. "So, did you find any positions in that book that didn't involve commitment from the partners?"

"Hmm. Doggy style?"

"I like doggy style," he said, leaning in to kiss her.

She tilted her face up for his kiss, and he brushed his lips over hers in a tender, almost butterfly-gentle kiss. He feathered his lips over hers, as if merely tasting her was enough, and the tenderness in the small caress was enough to make her toes curl.

"I need to make up for what I didn't give you last night," he murmured against her mouth. His hand slid up to cup the back of her head and then he was kissing her deep, his tongue sweeping against hers in a kiss that claimed as much as it pleasured. She moaned and leaned into the kiss, feeling shivers run up and down her body. And he kissed her endlessly, as if nothing existed but her mouth and her tongue, and they were there simply for his pleasure. When the kiss finally broke an eternity later, she was left panting and breathless. "Better?"

"Much," she said with a sigh.

"That was a no-strings-attached kiss."

"Mmm, those are my favorite kind." Hell, she was so thoroughly kissed she doubted she could even stand up straight.

He chuckled. "I figured as much." His hand slid between them, caressing the mound of her sex. "Is this ready for some no-commitment cock?"

"Oooh, it was born ready," she purred. "Though I don't mind if you keep giving it some no-commitment rubbing."

Grant's fingers slipped deeper, rubbing her piercing and clit. "Better?"

"Just like that," she breathed. "You know just how to touch me, don't you?"

"I do," he told her, an intense look in his eyes. "I watch everything you do. I see how you react. It's how it teaches me what you like."

A man who thought about what she liked in bed? Novel. "And what do you like?"

"Touching you."

"Oooh, good answer." She shivered when his fingers rolled her piercing against her clit. "Really good answer."

He leaned in and kissed her again. "I need to get a condom."

She nodded, her own need building even as his hand slipped away. She couldn't resist a small whimper of protest when he disappeared into the bathroom and emerged a moment later, condom in hand.

He returned to her side and brushed a hand over her ass.

"Get on the bed and on your knees. In a totally non-commitment way, of course."

"One non-committed pony ride coming right up," she teased. She moved onto the edge of the bed and went on her hands and knees.

Grant moved behind her. His hand slid between her legs and he began to rub her pussy again, until she was following the stroke of his hand and rearing backward with every touch.

"You wet for me?"

"As if you can't tell?" She was so slick and wet for him.

He slipped a finger deep and made a sound of pleasure. "Very wet."

She squirmed against his hand. "I need that non-committed cock inside me, Grant. Not your fingers."

"I can do that." He slid his hands to her ass cheeks and pulled her thighs further apart, until she was falling forward on the bed. And as soon as her chin hit the blankets, he was pushing into her, his cock sliding home.

Brenna moaned, clutching at the blankets. "Oh, Grant. That feels so good."

He pulled back, his hands clutching at her hips, and then he drove into her again. Then again, and again, until he was slamming into her with every quick, deep thrust. There was no control in his stroke, no leashed energy. He poured everything he had into each thrust into her body, and the intensity of the fucking made her toes curl.

And then his hand slid to the front of her and he began to play with her clit, even as he continued to thrust raggedly and wildly into her.

She came with a choked cry, her entire body tightening with the hard rush of need coursing through her. He bit back a curse and came as well, his strokes into her slowing down until he collapsed on the bed next to her. She could hear the snap of rubber as he took off the condom, and then he pulled her down next to him.

They lay there, panting for a moment. That had been a quick and dirty fuck, Brenna mused, but a good one. She was pleased.

"Well," Grant breathed. "That was certainly meaningless, wasn't it?"

She giggled. "Completely and utterly."

His arm wrapped around her and he dragged her in for a hug, and she snuggled into his arms, her eyes closing in utter bliss and relaxation.

Well, at least now he knew how Brenna ticked, Grant mused as he held her against him while she slept. Her purple bangs tickled his chin, but he didn't brush them away. She was sleeping soundly, her arms curled around him, and he'd be damned if he woke her up.

Her in his arms? Felt right. Their fun but slightly edgy sex? Felt right. The fact that Brenna had been wounded because he'd given her exactly what she'd asked for—just sex? Meant that she felt things for him. Probably the same torrent of emotions that he was feeling.

But instead of embracing them like he did, she preferred to pretend that they didn't exist.

Which wasn't ideal, but at least now he knew how to handle things. For starters, he wouldn't go around declaring that they should get married. Instead, he'd simply let Brenna call all the shots. His thumb brushed over one of her tattoos, grazing the soft skin.

If she felt like she was in control of things, she wouldn't get skittish. And if this thing between them continued to work out? They'd fall into a lifestyle so easily that Brenna wouldn't realize that she'd fallen into a committed relationship until it was too late.

Grant grinned. It was committed all right. He was crazy about her, completely and utterly crazy. The part of him that he'd thought was dead and gone after Heather had died? Wasn't dead at all. It was alive and kicking and full of piss and vinegar, especially when Brenna was around. Just being close to her made his heart race and made his protective feelings come to the forefront. He was in love with her. She was easy to love, with her happy smiles and carefree attitude.

But he couldn't tell her that, of course. He'd just go on letting her believe that what they had was nothing but meaningless fun for him, too.

Whatever it took to keep her in his arms? He'd do it.

Elise waited in the living room of the main lodge that served as the headquarters of the survival school. To pass the time, she checked her camera gear for the millionth time. It was a familiar and soothing sort of ritual, and was great for occupying her hands—and her gaze—when she was in uncomfortable situations.

Not that this was an uncomfortable situation at the moment. There was no one in the lodge, so there was no need to be nervous, but she'd been left in here by herself long enough that she was starting to get anxious. Where had Brenna run off to? Her brother's quirky girlfriend had mentioned something about finding her a test subject, and then had ran off, leaving her alone in the lodge.

She said she hadn't minded, but leaving her alone for an hour? She was going to lose the best light if they didn't get started soon. Elise frowned to herself and moved to one of the large windows, judging by the clouds in the sky. The best time to start shooting would be soon, if they didn't—

"You lost, Little Bo Peep?"

Elise gasped and turned, her hair whirling around her face. Someone was here. She saw the large, tattooed man who they'd just hired and her entire body shrank a bit. He was gorgeous and intimidating and looked just a bit wild—which meant that she wasn't able to look him in the eye. She was bad about that sort of thing. "B-b-bo Peep?"

He strode forward, and she was pretty sure he was smiling at her . . . or at least, she assumed that since she wouldn't look at him. "Yeah," he said. "You know. Little Bo Peep has lost her sheep and all that. Just kinda sprung to my head because you look all lost."

Oh. She didn't know what to say to that. Nothing clever sprang to mind. So she did what she did best—stared down at her shoes and wished the floor would swallow her up. *Stunning conversation there, Elise*, she told herself. *Just blow him away with your wittiness, why don't you.*

But it was hard to be witty around beautiful men. As a photographer and an artist (at least, she liked to think of her photography as art), she had a healthy appreciation for beauty and form. The fact that this tattooed man was sinfully gorgeous and moved like a dancer? Only fed her fantasies. She tried to remember his name and drew a blank. Something exotic and strong and elegant, like him. She hadn't thought to memorize it, though, because she'd figured she'd never need it.

Men like him didn't talk to girls like her. Self-conscious,

she let her hair swing in front of her face and straightened her shoulders again, careful to tilt the left one higher.

Silence fell in the lodge. Elise continued to stare at the floor, wishing that she could think of something to say to him that would be witty and clever, or outrageous and daring like Brenna. Heck, even something about the weather would be nice. But nothing came to mind at all, and so she began to pray for someone to return and distract him so she could admire him covertly from afar.

No rescue came.

"You're scared of me. It's obvious." His voice was scathing.

"I—" Her voice died into a squeak as she looked up at him. She wasn't scared of him. He was just way out of her league. He was stunningly beautiful, and he'd never look at a girl like her twice. "I'm not scared."

"Then why won't you look at me?"

Because you might see my scars. She forced herself to keep her gaze on his face, since he seemed offended by any less. And her heart fluttered when his hard mouth curved a bit on one side, hinting at a smile. It tugged at the piercing on his lip in the sexiest way.

"Not scared," she blurted again.

"You shy then, Bo Peep?"

Shy was only the tip of the iceberg. But it was hard to describe exactly how she was feeling when her tongue was locked to the roof of her mouth. She averted her eyes again, only to have her gaze alight on those arms corded with dark tattoos. His entire look was one of roguishness and utter sexiness. Totally forbidden.

Totally hot. He'd be in her dreams tonight, that was for sure, provided that she allowed herself to fantasize about a man like him being interested in a mouse like her.

He chuckled. "I'm going to guess that's a yes."

"Yes," she said, and the word was so quiet that she cringed internally.

"You don't have to be shy around me," he said easily. "I'm not anyone important."

Just the most stunning man who's ever talked to me, she thought to herself, but said nothing aloud.

The front door to the lodge banged, and Elise jumped backward a step, retreating away from him. Brenna wandered in.

"Well, Elise," she began, undoing the chin strap of her bright pink ATV helmet as she strode to her desk. "They're all in hiding from me, so unless you want Pop, we're going to have to do this thing without a model—" She stopped in her tracks at the sight of Rome and a beaming smile crossed her face. "Why, lookie there." Her tone became sugary sweet. "Hello, Rome, you sweet thing you." Brenna sashayed over, grinning like a madwoman. "Did Elise already tell you that she needs a man?"

Oh no. Elise felt her face get hot. She stared at the floor again, wishing it would swallow her up. Did Brenna have to word it like that? It made her sound desperate and lonely.

Not that she wasn't, of course. She just didn't want it to *sound* like she was.

"A man, huh?" Rome's voice sounded amused, but he wasn't laughing at her at least.

"For her photo shoot. She needs a male model and Dane and Colt are hiding out from us. You want to volunteer?"

Volunteer? Elise wanted to protest. Rome made her too uncomfortably aware of who and what he was. She needed someone like Dane, who she'd known since grade school and thought of more like a brother than a grown man. Or Colt, who'd be all business the entire time and never make her feel uncomfortable. Not Rome with his gorgeous eyes and long lashes and dark tattoos and that sexy lip ring. She had to concentrate for her photos and if he was distracting her, she'd get nothing but lousy shots.

And she really should have said some of this aloud. But her tongue remained glued to the roof of her mouth and she gave Brenna a mute look of appeal.

"Is this part of my new job?" Rome asked. "Cause if so, I suppose I don't mind."

"It is," Brenna told him firmly, her voice cheerful. "We require all our men to strip down and oil up."

"This a survival business or a strip joint?"

"Which one did you want it to be?" Brenna teased him.

Elise stood by mutely, listening to their banter. Brenna was so easy with Rome—so easy with all the guys, actually. Elise was wildly jealous of her. Not only was she pretty, she was fun and outgoing. Elise was none of those things.

Brenna could get a man like Rome. Not Elise. Boring, plain, unable to speak to men Elise.

"You sure you want to take pictures of me? I'm not exactly clean-cut," Rome said, and his hand went to his flat stomach and he idly scratched it.

"You don't have any scary tats, do you?" Brenna asked bluntly. "No obscene pickle-fucking or racist symbols or anything?"

Rome snorted. "Hell no."

"I think we'll need to see some proof," Brenna told him, and moved to Elise's side, elbowing her in camaraderie. "Right, Elise?"

A small squeak that might have been assent escaped her throat.

Rome looked over at her. "Was that a yes?"

She looked back at Brenna with mute appeal. But when

there was no help coming from that quarter, she turned back to Rome. "Um . . . okay?"

"All right, then." He reached for the hem of his tight shirt and pulled it out of his jeans, then dragged it over his head.

Elise was struck dumb at the sight of him without his shirt on. Big, brawny shoulders framed flat pectorals and washboard abs. A large, dark series of lines covered the front of his chest, going from collarbone down to below his pectorals. Skulls, knives, and other symbols were woven into the intricate design. It wasn't typical, but she was fascinated by it. And by him.

"Hmm. I don't know if that's too much for the photo. What do you think, Elise?" Brenna turned to her.

"Beautiful," Elise said softly, still staring at those tattoos. They were a work of art all their own, the way they flowed together. That chest tattoo even flowed to the ones covering his arms, so they were almost like another skin on him. And they were done with the greatest of care—that much was obvious. She wanted to run her hands over the tattoos and the hot skin they covered, just so she could admire them with her touch.

And then she realized she'd said he was beautiful aloud. Her face flushed and she took a step backward involuntarily. "I, um, have to set up my equipment," she told Brenna. "He doesn't have to do it if he doesn't want to."

Before she could hear Rome's answer, she grabbed her case of camera equipment and rushed out the front door.

So humiliating! Part of her prayed that Rome would decide he was too busy to fool around with the photo shoot. The other part of her wanted to get pictures of that gorgeous man so she could admire them at her leisure. It would almost be as good as the real thing. Almost.

"God, I wish I had your job," Brenna said to Beth Ann, sipping a straw as she sat in a folding deck chair, a big floppy hat on her head as she drank her blended homemade margarita.

Next to her in an identical chair and wearing an identical hat, Miranda lifted her bottle of beer to her lips, gaze riveted ahead. "I don't want her job. I like watching."

Beth Ann grinned and considered the man standing in front of her with a tilt of her head. "Do you think we need more mud or more mist?"

"More mud," Brenna said. "Baby likes 'em dirty. Rowrrr."

"I vote mist," Miranda chimed in, lifting her beer.

"Do I get a vote?" Rome asked. He stood next to Beth Ann in the midst of the trees, on a rocky outcropping situated just behind the lodge. He wore no shirt and his face, neck, and one shoulder were spattered with mud, as were the dark BDUs he wore, and combat boots. Two camo streaks had been painted under his eyes.

"No vote," Brenna said. "You are simply a canvas for greatness."

Rome snorted.

Beth Ann considered him a moment longer, and then spritzed him with another fine mist. "I think the gleam on the tattoos is a nice touch. What do you think, Elise?"

"Not too much mist," Elise said in a soft voice. She leaned over her camera tripod, adjusted the settings, and then moved forward to where Beth Ann stood. She reached for Rome's arm and positioned it carefully, just below his belt and on his hip. Then she adjusted his fingers, stepped back, regarded him, and then moved forward again.

"What's the problem?" Miranda asked.

"He's stiff." Elise frowned, staring at his hands.

Miranda tittered.

Elise jerked up, turned bright red, and staggered backward. "That wasn't what I meant. I . . . I . . . he's fine."

"I'll say he is," Brenna commented. "Rowwrrr again."

Elise shot her another mortified look and retreated back to her camera. She said nothing, but her hair hung in front of her face, as if she could hide behind a wall of long, swinging tresses.

Brenna wasn't deterred by Elise's shyness. How could she not stare at Rome's tatted-up hotness? Heck, Elise had even said aloud that she thought Rome was beautiful. That counted for something. He'd be good for her, provided she looked up from her shoes every now and then to notice what a gorgeous piece of man-meat was there for the taking. And Grant's sister was nice, but she was so uptight that she looked like she could use a few rounds in the hay with a much wilder guy.

Rome brushed a hand across his brow, absently wiping sweat—or spritzed water—from his brow. Immediately, Elise's camera began to whirr as she started snapping photos of the casual motion. "Remind me again," he said, "why I'm the one stuck out here getting basted in mud and squirted with water?"

"Because Colt and Dane are busy," Beth Ann said in an easy drawl, taking a step backward to proudly survey her handiwork as Elise continued to take photos.

"Busy hiding," Rome muttered, but then flexed and winked in Elise's direction, clearly not as miserable as he pretended. "What about Grant?"

Brenna was pretty sure that a choked little sound erupted from Elise, despite being shielded by the camera and her hair. "Yeah," Brenna commented, sitting up. "What about Grant? I could stand to see him a little filthy."

"I'm guessing you're an expert at seeing him filthy already," Miranda quipped.

"Maybe." But Brenna grinned.

Elise looked over at Brenna curiously. "I thought you guys were fighting?"

"We kissed and made up. Lots, and lots of kissing."

"Please don't tell me any more," Elise said, raising a hand in protest. "He's my brother."

Beth Ann came over, a wrinkle of surprise between her perfect blond brows. "You guys were fighting?"

"When are we not fighting?" Brenna said, taking another sip of her drink. "But I like to think of it as just a precursor to some really good makeup sex. It just means that the makeup sex is frequent, right?"

"I guess so, honey." But Beth Ann didn't look convinced. She shared a worried look with Miranda. "It's tearing up the boys, you know."

By "the boys," Beth Ann clearly meant Dane and Colt. And that made Brenna curious. "Tearing them up? How so?"

Miranda chimed in. "When you guys aren't speaking, they never know whose side to take. Grant's their buddy, but they look at you like a little sister. It makes things difficult for them."

Why was everyone suddenly interested in her sex life? Why had their casual sex started to affect others? Brenna began to feel that uncomfortable, smothering sensation of being trapped. They thought of her and Grant as a pair. That the health of their relationship suddenly affected theirs. And she felt the sudden, irresistible urge to escape. "I think I need a refill," she announced, ignoring the fact that her glass was still half-full. "Be right back."

Before anyone could volunteer to accompany her, she

hurried away. She needed a few minutes to herself, to get her head straight. Get a breath of air. Something.

But as soon as she walked back into the main lodge, Grant was there. And she sucked in a breath. Speaking of wet and delicious . . . he looked as if he'd just recently come out of a shower. His skin was lightly flushed, and his hair had been combed into slick waves that were only half-dry. He wore a dark Polo and khaki pants and was watching a stock report scroll across the flat-screen TV, remote in hand.

And even though Rome, who was far more her type with the tattoos and roguish attitude, was just outside? He hadn't done a thing for her. But seeing Grant in his straitlaced office wear? It made her instantly want him.

And a little sigh escaped her throat.

He glanced over at the sight of her, and a warm smile tugged his mouth. "Nice hat. You look ready for a day on the beach."

"Why, are you planning on taking me to the beach in November?" She gave him a saucy wink, her tongue lightly running over the end of her straw. All that worry about not being able to breathe because she was smothered? Kinda forgotten in the presence of Grant's dominating sexiness. He tended to make her forget all her resolutions when he smiled at her.

And she figured that wasn't entirely such a bad thing.

"I could be convinced," Grant chuckled, moving to her and looping an arm around her waist. "But you'd have to borrow a bikini from someone."

She made a mock-pout. "You mean I'd have to wear a swimsuit?"

"As much as I like to see you totally naked, you might want to save that for when we're alone." The words were admonishing, but the tone—and the teasing look on his face—was so affectionate and easy that it made her heart melt—and her pulse throb.

Let the others think what they wanted. She and Grant knew what they had.

TWELVE

Thunder crashed overhead, and the lights flickered in the main lodge. From her desk, Brenna looked up and winced, glancing over at Grant. "It's nasty weather today."

"It is," he agreed, seemingly unconcerned as he worked on a series of brochure proofs, his gaze intent on his computer monitor. "But our clients pay to get the full survival experience, remember? This is just part of the lessons—how to survive in the elements."

"But this isn't one or two elements," Brenna protested, hugging her coffee close and frowning at the windows. She moved toward one, staring out at the dark blue skies, and shivered at the wall of clouds that crackled with electricity. One of the trees near the gravel parking lot was nearly bent sideways with the wind. "This is like, all of the elements. At once."

Grant glanced over at her, a hint of a scowl on his face.

"It's Texas. We get bad weather all the time. What's got you all bothered today?"

She shrugged. "It's Rome's first class on his own today. I'm worried about him."

He got up from his desk and moved to her side. Coming up behind her, he wrapped his arms around her waist and nuzzled at her bare neck, her hair pulled up in a messy bun. "He'll be fine, Brenna. We hired him because he's good at this sort of thing. This is what he does. He's had intensive training for these kinds of situations, remember?"

There were a few fallacies in his thinking, which worried Brenna. First of all, she'd hired Rome because he'd showed up, not because he was the most qualified candidate. She figured he needed the job and he'd work all the harder because of it.

She hadn't been the only one to take Rome at face value. Pop had adopted the guy as if he was just another one of his sons who had shown up on the doorstep, looking for work. Colt and Dane had been leery about him at first, but when a few days had passed and no one had raised the alarm, she breathed a sigh of relief. Rome was a hard worker and a quick learner. If he was missing a few gaps in his knowledge, no one had noticed yet, and she didn't plan on ratting him out.

Of course, now that the weather had taken a turn for the worse, she was rethinking her brilliant plan. Rome had taken out a small group that morning, three men, all first timers. If something happened, she wasn't sure that any of them could take care of themselves.

A new bolt of lightning lit up the sky and illuminated a small group of men coming in from the woods. Brenna gasped and pointed. "Someone's come back."

Grant kissed her cheek and then moved to the coat rack,

grabbing his rain slicker. "You stay here. I'll see what's going on." He tossed it on, flipped up the hood, and then trotted out into the pounding rain.

Brenna pressed her face to the glass, trying to make out who it was as the trail of men came in from the woods. Her heart sank when four heads emerged, then two more, then two more. That was too many to be Rome's group, unless he'd come in with either Dane or Colt. She forced herself to wait, drumming her fingers on her arm impatiently as the men headed across the sodden clearing toward the main lodge.

When the men came inside, though, she saw her worst fear had been realized—Dane and Colt had brought their groups in and were chatting with Grant. "The river's flash flooding," Colt said. "It's not safe to hit our usual areas, and there's a chance of tornados. I'd rather wait a day or two and see how things shake out."

"First rule of survival's knowing when you're licked," Dane agreed.

Grant took in the conversation, grimly nodding. "You guys know best. We'll make arrangements for our guests, then." He gestured that the wet, bedraggled men should make themselves comfortable on the lodge couches. "Brenna can get some towels and hot coffee—"

"Brenna's busy," she butted in, moving to Dane and Colt's side. "Did you guys see Rome anywhere?"

Dane shook his head.

"The trail was pretty washed out," Colt said, rubbing his chin with concern. "We should go back out and look for him. He's not as familiar with the grounds as we are."

"I'll go with you," Brenna said, running back to her desk and grabbing the keys to the ATV shed. "Just give me a moment—"

"What? You're not going with them," Grant interrupted, a furious look on his face.

Brenna tilted her head, staring at him, then snapped her fingers. "You're right. We'll cover a lot more ground if we split up."

"No, I mean you're not going out in this weather." Grant moved to her side and grabbed her elbow. "Absolutely not. If it's that dangerous, I don't want you out in it."

She gave him an incredulous look. "Don't be ridiculous, Grant."

"Trust me, I'm not."

She ignored that, and the steely tone in his voice, and tried to simply move around him. He stood in the way, blocking her, and her jaw dropped in surprise. "Grant, I'm going after him."

"*No*, you're not."

On the far side of the room, Dane pointed at the door. "Colt and I are going to hike down to where his group was and see if they need any help."

"I'll be along, too," Brenna called over Grant's shoulder. "Give me a few minutes."

"No, she won't," Grant said. "I mean it, Brenna. You're not going anywhere. Not on my watch."

"You'll let them go out?"

"They're trained survivalists."

"I'm the assistant! It's my job to assist!"

"Not this sort of thing. Let the others handle it. Rome doesn't need you going after him."

"Funny, I'm not sure we agree."

"It doesn't matter if we agree. I want you staying here with me."

She stared at him for a long, searching moment, trying

to understand him. "Please tell me this isn't some sort of wacky plot to keep me here because you're jealous of Rome."

"Don't be ridiculous," Grant said, tight-lipped. "I'm not jealous."

"Then step aside and let me go out. I'll be fine."

"You're not leaving this lodge as my employee."

"Fine. Then fire me and I'm still going after Rome. You can't stop me."

"Goddamn it, Brenna!" His face was white with fury. "I won't let you get hurt!"

Exasperation swept through her. He was making her crazy. "No one said I was going to get hurt!"

"There's a million things that could go wrong. You could get a flat tire. Skid into a ditch. Lightning could strike your vehicle. You could flip over. Those things aren't safe. In fact, I don't want you driving them at all anymore."

She stared at him as if he'd grown another head. "Are you kidding me? Lightning striking the vehicle? I have better odds of a sinkhole opening up underneath me."

"Another very good reason why you're not going out there."

"Grant," she protested.

"No. Absolutely not." His mouth was tight, his gaze unforgiving. He looked ready to snap. Tension was vibrating off him in almost palpable waves.

She'd never seen him like this. "Why are you being so controlling?"

Grant's fists clenched at his side and he turned away from her. "You can go after him. But if you do, you're destroying any sort of friendship that we have between us."

Her jaw dropped. "That's the most ridiculous thing I've ever heard."

"That's how I feel. I don't give a fuck if it's ridiculous. But if you do, go ahead and leave, then. Clearly how I feel doesn't matter to you at all." And he turned and stormed out of the main lodge, heading for his cabin.

Brenna's mouth worked silently. She stared after his retreating back, wondering what the hell just happened.

One of the men in the lodge cleared his throat and gestured at the window. "Uh, miss?"

"Huh?" She turned toward him, her cheeks flushing. That strange argument with Grant had been witnessed by all of their clients. *How embarrassing.*

"There are a few men coming up the path right now." He gestured to the window.

Brenna rushed to it and counted heads. Three men in Wilderness Survival Expeditions slickers, and three men in various gear. Their missing campers. Perfect. She didn't have to go out after Rome after all.

Now she could go after Grant and figure out what the hell was wrong with him.

Irritation making her steps quick and crisp, Brenna marched out of the main lodge and down the path to Grant's cabin, ignoring the pounding rain that quickly soaked her to the skin. She pushed open the door to Grant's cabin and didn't see him in the living room. A quick peek up the ladder didn't show him either. On a hunch, she headed toward the bathroom and saw a narrow strip of light under the door. Just over the pounding rain she could hear the shower going.

Good. If he was just taking a shower, then they could still talk, because she had *plenty* to say to him.

She pushed the door open . . . and halted, her anger deflating at the sight of him.

Grant sat on the side of the tub in his jeans, his shirt tossed in the sink. The shower was running, but he wasn't in it. His head was buried in his hands, as if he were trying to compose himself. And when he looked up when she opened the door, there was such stark pain in his pale face that she forgot all of her anger.

She moved to sit next to him on the tub. "What's wrong?"

He shook his head, sitting up straight. "Nothing. It's nothing. I'm fine."

"You're not fine." Her hand moved to his and, to her surprise, he clasped it hard. "Talk to me. Is it Rome?"

A short, bitter laugh escaped him. "It's definitely not Rome."

"Then what is it? You can talk to me."

Grant scrubbed a hand over his face, but still said nothing, the tortured look remaining.

She stroked her fingers over his nape, rubbing him. "Something's clearly upset you deeply about the situation. Something deeper than what you're telling me."

"My wife . . . my first wife. I guess . . . I have strong reactions to unsafe situations." Each word seemed like a struggle for him to admit. He paused, then sighed.

"Go on," she coaxed gently. "What happened with her?"

"When we first got married, she was happy as could be. We were both going to college—I majored in business, and she majored in economics. We were very normal. And then for her twenty-first birthday, a friend took her bungee jumping. We thought it would be funny but harmless, something to laugh about afterward. I didn't realize it was going to change everything."

"How so?"

"Heather loved it. She loved it so much she went again the next weekend. And then after that, she went parachuting. And then extreme caving. Rappelling down sheer cliffs. And anything else that she could find within a decent drive from our apartment. And then she started doing stuff that involved longer than day trips. Scuba-diving with sharks in the Great Barrier Reef, rhino hunting in Africa, whatever she wanted to do that she could think of. Didn't matter if it was illegal or not, as long as she got a rush out of it. She was addicted to the adrenaline high, and it changed her. If she wasn't home, she was away on a thrill-seeking trip. And if she wasn't on a thrill-seeking trip, she was . . ." His voice trailed off and he swallowed hard. ". . . thrill-seeking here."

Brenna shook her head. "I don't understand."

"She brought home strangers because it excited her, and when I got upset, she promised she'd stop. And then she just met them at clubs. Two or three at a time, it didn't matter. Part of the excitement was the forbidden. I was pretty sure she was into drugs at some point, too. Not because she wanted them, but just for the high. After a while, she thought everything was boring—me included."

Brenna said nothing but simply rubbed his neck and let him keep talking.

"It got out of control and our marriage became miserable fast. I still loved her, but it was obvious that I wasn't enough for her anymore. Her trips got longer and more dangerous. It wouldn't matter if I told her no or that I worried about her. She just needed that next 'thrill' fix." His hand clenched tight in hers, clearly struggling with his thoughts.

"What happened?" Brenna asked gently.

"She died, of course." Grant's words were bitter with resentment. "Even though she had asthma, she got it in her head that she should climb Mount Everest. It doesn't matter that people have died repeatedly doing it. Someone told her that it was the biggest thrill you could undertake, and that was all Heather needed to know. She signed up to climb to the summit, and she declined an oxygen tank. It'd be more daring, she decided, if she went without one, and if it was more daring, it'd mean more to her. And those bastards who were supposed to be her guides let her do it. She died without ever reaching the summit."

Oh no. Brenna felt a sick clench in her stomach. "I'm sorry."

"What's the worst is that it was preventable. She didn't have to die. She could have put on an oxygen tank, but no one stopped her. We just all let her do whatever she wanted, because she was lively and fun and determined and so full of life that you never thought anything bad would happen to her." His mouth twisted bitterly. "I'm told that when she died, there were seven other people hiking to the summit, and that they all stood by and watched her collapse and die without helping her. Because helping her would have meant that they'd have to give up their chance at going to the top of the mountain, and they wanted that more than anything. She died surrounded by even more adrenaline junkies. And you know what I can't stop thinking about?"

"No, what?" Her words were achingly soft.

"It's not safe to pull bodies down from Mount Everest. The air's so thin that helicopters can't fly, and it's too risky for rescuers to drag the dead down. So they just . . . sit there. In the snow. Her body's still up there, somewhere. And everyone else who climbs the mountain just walks past it to get to the summit, because they need that fix, too. And meanwhile, I wasn't able to bury my wife because her thrill-seeking was more important to her than marriage."

Brenna said nothing for a long moment. There was so much self-loathing and self-hate in Grant's words that she wasn't entirely sure how to process it at first. Then, she gently asked, "So why do you blame yourself?"

"Because I didn't stop her. I didn't put my foot down

when she started putting herself in danger. Because I loved her and thought that she'd have enough common sense not to get into dangerous situations. Because I didn't tell her no. Because I cared for her and supported her even when she started sleeping around and doing drugs. Because I thought if I was patient, she'd grow out of the phase and we could go back to being just us again." He sighed heavily. "And because I wasn't exciting enough for her. I always wondered if I could have done more to make her happy."

"So you feel guilty?"

"I should, shouldn't I?" Grant's mouth twisted angrily. "But I mostly feel resentment toward her. She destroyed both of our lives, all because she needed some kind of fucking rush. That I wasn't enough to make her happy, and she fucked up my life, too. I think any love I had for her or her memory has been destroyed by resentment."

"Oh, Grant," Brenna whispered, her heart aching for him. "It wasn't you. It was never you. She was just looking for something that she didn't have inside herself. That's all."

His fingers laced with hers, still clutching her tight, as if he were afraid to let go of her. His gaze locked on their twined fingers. "So now you know why I seem a bit anal-retentive about things. Why I like order and schedules and precautions. Because those are what keep you safe."

And it was why he didn't want her going out in the rain on an ATV to chase after someone. Not because he was afraid she'd hurt herself—but that she'd get addicted to the rush that came with being in danger, and then he'd lose her, too. Brenna's heart softened and she pulled him against her, cradling his dark head against her neck. He was stiff against her for a moment, and then relaxed, his arms wrapping around her waist.

Brenna's thoughts were in turmoil. Grant had always seemed like he was so together, so in control. In reality? He seemed just as broken as she was. He just hid it even better than she did. Every day that she was with him, she found out he was more like her than she'd ever imagined possible.

Her hand rubbed his big shoulders, his skin warm. "Why don't you take a shower, baby? You'll feel better."

But he didn't move, though she felt his mouth press against her neck. "Take one with me?"

She nodded and wriggled out of his grasp, getting to her feet. "We need to get out of these wet clothes first."

A half smile crooked his mouth, almost wistful in its sadness. "Why does that sound like a pick-up line?"

"Because it is one? Now hush and let my fingers do the talking." She unbuckled his belt and pushed it aside, then went for his zipper. Her fingers rubbed up and down his groin as she slowly moved the zipper down, and she heard his swift intake of breath that told her he was paying quite a bit of attention to what she was doing. With a wickedly happy purr that she could turn him on so quickly, Brenna tugged at his damp clothes until they fell to his ankles, and leaned in and gave a kiss to his stiffening cock, then flicked him with her tongue.

He groaned, his hands going to her damp hair. "You're still dressed."

"Don't worry," she told him. "I plan on fixing that right away." And she stood up and shimmied out of her top, then peeled her wet jeans down her legs. Excitement was coursing through her, but more than that, she wanted to distract Grant, to comfort him and make him realize that he was wonderful and exciting to her, and that his first wife had been an idiot.

She kicked aside her wet clothes and sauntered past him to the still-running shower, leaning in to test the water. Still hot. "Come on, stud," she told him as she stepped into the water. "You are going to receive one primo rub down, courtesy of your lovely assistant."

"My assistant is more than lovely," he said in a low, husky voice, and cupped her cheek. "She's stunningly beautiful and kind." Another grin touched his mouth, this one easier than before. "She's a little weird but I'm learning to like that."

Brenna winked at him and poured a huge dose of bath gel into her hand, then rubbed her palms together. She planted them on his chest and began to rub vigorously, lathering him. She started out brisk, anyhow. The more she touched those slick, soapy muscles, the more fascinated she became with his body. After a few moments of washing, she began to slowly trace her fingers over his pectorals, then dragged them up and down his abdomen, dipping into his belly button. "You sure do have a sexy body."

"I have an even sexier assistant," he told her, leaning in to kiss her shoulder even as she reached behind him and soaped his hard buttocks. "I'm a pretty lucky guy."

"You are," she told him, and grabbed the bottle of bath gel again. She squirted a long rope of it over his shoulders, then tossed the container aside, putting her hands on him again.

"Are you using enough soap?"

"Maybe," she said in a low voice. "Maybe I just like putting my hands all over you." And she began to rub the streaming lather on him all over again.

He dragged a hand across his shoulders, scooping up some of the bath gel. "You've got enough on me that I could wash you, too." He began to rub her arms, then slid his hands to her front, flicking her nipples.

A hot rush of pleasure shot through her and Brenna moaned. "I think I need to get your back, baby," she told him, even as she stepped closer. Her arms went around his neck and she began to kiss him as she stroked soapy hands up and down his shoulders.

"You kind of suck at washing," he told her while caressing her skin.

"You were paying attention? I clearly need to up my game." And she dragged the tip of her tongue across his lower lip.

He groaned. "You're really good at that."

"Upping my game or licking you?"

"Both."

She ran her tongue along the hard line of his jaw as her hand slid to his ass and squeezed. "I could lick you all over, you know."

He held her to him, his hands running all over her body. "You're so beautiful, Brenna. When I'm with you, I forget about everything else."

For some reason, that made her absurdly pleased. And now she wanted to please him even more. She took her hand and wrapped it around the hard length of him, giving him a slippery stroke. Grant's breath hissed out of his mouth and then he clung to the shower bar, his gaze hot on her as she stroked his cock with her slick, soapy hands. Slow, excruciatingly tender motions. She took her time, not moving so quick that he'd come instantly. This was all about pleasure, and this was all for him. She wanted to make him feel better.

He leaned against the tile wall of the shower, eyes

closing when she increased the pressure of her fist as she stroked him. "Brenna, let up. Let me get a condom."

She stroked him as she considered it. Then she pressed her other hand to his chest to pin him in place, and she stroked her fist around his cock again. "Nah. I like it here."

His eyes grew dark with need. "You don't want me to touch you?"

"Oh, I do. But I like touching you so much that I'm kind of loath to stop." Stroke. "So I thought I might just continue to have my evil way with you." Stroke. "Until you lose control." Stroke. "Because I think I'd like to see that."

And she tightened her fist and squeezed hard. "Now say my name," she teased. "And tell me that you belong to me."

"Brenna," he bit out, his voice tight with desire. His gaze hadn't left her face for an instant, utterly focused on her. "I am totally and completely yours."

Oh, how she liked hearing that. It made her wet and excited all over again, and she stroked him again as a reward. "Tell me again?"

"Yours," he bit out, and then his hand wrapped around hers and he began to stroke his cock with her hand, using her hard and rough.

A moment later, he came on her belly, his gaze totally riveted to her. And she was about to come herself, just from watching him. It was a mixture of eroticism and satisfaction, and something else she couldn't quite name. Neither one of them moved for a long moment as he panted, trying to get his breath back, even though the water was growing steadily colder.

He hauled her close and wrapped his arms around her, burying his face against her neck and in her wet hair. "I love you, Brenna."

And she opened her mouth before she realized it, then snapped it shut.

She had almost said "I love you" back to him. That was the weird, niggling little sensation she'd been feeling all afternoon. It wasn't lust or pride or possession. It was all of those wrapped into one. And it was love.

Brenna was in love with Grant.

And that really, really freaked her out.

THIRTEEN

That evening, they lay in bed together. Grant was asleep, his arm wrapped possessively over her torso, one hand clutching her breast, his hips spooned against her own. Brenna, however, couldn't sleep. In her mind, she kept going over that afternoon.

Grant's first wife had been a selfish woman, Brenna decided. Oh, she'd been blond and cute and happy enough in the photos that Grant had of her, but she'd clearly made him miserable. She'd also made him think he was the problem in the relationship, even though every single sign pointed to something clearly unstable inside of Heather's head and not Grant's. What kind of woman went from mild-mannered college student to rhino-hunting, shark-swimming, Mount-Everest-climbing swinger who needed constant thrills?

The kind of woman who wrecked her husband in her

wake and didn't even realize it, Brenna thought, her hand stroking over Grant's larger one. She would never do that to him.

Her hand stilled. She had secrets of her own, though. Just as horrible and maybe even more embarrassing than that. Secrets that had fucked her up in the head and made it impossible for her to have normal relationships. So who was she to say that she'd be there for Grant?

She couldn't. Her life was the way it was because it was safest.

But for the first time, Brenna wanted more than what she had. And she didn't know how to handle that.

She needed to talk to Miranda and Beth Ann. Maybe they'd be able to help her see things clearly. Because right now? She feared things were doomed, and she was going to hurt Grant just as badly as Heather did, if not worse. If he knew her past he'd want nothing to do with her. He'd leave and she'd be left picking up the pieces.

And that thought hurt. A lot.

She crept out of bed a bit later, when she was sure that Grant was soundly sleeping and wouldn't wake up. She pulled on a pair of his pajamas and headed down to the main lodge, yawning.

Grant needed something to cheer him up, and she knew the perfect way to distract him. Sitting down at her desk, she pulled out the keys to the supply closet and headed there. Sure enough, at the bottom of the closet, there were a few rolls of cheerfully bright wrapping paper left over from Pop's birthday last month. They'd jokingly bought him the most childish, garish paper they could find, knowing he'd get a kick out of it. And there was plenty left over . . . and more than enough for her to cover Grant's desk.

Grabbing a bright pink roll of princess paper, she picked

up the scissors and set to work. Strange how she'd swap a few hours of sleep and hours of her time just to get a smile on Grant's face.

Yeah, she definitely needed to meet with her friends as soon as possible, because she had it *bad*.

At Brenna's request, Beth Ann and Miranda met her at Maya Loco for lunch and drinks. It was the busiest time for the restaurant, but it was also the only time Miranda and Beth Ann could both meet. Beth Ann hated leaving her salon for long periods of time, and Miranda closed the library for her lunch hour.

Brenna had simply left the main lodge while Grant had been out at the office supply store a few towns over. He'd come back and wonder where she was, but she'd left him a goofy little note. *Roses are red, violets are blue, went to lunch with the girls, but I'll come back and blow you.*

It wasn't the first time she'd abandoned her job midday, but the first time she'd left Grant a note so he wouldn't worry. Hell, it was downright domestic of her, and that was concerning. After all, now she was thinking about Grant's feelings and his emotions. She never had before. And even as she left him the note? She felt a little . . . anxious. Trapped. Worried. Because they'd gone from casual sex to emotional sex within the space of a week or two, and it was freaking her out. Two weeks ago, the last thing she wanted was a real relationship. Now?

Now she didn't know what to do.

She was the first one to arrive at the restaurant, so she ordered a margarita and then proceeded to down it in the space of a minute, between bites of chips and salsa. When the waiter asked if she wanted another, she made a rolling motion with her hand, indicating that he should keep them coming. By the time Miranda and Beth Ann showed up together, she was halfway through sucking down her third.

Miranda slid into the booth on the opposite side of her, her eyes wide at the empty margarita glasses. "Wow. Bad day? You fighting with Grant again?"

"No," Brenna said miserably. "We're awesome. That's the problem."

"Why's that a problem, honey?" Beth Ann slid in next to Brenna. "You both seem pretty happy lately."

"Oh sure." Brenna waved a hand, wishing she were drunker and the thought of their being happy together didn't hurt so much at the moment. "It's all fun and games until someone loses an eye. Or their heart."

"Huh?" Miranda shook her head. "You need to eat to kill that margarita buzz, or I'm going to have to drive you back to the ranch." She raised a hand for the waiter. "We need three coffees over here, please."

"Some of us are trying to get drunk, Miranda soon-to-be-Croft." Brenna glanced over at Beth Ann. "And Beth Ann Waggoner."

Beth Ann beamed at the mention of her new last name. "Has a nice ring to it, doesn't it?"

It did, and she was so ridiculously happy that it almost hurt to look at her. She and Colt had moved together seamlessly after their initial clash, and now they were so tight that it seemed like they'd always been a couple, instead of a fairly new one. She'd only been Beth Ann Waggoner for a few weeks now, and Colt's girlfriend for not much longer. But it was clear that they were deeply in love.

Brenna Markham, she tested on her tongue, but wasn't unhappy with it. Which only made her feel more jumbled inside.

"What's bothering you, Brenna?" Miranda asked as the three coffee mugs were set down in front of them.

"I'm just . . . not sure what to do."

"About Grant? It's clear he's crazy about you."

"He will be until he finds out the truth." Brenna couldn't help herself. She looked at Miranda's wrist to see if she was wearing her purple bracelet. No sign of it. For some reason, that made Brenna sad. She should have kept the bracelet. But keeping stuff led to other things, and those other things terrified Brenna.

Both Miranda and Beth Ann were giving her concerned looks, clearly waiting for her to go on. She didn't, though. They were her friends, but she couldn't tell them her deepest, darkest secret. She couldn't tell them any of it. So she deflected. "Grant told me some stuff about his first wife. Did you guys know her?"

"Heather? We knew her in high school, but they both went off to college together and we didn't see her again after that."

"What was she like?"

Miranda glanced at Beth Ann, then shrugged. "She was cute. Cheerful. Easily bored."

"A bit of a daredevil," Beth Ann added. "Remember we used to have slumber parties and she'd always be the one to suggest Truth or Dare? Girl never found a dare she didn't like."

"But she was nice," Miranda said. "Really nice. Everyone in town liked her. We were all sad when we heard she passed."

Couldn't even bury my own wife, Grant had said miserably. Because her body was stuck somewhere on Mount Everest, where people just climbed past it, heads full of their own daredevil quests. He'd thought he'd somehow not been enough for her and she'd turned to thrill seeking. But it seemed like the seed of it was there all along. She wondered if she should tell Grant. Would that assuage some of his guilt or just bring up old memories that he didn't want to relive?

"Why do you ask?" Beth Ann prodded, reaching into the chip bowl and nibbling daintily. "Grant say something about her?"

"A little," Brenna hedged. "He told me he loved me last night."

Miranda gasped and then clapped her hands in excitement. "Oh my gosh. That is so great! I've always wanted you two to be together! So you accepted his proposal?"

"Proposal?" Beth Ann looked shocked. "He proposed?"

This conversation was going from bad to worse. Brenna stared into her now-empty margarita glass, wishing she had another. "It's not great, and no, I didn't accept his proposal."

Miranda's excited clapping died.

"Why is it not great, honey?" Beth Ann asked softly, her voice gentle.

"Because I'm afraid of hurting him again," Brenna admitted, misery in her voice. She shoved aside her empty margarita glass and pulled the steaming coffee toward her. "Heather destroyed him. Totally broke him. It's awful. What if I do the same thing to him?"

Miranda and Beth Ann shared a look. "How would you do the same thing to him, Bren?" Miranda asked. "You planning on climbing Mount Everest?"

"Of course not." But she had secrets. Big, ugly ones. Just like Heather had. And those secrets were relationship destroyers. She'd seen it happen time and time again. Her mother's relationships had never survived it, and Brenna had the scars to show for it. "But . . . I just don't know what to do."

"About what? You're confusing me."

"I'm pretty confused myself, don't worry." Brenna sighed. "Let's say your past sucked, and you don't want Grant to know about it. What do you do, then?"

"You tell him," Miranda said.

"Let's say telling him is not an option."

"You tell him," Beth Ann said, reaching for another chip. "And if he's the one for you, he won't hold it against you."

"But what if he can't help but be freaked out by it? How can he not look at me differently?"

"This isn't about an STD, is it?" Miranda looked concerned. "Because you really need to tell him if that's the case."

"Gross! No. Not an STD." Brenna cupped her hands around her coffee, thinking. "Just something . . . unsavory in my past. I don't want him to look at me differently."

"Are you in love with him, too?" Beth Ann asked. "I was under the impression that things were just casual between you two and that was how you wanted it. No strings, no nothing."

"I thought that was how I wanted it," Brenna said glumly. "And then he told me he loved me and told me about Heather and now I can't stop thinking about things being different, and what it means for me."

"You have cold feet," Miranda announced.

Brenna straightened in the booth, frowning. "What do you mean, I have cold feet?"

"You are commitment phobic," Miranda told her with a grin. She grabbed a few packets of sweetener for her coffee and tore them open. "I feel the need to throw in a 'duh' here but thought that might be unfair."

Beth Ann gave a ladylike snort and sipped her coffee.

Brenna glanced at both women, uncertain. "You make it sound like it's a bad thing."

"It's not . . . unless you fall in love." Miranda's mouth quirked. "Take it from someone with experience."

"I never said I was in love," Brenna protested.

"You never said you weren't," Beth Ann told her in a softer voice. "Honey, if you think it's a big deal, just tell him about your past. Whatever it is, he'll accept it because he loves you. And if he doesn't, then he wasn't the man for you anyhow."

"Easy for you to say," Brenna muttered. "Colt doesn't have a shitty past. Pop's awesome."

Beth Ann gave another ladylike snort. "Are you kidding me? His past is weirder than you'll ever know."

"Oh?" Miranda perked up. "How so?"

But Beth Ann only shook her head. "It's Colt's story and he wouldn't want me telling it."

Miranda looked curious, but only shrugged. "The past doesn't determine everything. Heck, look at my past. I wanted to get out of this town because everyone talked to my chest and called me Boobs of Bluebonnet. And so I left, and then I came right back because I missed it anyhow. It wasn't that I missed being called Boobs. It was that I'd lose more than I gained by leaving. Like friends and family and Dane . . ." She had a pleased look on her face at the latter. "No one's called me Boobs since I got engaged. Having a big, muscular fiancé puts a new perspective on things for most people."

"Mine's worse than being called 'Boobs'," Brenna said glumly. "But I'll think about it."

"What do you have to lose?" Miranda asked.

Everything, Brenna wanted to reply, but she simply

shrugged. Because she'd seen it happen too many times in the past. There were things people could get past. And there were things that some people just couldn't get past no matter how much they claimed differently.

And she suspected she knew how things would fall if she exposed her past to Grant.

But it was either that, or continue as they were. In stasis. Grant confessing his love for her, and her demanding things be completely free and without attachments. How long would that last?

Not long enough. Glum at the thought, Brenna stared longingly at her empty margarita glass.

"None of that sad face now," Beth Ann told her with a pat on her hand. "So when are you going to come by and let me play with your hair?"

"Hmm?"

"Oh, I suggested to Elise that if she stays in town for a while, we try a joint venture. Pin-up photography. We agreed that since you have the Bettie Page bangs, you'd rock a serious retro look. We want you to be our test subject." She grinned and reached for another chip. "Basically we'll do your hair and makeup and dress you up in some glam clothing and take sexy pictures of you. Sound like fun?"

"What did you have in mind?"

Beth Ann popped the chip into her mouth, chewed, and then turned to play with Brenna's bangs. "We could curl these into a roll, or give you a retro upsweep. We'll experiment a bit."

Brenna shrugged again. "Sounds like fun. Can I wear it home? Surprise Grant?"

"Just don't have sex in the clothing," Beth Ann said. "Or you're paying the dry-cleaning bill."

"Great, now I'm picturing Brenna and Grant having sex, and I really didn't want to," Miranda lamented. "Now *I* need a margarita."

"So why all the business plans?" Brenna asked, sliding her bowl of salsa closer and digging into the chips. "I thought you and Colt were heading off to Alaska for a few weeks as soon as Rome's trained."

"We're leaving in two weeks," Beth Ann said breathlessly, practically bouncing in her seat. "I'm so excited to have a month of alone time with him. Between our schedules, it seems like one of us is always coming or going. It'll be nice to have a few days of nothing but lounging in bed."

Miranda gave her an odd look. "Clearly you have never been camping with one of these boys. I have, and I can assure you that lounging in bed is the last thing that Colt will have on his mind. He'll have you up at the butt-crack of dawn to go fishing or build a fire or something."

"I can be pretty convincing," Beth Ann said cheerfully, undeterred at the thought.

"What about your clients?" Brenna asked. "Can you leave without getting them all pissed off at you?"

"I'm stacking them and getting cuts in ahead of time," she told Brenna. "So I'm super busy this week and next week, but it'll be worth it." Beth Ann gave Brenna an amused look. "Since when did wild and careless Brenna start caring about business responsibilities?"

"Since I started sleeping with Grant," Brenna told her wryly. "Trust me, I'm as disturbed by it as you are. It's a good thing the man eats a fierce pussy, or he wouldn't be worth it."

Both Miranda and Beth Ann groaned as if in pain. Miranda pretended to scrub her eyes with her hands. "And there's yet another visual I'll never be able to shake. Thanks for that."

Brenna giggled. "You're so welcome."

"You sure you can't stay for longer?" Grant pushed his mother's designer carry-on into the trunk of his Audi. "I'm sure there's room at the Peppermint House if you wanted to stay another week or two. And it's good to have family around."

"You're sweet, Grant," Justine said, patting his cheek as only a mother could do to her grown son. "But Reggie wants to meet some friends for deep-sea fishing, and then we're heading to Florida to shop for beach houses."

Oh, to have such problems, Brenna thought wryly as she stepped forward to wave good-bye to Grant's parents. They were nice people—really nice—but they lived such a different lifestyle that she couldn't quite grasp it at times. Why did you need more than one house for only two people? It was bizarre to her, but she supposed that was what you did with your money when you had a lot of it. You bought stupid shit.

Which, of course, made her uncomfortable to think about. She watched Grant head into the main lodge to retrieve one last bag, thinking about all that money and how much pointless crap Justine and Reggie probably owned.

But Reggie and Justine were so very nice, and normal-seeming. Justine moved to hug Brenna and, to her surprise, she was immediately hugged by Reggie as well. "We're so happy that Grant has you in his life," Reggie told her, patting her on the back. "You're good for him."

"Thank you," she murmured, pulling away from the hug.

"I'm glad you worked out whatever it was," Justine told her with a beaming smile. "We like to see you two together."

"Thank you," she repeated again, because what could she really say? *Your son won't like me once he finds out the real me, so don't get too attached.* But all she said was, "I think he's pretty great, too."

Brenna turned to hug Elise, who was standing next to the car. But the quiet woman lifted a hand and grinned, seeming more at ease than when she'd first arrived. "You don't have to hug me. I'm staying."

"You are?" She couldn't hide her pleasure at that. She liked Elise.

"There's still the photo shoot to do, of course," Elise told her. "And I'm working on, um, a few other projects in the meantime. I can fly back whenever."

"Oh right. Beth Ann mentioned the pin-up photos."

"Yes!" Elise's face lit up with enthusiasm, light sparkling in her eyes. "They'll be a lot of fun."

"It'll be good to have you around," Brenna told her. "We can have a girls' night out this weekend. Or next weekend. Or every weekend."

Elise chuckled, the sound soft and shy. "How about we start with this weekend."

"Works for me." Brenna raised a fist for a fist bump.

After an awkward, almost-too-long moment, Elise fist bumped her back. *Getting somewhere, at least.*

Grant emerged from the lodge with the last suitcase, and his parents practically beamed with pride at the sight of him. Brenna had to agree that he was gorgeous. Silky brown hair fixed perfectly, wire-rimmed glasses perched on a perfect nose over sculpted cheekbones, and clothes that would make a model in *GQ* weep with envy. He always looked so perfect and put together, just like his parents.

His rich, rich parents with lots of stuff. Her stomach churned.

But the way that Justine and Reggie watched him? Their eyes were full of pleasure at the sight of their son, and happiness at *his* happiness. And Brenna realized with a sinking feeling that he would never understand where she'd come from.

But she needed to tell him anyhow. Because leading these nice people on wasn't fair. She liked all of them. They'd made her feel welcome and accepted from day one.

It was only right that she got all of her dirty laundry out in the open.

Something woke Grant from a sound sleep the next morning. He continued to lay in bed, still in a half doze, wondering what it could have been that woke him. The cabin was silent, the only sound the chirp of birds in the early morning light.

A finger poked him in the stomach again, then lightly tickled his sides. "Wake up, Grant."

Brenna. Delicious, warm, curvy Brenna. He dragged her closer, nuzzling her neck in a sleepy embrace. "It's early."

"I can't sleep."

He cracked an eye open, surprised at the tension in her voice. "What's wrong?"

Her troubled face gazed back at him, her purple and brown hair tousled. There were shadows under her eyes. She chewed on her lip, but was silent.

He was instantly awake, the need to soothe and protect her rising in him. To keep her safe from everything that upset her. Grant leaned up on one elbow and rubbed her shoulder. "What's wrong, love?"

A tear trickled out of her eye, falling onto the pillow. "We need to talk."

A horrible ache started in his gut. He forced himself to remain calm. "Talk about what?"

"About me. With you."

Immediately, Grant knew. He'd fucked this up again. He'd shown Brenna his vulnerable side the other day, in the shower. He thought things had been okay, but she was skittish when it came to commitment, and he'd been a dumbass and confessed his love to her. Still, when she hadn't panicked, he thought things were okay with them. That she was okay with him being in love with her as long as she could still say that she was in a no-strings-attached relationship. And he hadn't pressured her to say it back. He knew it was just a matter of time before she felt the same way.

Or so he'd thought.

But seeing her so distraught now? It tore at his heart. He wanted to make things better for her. Hell, he wanted to silence her with a kiss and make her forget whatever was worrying her. Anything to stop her tears.

"Brenna." He forced her name out of his throat and gently brushed away her tears. "Don't cry. It's okay. I'm not trying to pressure you at all. How I feel about you doesn't mean that you have to reciprocate. I know you don't feel the same way about me, and it's all right."

She stared at him, confused, and then burst into a few watery sounds that he couldn't quite tell if they were giggles or choked tears. "Oh Grant. Would you shut up for a moment? I said it's me, not you."

His heart stopped for a moment. "Then we're okay?"

"We're not okay," she said, and tears slid down her face again. "There's something wrong with *me*."

And just like that, his heart began to trip again, rapidly.

Relief mixed with unease. She was talking and he still didn't know what to think. "What do you mean there's something wrong with you? What's wrong?"

"I . . ." Her throat flexed, as if she couldn't say the words. "It's hard to explain."

Oh God. She was dying. He'd finally found the perfect woman for him—a woman who infuriated him as much as she made him happy. A woman as abandoned and easygoing in bed as she was out of it. A woman who made him feel like the king of the world instead of a worthless sack of shit that wasn't enough for her.

And she was dying. Had to be. That horrible ache returned to his stomach. He was going to lose Brenna as soon as he'd found out his feelings for her. Damn, fate was cruel. "Oh Brenna. Just tell me." *Tell me fast, so we can rip the Band-Aid off the wound and enjoy the rest of the time we have together.*

She looked so distraught that it broke his heart. But she tugged at his hand. "I have to show you something."

Shit, shit, shit.

As she sat up in bed, he realized she was wearing her pajamas. His pajamas, actually—flannel plaid pants that were double-knotted at her slender waist and his favorite Tulane T-shirt. But it wasn't like Brenna to sleep clothed. She liked to sleep naked and be curled around him. Which meant that she'd already gotten out of bed once, likely to prepare whatever it was that she wanted to show him.

That sick feeling in the hollow of his stomach felt like a black hole.

But she tugged at his hand insistently and, heart aching, he crawled out of their warm bed and followed her. He should have put on a pair of pants or boxers or something, but he needed to find out what was causing that look of anguish on her face first.

They descended down the ladder in silence, and he noticed his personal laptop had been fired up and was sitting on a video page. She tugged at his hand again, leading him toward the computer. Mystified, he sat down when she gestured for him to and tried to pull her into his lap.

But she resisted, her entire body tense. Instead, she leaned over him and clicked the mouse to start the video.

An ad played on screen, and Brenna's body vibrated with tension beside him. He scanned the Internet page, wondering what she was going to show him. Some sort of video describing fatal diseases? A home movie of some kind? But the video page had been put up years ago and had thousands of hits. The header read "S1 EP 14—the Atlees," but he didn't know what that meant.

All he knew was that it was going to somehow destroy Brenna to show him, and in the process, it'd destroy him, too. He loved her. He loved her wild exuberance and hated her tears. He tried to pull her close again, but still she resisted.

Theme music began to play, tinny through the laptop speakers, and he heard Brenna's breath intake sharply. Drawing his attention back to the screen, he watched the credits of one of those hour-long special reporting news shows roll past. A solemn news anchor in a gray suit sat on a stool next to a screen that read "Special Investigation: 2004."

"Thank you for joining us tonight," the man said in a deep voice, *"as we continue our series on a growing problem in America. Is this a disease? Something inherently wrong with certain people's minds that causes them to react*

differently than you or I? Or something else that forces these people to act the way they do?" He adjusted on his stool, gazing at the camera, and Grant thought his heart was going to burst from his chest in sheer anxiety.

What the fuck was it, already? He couldn't take much more of this. His mind was full of horrible images of Brenna suffering. Brenna stricken by disease.

"*This is an epidemic that is sweeping through many homes in the nation. As high as one in ten families can be affected. It destroys lives and everything it touches. We're talking, of course, about . . . hoarding.*"

Huh?

Hoarding?

Brenna wasn't dying? He wasn't going to lose her like he lost Heather? Relief washed over him, so powerful that he couldn't help himself.

He laughed.

Next to him, Brenna gave a horrified gasp and a choked sob. Before he could react, she reached out and slapped him in the face, then turned and ran for the front door.

"No, Brenna, wait—" Grant said, getting to his feet. *Damn it*, he didn't have any pants on. She was *wearing* his pants.

"Fuck you, Grant. Just fuck you!" Brenna slammed the door to the cabin after her.

Hell, he had to follow her. Explain that he wasn't laughing at *hoarding*—though it was absurd to think she was upset about it—but at his own wild relief that she wasn't dying of some mysterious disease. He searched the room for a blanket, but found nothing. Cursing, he headed for the ladder, intending to head up to his loft and grab a pair of pants.

A high-pitched voice from the computer stopped him.

"*I don't know when it started,*" Brenna's voice said. It

was high and girlish and held a troubled note. *"Our house has been like this for as long as I can remember. I grew up surrounded by bags and boxes full of stuff."*

Grant turned back to the computer. There on the screen was a much younger Brenna. Her face was skinny and her hair was long and untamed, a lighter, almost golden brown compared to the much darker waves she wore today. She wore a dirty T-shirt and hugged her arms to her chest, as if acutely uncomfortable. There was a look of shame on her face that he didn't recognize.

The Brenna he knew wasn't like this.

"Brenna Atlee," the reporter said, and Grant was startled to realize that he knew her under a different name, *"has lived under the shadow of hoarding all her life. Her mother, Agatha Atlee, is a hoarder. Her mother before her? A hoarder."*

Drawn back to the computer despite himself, Grant sat down in the chair. He knew he should have gone after Brenna, but the vulnerable, unhappy girl in the video had him riveted. He couldn't pull himself away.

The camera cut to the front door of a small ranch-style house in a run-down neighborhood. Brenna stood on the porch, her hand on a beat-up doorknob. There were large chips of paint missing from the red door, and a nearby window showed broken mini-blinds. She looked as if she wanted to run away. He'd seen that look on Brenna's face this morning. Then, with a nod, Brenna opened the door to the house.

Grant watched in horror as she pushed at the front door, shoving at it to get it to open enough to allow her in. She glanced back at the camera. *"Watch your step when you come in,"* she said, then began to step over piles of trash and boxes of junk to make her way into the house.

"Every inch of the Atlee house is covered in garbage,"

the narrator intoned, and the camera showed the reporter trying to follow Brenna into the house and having difficulty scaling the garbage. Teenage Brenna held aside a shopping bag of junk and assisted the reporter into a clear space in the house. *"Every room of this eighteen-hundred-square-foot house is filled, top to bottom, with things. The room we're standing in is the foyer. Brenna Atlee says her mother filled this room up last, though you wouldn't know it by looking at it. Boxes and bags of clothing, dishes, holiday gifts, and even the neighbor's garbage line the narrow walls of this cozy house."*

Brenna pulled open a bag and began to dig through the contents of it, showing the cameraman. *"She found this stuff at a thrift shop sale."* She pulled out a handful of tiny clothes and began to smooth them. *"It doesn't matter if she needs the stuff or not. She just buys it. These are baby clothes that she got for a few dollars. Boys' and girls' clothes. There are no babies here. I'm mom's only kid, and the neighbors won't take anything from us because they think we're dirty."* She pulled out another piece of clothing, a tiny red sweater. *"This is for a dog, I think. We don't have a dog. Can't have a dog. The city found a few dead animals in the house once and the neighbors called the cops on us. The fire department came in and cleaned out the garage once and found the carcasses of four dead cats. Mom was locked up for animal cruelty and my aunt had to bail her out. But once she was bailed out, she went through the garbage and took all her stuff back again."* Brenna's small hands smoothed the sweater. *"I always wanted a dog, though. I just figured it's not safe for them here."*

"Indeed," the narrator said. *"One would argue that the Atlee home isn't safe for humans, either. Yet this is where*

thirteen-year-old Brenna and her mother live, eat, and sleep every day. But Mrs. Atlee doesn't see a problem with her lifestyle."

The camera cut away from Brenna and moved to a woman who clearly had to be Brenna's mother. She was a slender woman with the same dark waves that he recognized from Brenna, and a thin face with a slightly longer nose. She also had deep lines on her face, as if the world had been cruel to her and aged her hard. She sat in a recliner, wedged amidst junk that was piled high around her, and her arm rested on a dry-cleaning bag still full of clothing. A small table next to her was covered with old magazines, dishes, and what looked like a rotten Halloween jack-o'-lantern.

The reporter handed her a box and squatted beside her in the mess, skirting the rotting pumpkin. *"Can you tell me a bit about the objects in this box, Agatha, and what they mean to you?"*

"Of course," the woman said in a reasonable tone. She began to dig through the box of stuff and pulled out the first thing. It was a baby food jar, black gunk stuck to one side. *"This would be good for keeping screws and things in it. I just need to clean it out."* She put it aside and pulled out the next item—a coffee mug with a broken handle. *"I just need to find the handle for this and it's good as new."*

"It's broken," the reporter protested. *"Why not just throw it out?"*

"It's perfectly fine," Agatha told him, a harder edge creeping into her voice. *"It just needs to be fixed."*

The film began a narrative montage as Agatha went through the box and pulled out item after item. A shoe with no match. A broken fan. A stack of waterlogged Post-it notes. A jar candle that had been burned down to the wick.

Useless crap, but Agatha Atlee had a use and an explanation for all of them.

Brenna's sad voice cut in again. *"It's like she can't see how to throw things away. She doesn't know how. She sees a use for everything and can't stand the thought of something being thrown out when there's still a need for it, somewhere."*

"But the rest of the world views it as junk," the reporter said. *"It's a viewpoint that has come between Agatha and her relationships many times in her life."*

"I first started collecting," Agatha was saying to the camera, *"when I was nineteen. I ran away from home to be with my boyfriend, got pregnant, and then he left me. I lived on the streets for a while, and then a program helped me get a job and my first house."*

"But by then," the narrator chimed in, *"the damage was already done. Used to living on the streets and having to scrounge for her next meal and the clothes on her back, Agatha found that she had a hard time acclimating to a normal life."*

"I just kept seeing my coworkers throwing away perfectly good things," she said, almost tearful with heartbreak. *"And so when someone would throw something away, I'd sneak in to their garbage and steal it back."*

"This stealing caused Agatha to lose that job. But by then, her baby, Brenna, was born, and Atlee qualified for assisted housing and food stamps. She bounced from job to job, and from relationship to relationship. No matter how strongly she felt about a man, the relationship inevitably ended once he got a look at her home life."

Grant's stomach sank. That sounded achingly familiar.

"I've never been able to give Brenna a real father figure,"

her mother said sadly. *"Most men say they can handle it, but when we move in together, it never works out."*

"Atlee has been married and divorced six times."

"My last husband," Brenna's mother was saying, *"didn't understand about my stuff. He told me we just needed to organize and clean up. One day, I came home and found him throwing out a bunch of my stuff. It was like he'd stabbed my heart."* She gestured dramatically at her chest. *"I didn't know how he could do that to me. I went to the dump and had to take some of it back, but I couldn't find all of it. I made him leave after that."*

"Each time Mom breaks up with someone, her hoarding gets worse," Brenna said, resentment and resignation in her voice and her dark, too-old eyes. *"Once she discovered the dump, it got even worse. She used to just take home one or two things every day. Now she takes whole carloads of stuff."*

"And family and friends are at their wits' end," the narrator intoned solemnly. *"Agatha's sister doesn't know what to do about her family, but she is concerned for their safety."*

The camera cut away to a woman with a deliberately pixelated face, clearly too embarrassed to reveal her identity. *"I don't know what to do,"* the woman said, her voice masked. *"Agatha doesn't see that there's a problem, and if you try to help her, she just gets worse. If I say something, she'll shut me out of her life entirely and Brenna will be the one who will suffer. I don't know how that kid can stand it, living in all that garbage. The other children make fun of her at school. They call her mom 'the trash lady.' They come and dump stuff on the lawn just to play mean pranks, and wait for Agatha to come and take it all inside, which of course she does.*" The sister's exasperation was evident. "*And poor Brenna has never gotten to be a kid. Growing up, she could never play at that house. She could never have friends over to spend the night. She's had to hide who her family is all her life. You know it has to affect her mentally. I just worry that she's going to turn out like her mother.*" She shook her head sadly. "*When she was younger, I couldn't go over because I'd constantly see that baby sticking garbage into her mouth. And Agatha didn't think it was a problem. I couldn't stand it . . .*"

The camera cut away and went into a long narrative about the psychological aspects of hoarding and how it affected those around them. They gave statistics on the number of hoarders in the United States, and Grant forced himself to listen with impatience. He just wanted to see the segment return to the young, vulnerable Brenna or her mother.

At the very end of the piece, sad music began to play, and they cut back to Brenna again.

"*How do you feel about all of this?*" the reporter asked Brenna. She sat in a small corner of her bed, the rest of it covered with junk, her room full. The floor was nowhere to be seen. "*Do you see your mother's things and feel like you need to collect as well?*"

Brenna gave a vehement shake of her head. "*I hate it. I hate all of it.*"

"*But your room is full.*"

"*This isn't my stuff.*" She looked almost offended at the thought. "*My room has always been clean. But when Mom ran out of space, she started putting stuff in my room. It doesn't matter what I do—her stuff invades every inch of my space.*"

"*And how does that make you feel?*"

"*Like I need to run away. I just want to throw it all away.*"

All of it. It's not necessary, you know? It's just stuff. And I hate stuff. I wish I could just get away from all of it. That's all I've ever wanted."

The camera faded to black on Brenna's words.

Grant sat, stunned. Before he could turn off the video, the screen flashed over and began to play the same music. Another segment about a hoarding family played. Fascinated and horrified despite himself, Grant watched it, hoping for another glimpse of younger Brenna, but this was about an elderly couple who acquired things from thrift shops. The next segment was a middle-aged couple with two boys.

He watched every segment. Then he went back to the beginning and watched the prior episodes. Mentally, he was trying to grasp what it must have been like for Brenna.

Her shame and frustration at her mother, at her home life. The bitterness in her voice. *It's just stuff. I wish I could just get away from all of it. That's all I've ever wanted.*

He'd never understood why Brenna was the way she was before. Why she was such a flake when it came to things like scheduling. Why she insisted on having a no-strings-attached relationship. Why she'd so quickly given up her cabin to Rome and planned on sleeping on the couch in the lodge, more or less without a space to call her own. Why, when he'd dug through her things, he'd found only the barest amount of clothing.

Why she'd given away his presents.

It's just stuff. I wish I could just get away from all of it. That's all I've ever wanted.

Everything made sense now. She'd shown him this video because she wanted him to understand how she was. The look in her eyes this morning had been full of terror and misery. As if she expected him to see the truth about her past and do the same thing that every other man had done—pack up and leave once the truth was uncovered.

And he'd laughed in her face, relieved that it was *just* hoarding.

God, he was an asshole.

Grant darted away to get some clothes. He had to go after her.

FOURTEEN

B renna slammed a fist down on the dashboard of her beat-up Sunfire. When that didn't make the engine start again, she leaned forward, resting her forehead against the steering wheel and wishing that today would just disappear.

She turned off the car, waited thirty seconds, and then turned the key in the ignition again. Nothing. Figured. With one fingernail, she tapped the gas gauge. The needle moved wildly. *Well, that might be a problem.* Or was it the battery? When was the last time she got a new battery? Probably the last time she got the oil changed. 2009? 2008? She couldn't remember. Didn't matter. The car was a piece of crap. She kept it exactly because it was a piece of crap—that meant it was easily abandoned.

But for some reason, that didn't sit well with her.

Brenna took the keys out of the ignition one final time, then pocketed them. Her purse was still back at the office.

Double-figured. She wiped her eyes, sniffled loudly, and then got out of the car. There was nothing to do but walk. Luckily she was close to town. From over the trees, she could see the roof of at least one building a block or two away. And the weather was decent.

It was just the rest of the world that was crapping on her lately.

Tears began to well in her eyes again, and Brenna swiped them away. She jingled her keys in her pocket, then tossed them on the ground. She didn't really need those anymore, did she? Her car was dead.

Dead like her freaking heart, now that Grant had stomped all over it.

She'd confessed her big ugly secret. Finally told someone the truth about who she was, when she had never told another soul. She'd changed her last name to get away from her past, ran away from home at the age of sixteen and cut off contact with all family, all because she'd been so desperate to escape. And once she was gone? She'd hitchhiked to Alaska, started fresh, and lived a life of no clutter and no worries. She'd buried who she was so deep inside she didn't even talk about it to herself.

But after years and years of careless living, she'd finally found something she wanted—Grant. And she'd been terrified of what he'd think. Would he be disgusted? Revolted? Permanently unattracted to her since she was a "trash girl" like she'd been called for so many years? Or would he not care?

She'd never in a million years thought he'd *laugh* at her.

And that had hurt so badly. It had been like a rush of cold water in her system.

So she reacted like she always did when things got to be too much—she ran away.

Of course, she hadn't run far. Brenna had contemplated getting in her car and just driving as far as she could. See where the road took her. Start over. She'd done it before.

Turned out the road hadn't even taken her as far as Bluebonnet.

Luck was definitely not on her side. Brenna kicked a rock in the road, and then she noticed the crunch of nearby footsteps.

She looked up at the same time that Elise Markham turned the corner and waved.

Brenna groaned inwardly. Elise was the last person she wanted to see at the moment . . . well, second to last person. Not that it was Elise's fault her brother was such an unfeeling douche. "Hey, Elise."

Elise headed for her, her smile fading a little as she studied Brenna's pajamas. "Why are you walking into town in your pajamas?"

"I'm running away."

Her brow furrowed. "From what?"

Brenna's eyes began to water all over again. "From my life."

Elise's soft gaze moved over her sympathetically. She went to Brenna's side and wrapped an arm around her shoulders. "You want to grab some coffee? We can sit down and talk."

"I can't drive anywhere," Brenna blubbered. "My car's dead."

"That's okay. Emily was baking when I left this morning. We can head back to the Peppermint House and have muffins." She nudged Brenna down the road. "Come on."

Numb, Brenna followed her.

The Peppermint House Bed and Breakfast was only a block away, so it wasn't a long jaunt. And to Brenna's relief,

Elise wasn't the kind to ask all sorts of prying questions. She just simply hugged Brenna close and offered quiet support. That was good. That was exactly what she needed right now. No questions, just friendship.

When they walked in the door of the Peppermint House, Emily came out of the kitchen with a smile on her face. It faltered at the sight of Brenna's red eyes and wet cheeks. "You poor thing," she exclaimed, moving forward to hug Brenna. "Are you okay?"

Brenna sniffed. "Just dandy."

"I just pulled some muffins out of the oven," Emily told her. "Why don't you sit down and eat? I'll put on a fresh pot of coffee."

Brenna nodded and let Emily drag her to one of the barstools in the breakfast nook. She sat down, Elise sitting right next to her. Immediately, Emily pushed a plate heaping with muffins over to her. "I'm making a batch for the firefighters, but you two can eat these and I'll make some more. What they don't know won't hurt them." She began to pull out coffee cups, plopping them on the counter with determination.

That brought a hint of a smile to Brenna's face. Every time she'd met Emily Allard-Smith, she was feeding someone. Even though Emily was only a few years older than her, the other woman acted like the entire town was hers to mother and feed. It was cute. All the guys in town loved her because all you had to do was mention your favorite type of baked goods and she'd make you some. Brenna secretly thought Emily had missed her calling of running a bakery shop, but a bed and breakfast was a decent substitute. She plucked a muffin off the heap and bit the top. It was a delicious chocolate pecan.

"Her car's broken down," Elise said softly. "Should we call a tow truck?"

"Don't bother," Brenna told her, her mouth full. She swiped at her lips with the back of her hand, then took the napkin that Emily pushed in her direction. "It's dead. I'll just leave it."

"Leave it?" Emily looked scandalized at the thought. "Is someone coming by to pick you up, then?"

"I sure hope not." Brenna took another big bite of muffin to forestall any questions.

Emily and Elise exchanged glances.

"You want to talk about it?" Emily asked.

"Not really." Brenna shrugged miserably. "Don't know what there is to say."

Emily gave Elise another look and passed two cups of coffee. "Why don't you two finish eating? I have decorators coming by in about an hour and I want to make sure I have my swatches ready for them." She gave the counter a little pat, and then bustled away. "Just yell if you need anything."

Elise watched Emily disappear into the back of the old Victorian. She said nothing until the door shut behind her, then glanced back at Brenna again. "You sure you're okay?"

"I thought Emily was renovating this place on her own."

"She is. She's just lying to give us some time to talk if you need it."

"Oh." Brenna's lower lip stuck out despite herself, and she couldn't help but confess just a teeny bit to Elise. "Your brother's kind of a dick."

"He can be," Elise said with a subtle smile. "What did he do?"

Oh God. She was not telling Elise the full story. Not at all. She'd learned her lesson. Uncomfortable, Brenna grabbed another muffin off the plate and began to slowly peel the wrapper down the sides. "I told him a really personal secret and he laughed in my face." She crammed the muffin into her mouth and began to chew, her cheeks ballooning out like a squirrel's. She knew she was acting childish, but she didn't care. "He's a jerk," she said between chews, her mouth full.

Elise sipped her coffee, seemingly calm, though her brows drew together in a faint frown. "That doesn't sound like Grant."

Brenna snorted.

"I'm serious," Elise said. "Grant is a lot of things. He's kind of a control freak and completely unmovable when he thinks he's right. He can be incredibly overbearing. And he's arrogant at times. But he's never out and out cruel." She shook her head. "That really doesn't sound like him. I'm sorry."

The delicious muffin stuck to the roof of Brenna's mouth, and she had to work to swallow. She grimaced and then shook her head. "I didn't mistake it. There was a definite laugh."

"So strange." Elise gave her a helpless shrug. "Maybe you bring out the worst in him?"

Well, that was certainly true. Brenna said nothing, just slid another muffin toward her. Maybe she could take some with her for the road. "It doesn't matter. I'm done here."

"Done here?"

"I'm leaving. Maybe I'll go back to Alaska."

Elise looked her up and down. "In your pajamas?"

"I don't have anything I want to take with me."

"How about a pair of pants?"

Brenna shrugged again.

Elise looked concerned. "You sure you're okay?"

She wasn't okay. Not by a long shot. But she'd scraped herself off the floor before and started over. No reason why she couldn't do it again. "I really just don't want to talk about it."

"Fair enough. Is there anything I can do to help?"

Brenna thought for a moment. "Wanna give me your pants?"

Goddamn it, where were his keys?

Grant tore through the main lodge, digging through his desk drawers again and then tearing through Dane's normal spot and then Brenna's desk. They were nowhere to be found, which meant she'd probably hidden them in one of her playful pranks.

Except she hadn't seemed playful. She'd seemed betrayed. And he desperately needed to find her. Grant growled under his breath and headed into the kitchen, digging through the dishwasher and any bowls he could find. She'd hidden his keys in a bread pan once.

The kitchen door swung open and Grant looked up, hope in his eyes. But it was only Colt and Dane, somber expressions on their faces.

"Have you seen my fucking keys?" Grant tugged out the silverware drawer, and then slammed it shut again. "I can't find them anywhere and I've got to go after her."

Silence.

Grant looked up, only to find that both Dane and Colt had their arms crossed over their chests, and they were both scowling at him.

"What exactly did you do to Brenna?" Dane asked.

"I know you blow hot and cold on her, but she's like a little sister to us," Colt added.

"And Miranda just got a text from Elise saying that Brenna's been crying. She's in her pajamas and she's crying."

Grant raked a hand through his hair, that frantic panic billowing up in him again. "That's why I need my keys. I have to go after her and explain. I wasn't laughing at her—"

"You were laughing at her?" Dane's normally easygoing features were set into a scowl.

"No," Grant snapped. "But she thinks I was. I was just fucking glad that she didn't have cancer."

"Cancer? What the hell are you talking about?" Colt's tone was irritated. "You're not making any fucking sense."

"I know. I don't care. I just . . . I need to find her and explain." He didn't want to share her secrets. The way she'd reacted when she'd told him? He knew that if he ever told a word of it to Colt or Dane, it'd be unforgivable in her eyes. And he wouldn't do that to her. "I can't talk about it."

"And what makes you think that we're going to let you off the hook without explaining what's going on?" Colt asked in a surly tone.

"Because you've known me for twenty goddamn years," Grant snapped. "And I don't say this sort of shit lightly, but I love her and want to make things right. And I'm not telling you her secrets, because they're hers, so fuck off about it. Either help me find my keys or get out of my fucking way."

"Hoo-rah," Colt said, apparently pleased by that response.

Dane grinned and held up a hand. Grant's keys were dangling off his finger.

"You stole my keys?" Grant's hands curled and he stormed toward Dane. "You asshole! I've been looking for them for twenty minutes!"

"Wanted to make sure your head was in the right place

before you took off after Brenna," Dane said simply. "You want us to go with?"

He snatched the keys from his buddy. "Hell, no. I can talk to my girl myself."

"Cause you did so well in the past?" Colt drawled.

"Fuck off."

His friends just laughed.

Grant tore into Bluebonnet at top speed, his tires screeching at every stop sign. He slammed to a halt in front of the Peppermint House, just as Brenna and Elise were heading down the front porch stairs. Brenna still wore his Tulane shirt, but her hair had been tugged into a clip at the back of her head, her purple bangs brushed, and she wore a pair of jeans that were too loose on her and sagged.

Both women looked his way as he jumped out of his car, and he could have sworn Brenna's jaw dropped in surprise.

She looked over at Elise with a betrayed look. "You told him I was here?"

"I didn't tell him to come over here," she protested, putting up her hands. "I just gave him a little text-shaming from afar for making you cry." But she didn't look displeased at all.

"Likely story," Brenna told her with a faint scowl.

Grant was so relieved to see her that he bounded up the stairs, reaching for her . . . and stopped when she shied away.

"I don't want to talk to you," Brenna told him in a cool voice. "In fact, I was just leaving."

"Leaving? Where are you going?"

"Anywhere that you're not!"

"Why?"

"Because I don't want to be around you anymore!" The look on her face was stubborn. "I thought I could trust you and it's clear to me that I was wrong. So I'm done here. Time to scope out the wild blue yonder once more."

Panic assailed him anew. She was pulling up roots and leaving? Then again, this was Brenna. She didn't believe in roots. "You can't leave."

"Why can't I?"

He moved toward her again, ignoring the fact that she shied away from him. "Because I love you and I want to be with you."

"You have a funny way of showing love, Grant Markham."

He looked over at Elise, who stood watching their exchange, a faint frown on his sister's face. "Can you leave us alone to talk, Elise?"

"Will you be long?" his sister asked.

"We might," he admitted. "However long it takes to get through to Brenna's stubborn brain."

"Insulting me is not the way to win me over," Brenna announced.

But Elise grinned and wiggled her fingers at him, turning around and disappearing back into the bed and breakfast. After the door swung shut, it was just him and Brenna, alone on the big wooden stairs.

Brenna crossed her arms over her chest and gave him a blatantly unhappy look.

"Just let me talk," Grant soothed. "I promise I'll explain everything."

"This should be good," she muttered. But she didn't leave. That was a start.

"You were right to slap me for laughing," he told her, since he knew that would get her attention. And he was correct because she perked up a little after that. "But," he continued, "you should have heard my reasoning before you ran off." When she said nothing, he decided to plow ahead. "It wasn't that I was laughing at you. It was just that you and me were too perfect together. I guess it reminded me of how things were back when Heather and I first got married. I was so happy with her, and then it felt like everything turned upside down overnight. I suppose I was worried that it would happen again. Once your life goes down the drain once, you get gun-shy and afraid it'll happen again."

She still said nothing. But that scowl was gone from her face.

"This entire time, you've been telling me that you can't commit. You won't commit. That there's no future for us except for no-strings-attached sex. And I kept wondering why, because I've fallen for you so hard that my head is spinning, and unless I missed my guess, I thought you had fallen for me, too."

"You know what they say about assuming, Grant." She tried to make her voice light, but there was an unsteady wobble in it. And she glanced away, avoiding eye contact.

"I know," he told her. "I am assuming. But that was how I felt. And then you woke me up in the middle of the night, crying, and telling me that you had a massive secret. And I thought my heart was going to splinter right in my fucking chest." He clenched a fist against his breastbone as if to demonstrate. "What could be so awful about someone as wonderful and vibrant as you? What on earth could possibly destroy what we've got together? What would make you so miserable that you'd be unable to sleep and make you cry? So I thought it must have been something fatal. Like cancer. Or a terminal disease."

She looked confused. "Cancer?"

"Cancer," he agreed. "My mind went right there, assuming the worst possible. How could I know?" He shrugged helplessly. "So when you showed me the video about—" he glanced around to make sure no one was nearby "—about hoarding, I was so relieved that you weren't dying that I couldn't help it. I laughed."

Her face softened a little. "I thought you were laughing at me." There were leagues of hurt in her voice. Hurt that he'd caused.

He reached for her, and she didn't pull away. *Thank God.* He stroked her arm. "Brenna, I would never laugh at your past. I was laughing because I was so damn relieved that I could hardly stand it."

She stared at him. "Cancer," she repeated.

"Crazy, I know. But I kept thinking, what possible reason could you have for not wanting a permanent relationship?"

"Because there's no such thing," Brenna exclaimed. "Not for people like me."

"I watched all those videos. You're not like your mother. Not like any of those people."

"Because I fight it," she told him, her posture stiffening again, as if she could protect herself. "I fight it every day. Did you know that most children of hoarders grow up to be hoarders? Because they don't know any better. Because that's how they're raised."

"And yet you live in a way that would make a Spartan envious. I've seen your possessions, Brenna. I know you have hardly anything."

"Because people don't need a lot of stuff to be happy," she told him patiently. "Surrounding yourself with pointless garbage is stupid. Even your cabin is filled with all kinds of knickknack crap that makes me uncomfortable. That's why I'd rather live in the main lodge."

"With no place where you can possibly acquire a bunch of crap," he said, suddenly starting to understand how her mind worked.

"Exactly," she told him with relish.

"And that's why you borrow everyone else's stuff," he guessed. "Because they'll always want it back."

She nodded triumphantly. "None of it sticks around."

"It's actually a pretty genius system," he said slowly. "But there's one major flaw in the plan."

"I know," she told him, looking disgruntled. "Oil changes."

"Huh?"

"Oh, that wasn't what you were going to say?"

"I was going to say that the flaw was love." He took her hand in his and raised it to his lips, kissing the backs of her knuckles. "What do you do when you fall in love?"

"Run away," Brenna said promptly. "Start over."

He might have gripped her hand a little more tightly just then. Just a little. "What if I don't want you to run away? What if I want you to stay?"

"Staying never works out," she said sadly. But she didn't pull her hand from his. Her gaze was on his mouth, where it hovered just above her knuckles. It was as if she wanted desperately to believe him, but didn't trust herself. And that was close to breaking his heart all over again.

"How do you know?"

"Because I saw my mother get married and divorced six times. And every time, they swore it would be different. And every time, it wasn't." Her face grew soft. "The last time you were married, it devastated you when things went wrong. Why would I do that to you again if I cared for you?"

He tensed. "Did you just admit that you cared for me?"

She put her fists to her forehead and closed her eyes, as if frustrated with him. "Are you listening to me, Grant? It doesn't matter if I do or not. It won't go anywhere!"

"Why don't you let me decide that?" He pulled her hands away from her face and kissed one fist. "As long as we love each other, nothing else matters."

"Do you know where my mother is now?" she asked him desperately. "She's institutionalized. The last time I saw her, she begged me to bring back her things. She's completely lost it."

"I'm sorry," he told her, wrapping his arms around her so she couldn't escape. "I'm sorry that it was so hard for you, but that doesn't change how I feel about you. You're not your mother."

Worry and panic flitted across her face. "Do you know that she used to feed me from the garbage when we ran out of money? She thought people were throwing away perfectly fine things, and so when I was too little to know better, we ate from Dumpsters."

"It must have been hard growing up like that," Grant told her, and leaned in to kiss her soft, worried mouth. "But I still love you and want to be with you."

She was stiff in his arms and anxiety was etched into her lovely face. "You're not listening to me, Grant."

"I am, actually. I'm listening to everything you say. It's you who's not listening to me." He put a hand to the back of her neck and gently tugged at the knot of her hair until she tilted back to look up at him. "I love you, Brenna. I want to be with you. I don't care about your past. It helps me to understand who you are, but it doesn't change how I feel about you." He leaned in and kissed her again, his lips brushing over hers to silence any protest. "Just like you don't care about my past."

Brenna rolled her eyes at him. "Like your past is as weird as mine. You just married someone who was awful to you. That doesn't have anything to do with you, Grant. It didn't shape you into a freak."

"Didn't it? Did you not notice how I panic when it comes to the thought of you doing something dangerous? Did you not notice how overprotective I can get? And that I can get really overbearing at the thought of you getting hurt?"

"Well, yeah," she said slowly. One finger reached out and lightly traced his unshaven jaw. "But I thought that was kind of sweet."

"You say sweet, I say overbearing and crazy." He shook his head. "What I'm trying to tell you is that the past made us who we are today. I don't hold your past against you, and you don't hold my past against me. That's what makes us good together, Brenna. We're both freaks."

A small giggle escaped her throat.

"That's what makes us work, love. I don't care that you're not perfect. I like you wild and unpredictable and just the way you are. That's the woman I fell in love with." His mouth curled into a half smile. "I'll just hide the garbage cans from you."

She punched him in the arm. "Not funny." But she was relaxed, her expression amused.

"I'm willing to compromise, though. If you find my cabin uncomfortable, I'll change it. I want you to be happy there, because I want you there. With me. In my bed. Always."

Brenna considered this for a moment. Then, in a small voice, she asked, "You'll toss out all the junk I point out?"

"I'll give you free reign to toss out anything and everything you don't like. None of it means a thing to me." He leaned into her tracing fingers. "But you? You're everything to me."

"I'm scared," she admitted, moving closer to him. "Scared it won't work out and I'll have to run again."

His arms tightened around her at the thought of her running. "I'm not." At her curious look, he continued. "Thing is, I know that you're amazing and brilliant and just a bit wild and untamed. I like that. You're my opposite, and that's just what I need. Just like I'm what you need. Please stay." He wanted to add what he was truly thinking—*I couldn't bear it if you left me.* But he knew that would be unfair to her if she truly wanted to go. The last thing Brenna needed was more guilt.

She was silent for so long that he began to worry. His grip tightened on her, pulling her closer. *Please, please stay with me,* he thought, the words repeating in his mind over and over again like a mantra.

She looked up and gave him a tiny smile. "Just so you know, if you bring home anything I don't think is necessary, it's going in the garbage."

He grinned widely. "Just so you know, if we do this, every time it rains, I probably won't let you leave the house for fear of you skidding off into a ditch or something equally frightening."

She patted his shoulder. "We'll talk about that."

"Do I need to hide the ATV keys from you on cloudy days?"

"You might need to," she said, and her voice was her familiar sassy self. She pinched his chin and gave his head a little shake. "You know I'm no good at listening to rules."

And that was part of what terrified him—and made her

so exhilarating to live with. "I guess I'll just have to keep you busy on those days."

"Is that so?" She snuggled closer, fitting her body against his.

At the feel of her against him, his cock began to stir. No one but Brenna could drive him that quickly to desire. This wild, untamed girl was his. And he loved that. "Very busy," he told her in a husky voice. "Maybe I'll bring home some extra stuff just so you can throw it out. It'll keep you busy."

She snorted at the thought. "You're getting to be quite manipulative."

"Don't worry. I'll reward you nicely."

"Oh?" Her voice took on a husky note, and that made him have a full-on erection. "What did you have in mind?"

"Well," he began, nipping lightly at her lower lip. "All that cleaning is a lot of tiring work. I think I'd have to give you a nice, full-body massage to relax you and make you comfortable."

"Mmmhmm," she murmured, wrapping her arms around his neck. "Go on."

"Then I'd have to lay you down in my bed and make sure you're totally relaxed. I'm thinking maybe a half hour of oral sex. Just to take the edge off."

"Why stop at a half hour?" she asked playfully.

"No need. I can keep going as long as my tongue does."

"You do have a good tongue," she agreed breathlessly, her gaze moving to his mouth as if imagining things. "God, it makes me wet just thinking about it."

And the thought of her wet? It made his cock as hard as a rock. "I love it when you talk dirty."

"You love everything I do," she purred.

"It's pretty much true. But I really love the thought of

getting my mouth on that wet pussy of yours and licking the hell out of that piercing."

She sucked in a breath, her fingers digging into the sleeves of his shirt. "You sure do know how to sweet talk a girl, Grant Markham."

Behind them, someone cleared her throat.

Grant kept Brenna pulled against him to hide his erection, and because he was never letting her go again. He turned to view their observer.

At the top of the stairs stood Elise, the expression on her face amusement mixed with horror. "I was going to ask if everything was okay out here. Now I'm a bit mortified that I did come out, because I think I heard way too much."

"Your brother was just telling me how he's going to lick me into next week," Brenna said, gazing adoringly up at Grant while she toyed with his hair.

"Oh, I heard that." Elise looked revolted. "I'm going to assume that things are fine between the two of you now?"

Grant looked at Brenna. She was soft in his arms, the look on her face aroused. But that weird tension and unhappiness was gone. And if she hadn't told him she'd stay yet, that was okay. He knew she wasn't the type for verbal commitments. He'd just have to coax the words out of her.

And coaxing the words out of her would be a *most* enjoyable task.

"We're good," Grant told Elise, not taking his gaze off Brenna. "You can go now."

"I plan on it," Elise said. "And I'd like to suggest that you two get a room, but I'm guessing you're already planning that."

"Absolutely," Grant said.

"Bye now," Brenna said dreamily, not looking at Elise. Her hand slid between them, and she cupped Grant's erection. "So, are you giving me a ride home? My car's toast, and your car's better for blowjobs. Nice big front seat."

Grant barely heard Elise's strangled good-bye. Brenna's hand on his cock was distracting him a bit too much. He didn't care that they were on the steps of the bed and breakfast. He didn't care that they were in downtown Bluebonnet for anyone to see. He did, however, care that her car was dead. "What happened to your car?"

She shrugged. "Don't know, don't care. Take me home?"

It was on the tip of his tongue to protest, that they should retrieve her car because that would be the sensible thing to do. He could get it towed for her, or take a look at it himself and determine what was wrong with it. He wanted to take care of it for her.

But then she squeezed his cock, and he pretty much forgot about everything but taking her home and fucking the hell out of her. "Let's go home, then."

Thank God his car was only steps away. Grant wouldn't have been able to walk far otherwise, not with his raging hard-on. He reluctantly released Brenna long enough to open the passenger-side door for her, and when she slid in the car and he was positive she wasn't fooling him and wasn't going to run away, he breathed a sigh of relief, closed the door, and headed to the driver's side.

As soon as he slid in the car and put his key in the ignition, she reached for his cock again.

Grant groaned, leaning his head back against the headrest. "Brenna, I won't be able to drive if you keep grabbing me."

"Sure you can," she teased, stroking him through his pants.

He gave her a quelling look. "I love you, but I'm not running off the road because you can't wait until we get home."

She bit her lip and gave him an innocent look, moving back to her own seat. She slid her hands between her legs and trapped them between her knees, as if to prove that she'd be good for him. "Better?"

"Not really, but it'll at least allow me to drive," he told her. And because she was looking so delicious, he leaned over to kiss her. It was going to be the longest drive ever.

He'd no sooner turned the car around and headed back down the farm road when he heard her give a low, soft moan. His cock immediately jolted, and he looked over at her.

Brenna had her hands between her legs, and she was rubbing herself through her jeans. Her eyes were closed and she had her head resting on the seat, her expression one of utter pleasure.

"What are you doing?" Other than driving him crazy, of course.

"You won't let me touch you," she murmured, her tone blissed out. "So I figured I'll just touch myself while you drive."

Ah, fuck. That was incredibly hot. And incredibly, incredibly distracting. He forced himself to stare out the windshield at the road ahead of him. Luckily, Bluebonnet was a small town and the roads in and out weren't busy. He had a feeling he would have driven anyone nearby off the road, because he swerved again when she made a soft gasp in her throat. "Stop that!"

"I can't," Brenna told him. "I need you so bad and you won't let me touch you." She gave another shuddering little gasp, and he heard her zipper go down. "Oh God, I am totally wet."

He groaned, picturing her flesh silky and slick with need.

"Maybe you should touch me," she offered. "You can keep one hand on the steering wheel, and one hand on me."

Damn it. He shouldn't. It wasn't safe. Common sense warred with need, but when she made another one of those breathless sounds, he slid a hand toward her, his gaze still firmly glued to the road.

She grasped it and dragged his hand between her thighs.

Immediately, his fingers were enveloped by soft, sweet, achingly hot flesh. She was extremely wet, and his own cock gave a jerk in response, the head already beading with pre-cum and causing his boxers to stick to his skin. The sensation of her slick pussy around his fingers was driving him mad, and when she tugged at his hand insistently, demanding that he move his fingers, he rubbed, and she went wild.

Brenna cried out, and her nails dug into his forearm. "Oh God, Grant. Keep doing that! You're so fucking dirty, fingering me while you drive."

More dirty talk. It made his eyes practically cross with lust when she did that. He was weaving all over the damn road, distracted to hell as he continued to rub her pussy. It was impossible to drive and pleasure Brenna at the same time, he decided a moment later, and he jerked the car over to the side of the road, pulling off into the grass.

"What are you doing?" she asked breathlessly when he slammed the brakes on and threw the car into park. Her glazed eyes watched him, her breasts heaving with need.

"You want to be pleasured?" he growled. "I'll fucking pleasure you."

And he reached over between her legs and threw the seat release. She fell backward with a yelp, almost lying down in the passenger seat.

He bent over her, one arm on her stomach to hold her down, and leaned in to that damp pussy. "You want me to give you some attention before we get home?"

"Oh yes, yes I do," she said, her voice shaky with excitement. Her fingers twined in his hair, and instead of pushing him away from her, she pushed his head toward her waiting flesh. She didn't give a shit that they were on the side of the road, where anyone could find them. His Brenna just did what she wanted, when she wanted.

It was what made her so damn perfect for him.

Grant buried his face between her legs, delighting in her surprised squeal of pleasure. His tongue stroked at the soft lips of her sex, and he lapped at her, tasting her sweetness. She moaned when his tongue slid across the piercing, rubbing it against her clit. He pushed with his tongue, then began to circle slowly, dragging the tip across her sensitized flesh.

Her hands curled into fists and she clutched at him desperately. She was making wild, incoherent noises in the back of her throat, and those were making his cock so hard that he felt he'd burst. He wasn't going to make it until they got home. No fucking way. He didn't give a shit, either. He'd happily change his pants as soon as he got in the door. Didn't matter. All that mattered was pleasing her.

Slipping a finger down between her legs, he pushed past the bunched fabric at her thighs and stroked at the wet lips of her sex with his forefinger before sinking deeper, seeking her heat. He sank it deep and then moved his mouth back to her clit, sucking hard even as he began to drive his finger in and out of her.

She whimpered, her thighs quivering around him. "Oh, Grant. Oh, fuck yes."

Brenna was close. He could tell by the way little quivers were beginning to drag at his finger deep inside her. His tongue picked up the pace, slicking and teasing at her clit faster than before. His finger slammed into her warmth. She clenched around him and gave a high-pitched scream, and he felt her clenching and dragging at his finger, the power of her orgasm making her entire body shake. He continued to lick her, dragging every ounce of pleasure from her that he could, until she was heaving for breath and pushing his face away.

"Oh wow," she breathed after a long moment. "Oh wow. Just wow."

He sat up slowly, his own need a fierce ache, and watched her with intense pleasure. She looked flushed and delicious. Her hair had fallen from her clip and was strewn about her shoulders, and her jeans were bunched down on her hips, her shirt tugged up, revealing her pale, smooth belly. Grant licked his lips, tasting the remnants of her pleasure. "Feel better?"

"God, yes." She gave a sensual stretch, grinning at him. "That was just what I needed to take the edge off things." Her gaze slid to his lap. "You must be positively aching, though. Want me to fix that for you?"

And she slid toward him, her hand going to his tented pants, a sultry smile on her lips.

Grant sucked in a breath, entranced by that wicked look on her face. "You don't have to—"

"Duh." She leaned over toward him and rubbed a hand up and down his length. "But this monster's calling to me, I admit. And it's only fair that I take care of you, don't you think? Then we can get home and really have some fun."

He wanted to. More than anything. His gaze went to the empty road. A few cars had whizzed past, but no one had stopped to assist. No one would see, just like no one had seen him going down on her moments ago. So why was he hesitating?

She made up his mind for him. With a wicked giggle, she reached for the release on his seat, and he went backward with a thump. Then her hands were on his belt and she quickly undid it and his zipper. Moments later, she was pulling his cock out of his boxers with a satisfied sigh, and she swiped her tongue across the head.

Pleasure burst through him at her touch.

"Poor dear. You're so very hard for me, aren't you? Look at how much this cock aches," she murmured, dragging her tongue over his length and licking him like a delicious treat. "It needs relief."

"Good thing you're here," he said raggedly. His hand stroked her cheek, even though he desperately wanted to push down on the back of her head and cram his cock into her mouth, watch her take him deep.

As if sensing his thoughts, she gave him another small smile and then opened her mouth, sinking down on him.

He groaned at the fierce wash of pleasure that shot through him, unable to stop watching her as she sucked him deep. Her cheeks hollowed, and he felt an incredible suction on his cock. Unable to contain himself, he pulled back against her head. "I'm about to come, Brenna. Don't—"

She popped off him immediately, looking up at him in surprise. "Don't what? Deep throat you? Really?" Grant reached for his cock to stroke himself off, but she stopped him. "Don't you want to come in my mouth?"

"More than anything."

Brenna moved down so close that her breath hummed along his skin. "Don't want me to take you deep in my throat?"

"Brenna," he rasped. "I'm close—"

"Or maybe you wanted to come on my face?" She leaned

in so her lips brushed his cock while she talked. "Get your come all over my lips and my cheeks—"

A snarl broke from his lips and he pushed at her head. Eagerly—almost greedily—she took him into her mouth again, and he pushed at the back of her head, sinking his cock deep into her mouth. Her throat worked around him and it was too much—he came with a rush, groaning out her name as his cum flooded her mouth. That evil, evil suction broke and she released him, her throat working to swallow. And Grant fell back in his seat.

Damn. That had been amazing. He gave her a stunned look.

Brenna sat up, wiping the corners of her mouth with delicate fingertips and looking extremely pleased with herself. "That was so sexy, Grant. You're making me turned on all over again." And she gave an excited wiggle in her seat. "Now I want to have sex again."

He bit out a laugh. "We're never going to get home at this rate."

"Oh, I'll let you drive the rest of the way home," she said languidly, and ran her hands up her front, cupping her breasts. "But the rest of me is going to want some attention when we get there."

"I can do that," he murmured, then flipped his seat back into the upright position and started the car again. "Buckle up, because we're going to drive fast. We're even going to go the speed limit down this road."

"You wild man, you!" Her throaty laugh of pleasure only spurred him on.

They made it back to the cabin in record time. By the time he pulled into the gravel parking lot, his cock was hard again and Brenna was squirming in her seat, telling him all the dirty things she wanted to do to him. The woman didn't know the meaning of patience . . . and that was just fine with him, really. More than fine.

He hauled out of the car, not caring that he hadn't parked straight, and then Brenna was jumping out of the car next to him, before he could open her door. She gave him a mischievous smile and held out her hand.

He took it and instead of holding her hand, he hauled her into his arms, swinging her legs over his elbow.

She squealed in protest, her arms going to his shoulders. "What's this for?"

"So you don't get away."

"After that car ride? I'm not going anywhere."

"Good."

Grant strode across the grounds, Brenna cradled in his arms. When he got to his porch, he turned so she could twist the doorknob for him, and then he pushed the door open with his foot.

"Home sweet junky home," Brenna announced. "Get ready for a makeover."

He grinned, pleased as hell that she thought of his cabin as home. He didn't even mind that she thought his house was junky. He kept it clean, but that wasn't what bothered her. He'd had a decorator come in and make it look like a home, so as a result, he had some useless items—like decorative spheres made out of dyed grapevine that sat in a wooden bowl on a coffee table—but none of it meant a thing to him. Brenna's happiness was what was truly important. She could toss it all away and he didn't care, as long as she was smiling and in his arms. "You do whatever you like to it."

"Oh, I plan on it. Right after I do whatever I like to you."

She ran a hand down his chest. "Put me down so we can go upstairs?"

He did, setting her feet down. Before she could slide away, he kissed her again, his lips moving over hers in a gentle caress. Nothing deep or searing, just a simple, gentle affirmation of how he felt about her. And he loved the smile that blossomed across her face as a result.

"You're trying to distract me away from sex with kissing and cuddling, aren't you? You fiend."

"Never," he told her, unable to stop touching her. His hand dragged through her hair, brushing it off her neck, and he began to kiss her lightly on her jaw and neck. "We'll still have sex. Don't you worry."

"Good," she told him, sliding her hands under his shirt and running her hands along his spine. "Because I like cuddling, but I'm an even bigger fan of a deep dicking."

She had such a filthy mouth sometimes. It shocked him, but he also liked it. "So a bit of cuddling and then a deep dicking? I can handle that."

"Oh, I approve. You're so good at both."

He grinned against her neck and lightly nipped at the skin there, enjoying her shiver of response. "So I should stop with the cuddling and the foreplay?"

"Mmmm. I'm debating." She cycled a hand in the air. "Keep going and I'll let you know what I decide."

His hand moved to her breast, cupping it through the fabric. No bra. He felt her nipple harden against the brush of his hand, and then he began to tease it as he kissed her neck. "How's this?"

She made a soft sound, then spoke. "It's . . . it's really good."

He licked at the smooth skin of her neck, and then pushed

her shirt up, his hand sliding under the material to caress her bared breast. The curve of it was the perfect fit to his hand, and he thumbed her nipple, rolling it back and forth into stiffness. His other hand slid to her other breast, and when he began to play with both nipples, she moaned.

"Still down for some more cuddling?" he asked.

She shivered, but her breasts pressed against his hand. "What else did you have in mind?"

He cupped one of her breasts and tilted it so the nipple was pointed toward him. Then he leaned in and brushed his lips over it.

Brenna cried out softly, clinging to him for support.

He tongued her breast, circling the stiff nipple and then licking it. He sucked on it for a long moment, then turned to look up at her. "More?"

"Actually," she breathed, panting hard. "I think I'd really like my deep dicking now."

He thumbed her nipple again, then smacked her ass. "Then let's get upstairs."

She shimmied up the ladder with a wiggle that drove him crazy with lust. It didn't matter that she was wearing someone else's cast-off jeans and one of his shirts. She was outrageously sexy to him. It was evident in her smiles, her playful tone of voice, and just the way she looked at the world. He couldn't get enough of her. Never would.

Once they were both up the ladder, she headed straight for the bed, tearing off her clothing. He grabbed a condom from the dresser and began to get rid of his own clothes, tearing them off in his haste. He'd never learned to undress so fast as when he was with Brenna.

She finished undressing first and came over to his side, helping him take off his clothing as she leaned in for another kiss. He kissed her, letting her tug at his shirt even as he played with one of her bare nipples, loving how distracted she got. In every other aspect, she could distract him within moments. It felt glorious to turn the tables on her. His fingers tugged at her nipple, coaxing and teasing it, and she whimpered when he leaned down to bite at the stiff tip. All her playfulness had vanished and was replaced by sheer need. "Grant," she panted. "I need you. Need this."

He let his half-torn shirt slide off his shoulders and shook it to the ground. Condom still in hand, he tore the package open and began to roll it on as Brenna ran her hands on his chest. When it was on, he grabbed her and dragged her to the bed. They fell in a heap together, and then Brenna's hands were all over him, hungrily clutching at his skin. Her hand slid to his cock and she spread her legs wide, trying to guide him into her. Grant's hand covered hers, and he guided himself in, then slammed home.

"Ah!" Her first cry was a shriek of delight, and she wrapped her arm around his neck, holding him against her. "Yes!"

"Is this what you wanted?" he gritted between thrusts, driving into her.

"Oh God, yes. Fuck me so deep." Her head threw back, her mouth half open with pleasure.

Grant began to thrust harder, pounding into her with as much speed and power as possible. He'd have been afraid that he was going to hurt her with the force of his thrusts, but she clung to him and kept asking for more. Harder. Stronger. So he complied, each stroke sinking deep, only to pull back and roughly pound into her again.

Brenna clung to him, crying out with each wild thrust. She hooked her legs around his waist and lifted her hips with each thrust, demanding more.

Grant's control was close to shattering—it wouldn't be a

long fuck, but a short, violent one. He held off, determined to make this as good for her as he could. He wouldn't be able to stand a long, slow, torturous fucking. They were both too worked up. Even now, Brenna was nearly insensible, softly crying out his name over and over with each thrust, her nails digging into his back so hard that she was drawing blood.

And then, he felt her pussy spasm around him, clenching hard. "Oh God," she moaned. "Oh, I'm coming. God, I love you."

His heart skipped a beat at her wild admission. She loved him? It was the first time she'd ever admitted it. He was so startled by it that he lost his control. The orgasm he'd been fighting back rushed over him and he came with a muttered curse and collapsed on top of Brenna.

She clung to him, her skin stuck to his, and gave a long, drawn-out sigh of pleasure.

Grant kissed her one last time, breathing hard. "Did you mean it?"

She blinked at him, still dazed from her own wild orgasm. "Mean it?"

"That you love me?"

"Oh." Her eyes got soft and she smiled at him. "I do. Is that so bad?"

"It's not bad at all. I love you, too."

She snuggled closer to him, pulling off his now smudged and completely askew eyeglasses and tossing them on the nightstand. "It freaks me out a little, I admit. I'm still scared to be in love."

"I won't hurt you," he told her, stroking a hand down her arm. "I'd never hurt you."

"It's just . . . vulnerable."

"It is," he agreed. "But it's also incredible. When I'm with you, I'm happier than I've ever been."

"Ironic, isn't it? You used to hate working with me."

"Oh, I still hate working with you," Grant said, grinning. "You're a shitty employee. But you make an incredible girlfriend."

"So much for just pretending. I guess we're not very good at that."

"Nope. I'm not complaining."

She gave another blissful sigh. "Me either."

Grant stroked her hair. She was so beautiful after sex, all sleepy and tousled. Purple strands of her bangs stuck everywhere. "I still want to marry you."

Brenna considered this for a moment, then tucked her head against his shoulder. "Would I have to wear a ring?"

"Not if you don't want to."

She thought about it, and then shrugged. "Make it a shitty ring, so I won't feel bad if I lose it."

"I . . . can do that. Is that a yes?"

She gave him a mischievous look and then licked his chin. "It's not a no."

"I'll take that," Grant said, and leaned in to kiss her again. "One shitty ring, coming right up."

FIFTEEN

"Y ou're going to have to take that piece of crap off for the photo shoot," Miranda told her. "It doesn't match your outfit."

Brenna protectively held her hand close to her breast, scowling at her friend. "It doesn't matter. It's my engagement ring."

"It came from a candy machine," Miranda pointed out. "I can't believe that Grant's a millionaire and he cheaped out like that on your ring."

"I asked him to," Brenna said, beaming as she extended her hand and admired her ring again. It was a cheap piece of crap, but it was *her* cheap piece of crap. They'd gone out to dinner to celebrate, just the two of them on their first official date. As they'd entered the restaurant, they'd noticed a candy vending machine full of plastic bubble packs with a toy inside. Grant had stopped in his tracks and started to search his pockets for change.

"What is it?" she'd asked, and he'd pointed at a small play ring at the front of the vending machine. And he'd sank a quarter in and tried to get it for her. Three quarters later, and he'd had to go inside for change. Twenty-seven quarters later, they'd handed out the extra toys to kids who passed by with their families, and Grant had finally retrieved the ring. It was a total piece of junk—the back was a plastic c-clasp obviously meant for smaller fingers, and the purple stone was more of a gaudy bead.

But she'd loved it, and she loved that he took her hand and slipped it onto her finger as if it were the most important thing in his life. And he'd told her he loved her all over again.

Brenna had told him that she wanted a cheap ring because it wouldn't bother her if she tossed it. But now that she had her ring? She loved it, and she'd be damned if she switched it out for anything. It made her happy just to see it.

"Elise, tell her that ugly ring is going to ruin the shot," Miranda insisted. She leaned out of her chair, the huge pink curlers in her dark brown locks sticking up wildly. In front of her, Beth Ann wielded a can of hairspray, enveloping her in a cloud of fine mist and then waving a hand to dissipate the smell.

Her name called, Elise dutifully came over to the other side of the salon, where Brenna and Miranda sat. They'd volunteered to be the test subjects for the pin-up photo shoot, and had arrived for an early morning of pampering. Brenna's hair had been curled and pulled back on the sides in a mimic of Bettie Page's hairstyle from an old photo, and she wore a pink and black diner T-shirt and a short, pleated black skirt that barely covered the frilly, pink ruffled-rump pant-ies she was wearing underneath. Her legs were clad in pink thigh highs and she wore black high-heeled Mary Janes. Atop her head, a paper diner hat had been artfully perched, and her makeup and nails had been perfectly done, thanks to Beth Ann's ministrations. Looking in the mirror, Brenna had to admit that she did look a lot like a pin-up model.

At her side, Miranda sat in a tight white sweater with a blue peter pan collar and matching blue poodle skirt. Her hair was being carefully teased into several large rolled pin curls atop her head.

Elise studied Brenna's ring for a long moment, then shrugged. "It's whimsical. It's not like it won't fit the theme. If she wants to keep it on, she can."

Miranda made a face at Elise. "Party pooper."

Brenna stuck her tongue out at Miranda, then grinned and hopped out of her chair. "Are we ready now? All this lipstick's driving me crazy." For the shoot, Beth Ann had slicked Brenna's lips with a bright red gloss that looked gor-geous, but tasted awful. And of course she kept licking her lips by accident.

"We're ready," Elise told her. "I need you to go stand in the center of the sheet."

Brenna trotted over to the area that had been staged for the photo shoot. Beth Ann's tiny salon had been temporar-ily transformed. Pale beige sheets had been draped over the windows and across the flooring, creating a neutral area for the shot to be set up. The barber chair had been pushed to one side, and a white stool sat in the midst of the sheets. On the far corners of the room, lamps had been set up on tripods to make sure that the room would have the best lighting possible.

"So do I just sit on this stool?" Brenna asked, dusting her

hands over the ruffles on the backside of her panties. They were so ruffly and her skirt so short that it kind of stuck out in the back, almost like she was wearing a crinoline.

"Actually, the stool's for Miranda." Elise hurried forward and moved it out of the way. "If you're up for a slightly racier shot, I have a few ideas to go with your waitress costume."

On the far side of the room, Beth Ann squirted more hairspray over Miranda's curls and laughed. "Up for a slightly racier shot? Do you know who you're talking to?"

Brenna rubbed her hands gleefully. "I am so ready for something dirty. Bring it on."

"Well, these are pinups," Elise told her, bustling to her prop box on the other side of the room. She tore open some sort of plastic package, the rustling filling the room. "The idea is fun and naughtiness more than blatant dirt." She glanced over her shoulder and smiled at Brenna. "Not that you couldn't make that work."

"You know I could," Brenna said, and flexed her arm, grinning.

She was glad Elise had stayed in Bluebonnet. The girl had seemed so lonely when she'd arrived. But since undertaking her new business scheme with Beth Ann, she'd been blossoming out of her remote shell. Now when the girls got together for drinks and girl chat, Elise was usually with them. They made a fun foursome, and Elise's quiet personality was a good foil to Brenna's brashness—not that Elise didn't occasionally zing them with a mouthy quip of her own.

She fit right in, Brenna thought. And Grant seemed to like having his sister around, which was nice, too. Elise did spend a lot of time at the ranch lately, but that was to be expected, Brenna supposed. She just hoped Elise didn't accompany her back to the ranch today, because she was feeling mighty amorous in her cute spanky panties, and the guys were all out on runs with clients . . . which meant that she and Grant would have the lodge entirely to themselves.

And they hadn't quite christened the shed yet. The kitchen, yes. Grant's desk, yes. Her desk, oh yes. The sofa? Yep. But not the shed. Seemed a crime to not include it.

"All right," Elise said, brandishing a long, thin stick at her. A shish kebab skewer. "I'm going to need you to hold this."

Brenna frowned at it, curious. "What am I supposed to do with it?"

Elise stuck a hot dog on the end of the skewer. "Bend over and pretend to eat that."

Brenna eyed it, then Elise. "You dirty, dirty girl. I like the way you think." She winked and leaned over, flipping her skirt up so her panties were on full display, and pretended like she was about to take a bite out of the hot dog. In the background, she could hear Miranda giggling.

"Perfect," Elise said, and put out a hand. "Now hold that pose."

"And don't deep throat it," Miranda called out helpfully. "It's not Grant."

"Of course not," Brenna called back. "It's much too tiny. Grant's got a lot more meat on his hot dog."

Behind the camera, Elise made a gagging sound.

Brenna just grinned and slid her tongue out as if to lick the frank poised against her lips.

Brenna pulled Grant's car up to the main lodge and pulled the bag of hot dogs out of the seat. Water was leaking from the opened package, and she winced at the sight of the droplets on the leather. She looked around for a napkin, didn't find one, and shrugged and headed out of the car. She'd be back to wipe it later, or Grant'd be wondering why his lovely Audi smelled like wieners. A hot dog cookout for dinner sounded nice, though, so she'd taken the extras home.

She was still dressed in the pinup girl outfit, though most of her thick lipstick was gone. They'd gotten some fun shots, and Elise promised to email her some later after she'd touched them up. Brenna wanted a print of one of the hot dog ones so she could frame it and put it on Grant's desk to replace the picture of Heather that had been permanently retired. Thinking of Grant put a bit of a bounce in her step as she imagined what he'd think of her frilly panties. And how he'd strip them off her.

When she got into the lodge, she looked around in surprise. Grant wasn't at his normal seat, and it was during office hours. "Grant?" she called out, curious.

His head popped up over the couch. "You're home?" His gaze went to her outfit and hair. "Holy shit."

She grinned and gave her skirt a saucy little flick. "You like?"

"Definitely." He looked extremely appreciative, his gaze moving up and down over her body. "Damn. I can't wait to see those pictures." He seemed momentarily distracted, then shook his head. "I didn't know you were coming home so early, though—"

She started forward, amused. "Were you taking a nap? Because I can think of a few other uses for that couch right about now—"

A high-pitched yap interrupted her.

Brenna blinked in surprise, stopping short. "What was that?"

Grant hefted a small, squirming beige bundle into the air. "Your surprise."

"My surprise?" She started forward again, staring at the

squirming puppy in Grant's hands. Short, fawn-colored fur covered a wriggling sausage body and tiny paws. Two bug eyes stared out in opposite directions from a wrinkly black muzzle. It was hideous. It was so adorable it made her want to pinch it. "You . . . got me a puppy? Why?"

He got to his feet and headed toward her. When he got to her side, he pushed the tiny puppy into her hands. It immediately began to lick her chin, then her fingers. "Because I remembered in the video that you showed me that you said you always wanted a dog. And I thought it might be a good way for you to get your feet wet with the whole 'being tied down' thing. This dog's small enough that you can take him anywhere."

Tears burned her eyes. He'd remembered that she'd said that? She hadn't even remembered it. The puppy continued to lick her, and Brenna pulled it away from her to get a good look at it, and laughed through her tears. "It's really damn ugly."

"It's a pug," he told her, pleased at her reaction. He wrapped an arm around her waist and pulled her close to him as she snuggled the puppy against her again. "They're supposed to be very interesting personalities."

"His eyes aren't even facing the same direction," she blubbered happily, unable to stop crying. Luckily, the puppy was there to lick away her tears. "He looks like Gollum from *Lord of the Rings*."

Grant laughed. "Sounds like as good a name as any." He leaned in to kiss her cheek, and then pulled away. "Why do you smell like hot dogs?"

"Because of the photos," she told him, entranced with the puppy. "You got me a present?"

"Of course. I'll get you a present every day for the rest of your life, if you like. But I know you wouldn't like that."

She smiled. He knew her well. Within twenty-four hours of the okay from him to "redecorate" his cabin, she'd removed all the furnishings except the bare essentials, and had denuded the house of most everything except a framed photo or two. She'd even cleaned out his cabinets, tossing extra canned soups and power bars. Hell, he could have sworn that he'd come in for breakfast yesterday morning and caught her throwing away plates.

It didn't matter. She was more at ease in his newly spartan home, so he didn't care if a few throw rugs or decor pieces were gone. The furniture was there, and Brenna was there. He had everything he needed.

"Gollum it is," she said with a happy grin, and then leaned over to kiss him. "You're the best man I've ever known."

"I can't say I don't have an ulterior motive."

"Oh?" She smiled, still cuddling the squirming puppy to her. "I think I can live with giving you a week of morning blowjobs."

"That . . . wasn't what I meant, though I'll definitely take it." Grant grinned and tugged at a curled purple lock of hair. "I was talking about your smile."

"Oh." She laughed. "Well, I suppose that's important, too." This was a good segue, though. "I bought you a present, too, but it's not here. We're getting it this weekend."

He looked surprised at her words, and a pleased look crossed his face. "You got me something?"

"Something as big to you as this puppy is to me," Brenna told him, holding Gollum aloft so he could lick Grant's chin.

"Uh-oh," Grant said warily. "Am I going to like this present?"

"Probably not," she told him. "But I'll be strapped to you the entire way down."

"Entire way down?" His eyebrows shot up and a look of horror crossed his face. "What did you do?"

She gave him an innocent look. "I might have signed us up for a tandem skydiving session to get you over your fear of control."

"You *what*?"

"Don't shout." She shoved the puppy in his face. "You're going to scare Gollum."

"Brenna," he said in a warning tone.

"It'll be good for us," she said, leaning in to kiss him. "Don't you want to be tied up to me?"

"Not if someone's going to push us off a plane," he grumbled.

She gave him a mock-pout and held the puppy up again. It began to lick Grant's glasses. "Then I guess you'll have to take Gollum back."

He pushed the puppy's head away and gave Brenna an exasperated look. "You really want to do this?"

"Well, no," Brenna said, pulling the puppy close and tucking it under her chin. She began to rock it against her chest. "I've never given it much thought. But since we're all about conquering our fears to make ourselves better people, if I can get a puppy, you can go skydiving."

"I'll go," he said slowly. "On two conditions."

"What's that?"

"First," he said, and pulled up the edge of her skirt. "That you wear those panties for the rest of the day, because they are smoking hot."

"Deal," she said with a grin. "What's the second condition?"

Grant gazed down at her with a look of infinite tenderness. "That you tell me you love me again."

"I'll tell you every day for the rest of our lives," she vowed to him, and leaned in to give him a kiss.

"You still smell like hot dogs," he murmured against her mouth.

"You sure do know how to sweet talk a woman," she said.

And then no one spoke for a good long while.

Read on for a special preview of

the next Bluebonnet novel

THE VIRGIN'S GUIDE TO MISBEHAVING

Coming soon from Berkley Sensation!

There were days, Elise Markham decided, in which the world seemed to be hideously unfair.

If the world was fair, she wouldn't have been born with that awful port-wine stain on her entire left cheek. It didn't matter that she'd had it lasered away in her teen years. When she looked in the mirror, she could swear she still saw traces of it there. And if she saw it, so did everyone else. If the world was fair, karma wouldn't have then turned around and slapped her with scoliosis during puberty that involved wearing a bulky back brace and made her even shyer.

If the world was fair, that would have been enough and she wouldn't have had to go through the other awful things teenage girls did, like pudgy thighs and pimples and braces. But she had.

All of which had told Elise by the age of thirteen that the world wasn't fair, and she needed to stop wishing it was.

Because if the world was fair? Her new friends would not be trying to set her up on a blind date.

"What about that really quiet, tall officer?" Miranda asked, raising her margarita glass and licking the salt from the rim. "The one that's the sheriff's son. He's not bad-looking. He gave me a ticket last month for speeding and I thought he was kind of cute. In a law-officer sort of way."

Miranda and Brenna sat across from Elise in a cozy booth at Maya Loco, the only restaurant in tiny Bluebonnet. Beth Ann was at the bar, getting a refill on her drink and chatting with a friend. It was busy in the restaurant, a noisy hum of voices and clinking forks making it difficult to hold a quiet conversation.

Not that it stopped the women she was seated with. At her side in the booth, Brenna shook her head. She twirled her short red mixing straw in her drink as she spoke. "He hooked up with that weird blogger chick. Emily's sister. You're a few months too late."

"Oh. Rats." She screwed up her face. "I know this is a small town, but Jesus. There have to be some hot eligible men around here."

"It's really okay," Elise said, but her voice was so quiet over the din of the restaurant happy hour that she wasn't sure anyone heard her. "I don't need to date."

"I stole the last hottie," Brenna said with a sly grin. She winked at Elise and adjusted her purple bangs on her forehead. "Lucky for me he's into tattoos and kinky sex."

Elise made a face at the same time that Miranda did. "Um."

"That's her brother, you sicko," Miranda said. "Gross."

"Doesn't matter. She'd do him. He's hot. Those uptight clothes and frumpy glasses? Mmm." She fanned her face.

"Still her brother," Miranda said.

Elise nodded. Brenna was weird. Sweet, but weird. No one could predict the things that came out of her mouth, so it was best for Elise to just sit back and let someone else correct Brenna when she spouted off. Not that Elise would ever say something to hurt Brenna's feelings—her brother's fiancée was strange, but Elise loved her. Brenna played to the beat of her own drum—she wore old T-shirts and ill-fitting clothing more often than not. Actually, most of the time it was Grant's clothing, which was odd to see. But her uptight, once-lonely brother worshipped Brenna, and for that, Elise adored her as well.

"There's got to be someone," Miranda muttered.

"Someone for what?" Beth Ann slid into the booth next to Elise. Self-conscious at the appearance of the statuesque blonde, Elise straightened, careful to raise one shoulder above the other so it wouldn't look like she was slumping. Of her three new friends, Beth Ann was the most intimidating. Miranda was pretty but scholarly. Brenna was cheery and strange, and dressed like a slob. But Beth Ann? Beth Ann was completely perfect, from her delicately manicured nails to her faint tan in November and her immaculate blond hair. She was also dressed in a dainty gingham dress topped with a matching cardigan and slingbacks.

She was intimidating, all right. But Beth Ann was also the sweetest person that Elise knew, and her partner in a new business venture.

"A man for Elise to date," Miranda offered, delicately licking a large grain of margarita salt off of one finger. "Since we're all paired up, we thought it might be a good idea to find Elise a man, too."

Elise shook her head, voice whispering. "I really don't—"

Miranda snapped her fingers, cutting off Elise's thoughts. "I know! What about one of Colt's brothers?"

"Oh, honey, no," Beth Ann said in her sweet drawl. "Berry's the only one close to her age and he's not right for her. At all."

Brenna leaned across the table toward Elise and gave her a mock-conspiratorial whisper. "Colt's brothers are all named after guns. Berry's short for Beretta. It's all very redneck."

"Honey," Beth Ann said again, "she knows that. She grew up here, remember?" Of the four of the women at the table, only Brenna wasn't originally from Bluebonnet.

"Actually I don't know them all that well," Elise said in a small voice. "I went to boarding school as soon as I was old enough." And she'd never left the house much before that, too ashamed of the gigantic purple mark that had disfigured her cheek. Even now, she had to fight the urge to drag her long hair over that side of her face to hide it. "But it's okay." She did remember Grant's stories about Colt's poor-as-dirt family growing up. Not that she was a snob, but when Colt didn't even want to associate with them, it was bad.

Beth Ann patted Elise's hand. "We'll find you a good man, honey. Don't you worry. I have a few single clients. Let me think."

God, she didn't want anyone. Or rather, no one would want her. But her friends seemed determined to find her a man, which made her want to cringe and hide. She felt like a charity case, which only made things worse. *Our poor ugly, shy friend can't find a man? We'll just have to find one for her.*

The worst was that she knew they meant well, but it still hurt. It hurt that she was ungainly and unattractive enough to have to resort to charity. Being single and alone was so much easier. No hopes to get up. "I don't really want to date right now, Beth Ann," Elise said in a low, soft voice. "I just don't think—"

"Nonsense," Brenna interrupted. "You just sit in your room every night over at the bed and breakfast unless we drag you out. That's not healthy."

"That's not true," Elise protested, then bit her lip. Okay, so it was a little true. "Sometimes I go out and take photos." But only at times that she wouldn't risk running into too many of the nosy, well-meaning people of Bluebonnet. People that would stop and try to have a conversation with her.

Elise wasn't good with conversations. Actually, she wasn't good with small talk, period.

"You don't want to date?" Miranda looked crestfallen. "Really?"

"I'm concentrating on business right now," she said. "And besides, like Beth Ann said, I grew up here. There's no one in town that interests me. No one here is my type."

"So what's your type?" Brenna wanted to know.

Her tongue felt glued to the roof of her mouth. Should she lie? She was a terrible liar. Really, the only thing she was excellent at was taking photos and avoiding people. But admitting her type would make it pretty obvious who she liked. More than liked, really. She had a schoolgirl crush on a man that was tall, dark, and handsome, covered in tattoos and had piercings, and drove a motorcycle.

But only one man in Bluebonnet matched that description. So Elise said nothing, because speaking would have betrayed her thoughts, and she had no desire to be humiliated like that. She simply shrugged her shoulders.

"Do you like tall men?" Brenna prompted.

"Let it go," Beth Ann said, coming to Elise's defense with a laugh. "If Elise doesn't want someone in town, I can't say I blame her."

"We could always get her an out of towner," Miranda said with a sly glance in her direction. At her side, Brenna gave a chortle and elbowed her, then nodded in the distance.

Beth Ann and Elise turned.

Coming across the crowded restaurant, beer in hand, was none other than the object of Elise's crush, Rome Lozada. *Oh no.* Elise immediately turned away, feeling her face turn a bright, beet red that would make the remains of her old scar whiten on her face. *Please no.*

Oblivious to Elise's distress, Brenna waved a hand. "Rome! Hey! Come sit with us!"

Elise whimpered in her throat. Luckily, the restaurant was too noisy for it to be overheard. She stared down at her iced tea, unable to work up the courage to lift it to her mouth, lest someone notice her movements. Maybe Rome was meeting friends and wouldn't be sitting with them.

To her dismay, he came and stood at the end of their table. "Ladies." He gave them a gorgeous smile, and Elise felt her pulse flutter. No man should be that pretty. It was unfair. "Am I interrupting girls' night out?" He glanced at their group, and his gaze seemed to linger on Elise.

She averted her gaze, staring at her drink. With a quick shift of her chin, her hair fell forward.

"We're just trying to find Elise a man," Miranda said, a hint of slurring in her voice. Too many margaritas for her. "You know of any good pieces of man meat?"

"Other than yourself," Brenna said and gave him a wicked, lascivious look. "You're the best man meat we have in town. Other than all the ones that are taken, of course."

"Am I?" Rome laughed at Brenna's outrageous comments. "Maybe I should volunteer to be Elise's man meat, then."

Elise wanted to crawl under the table. She shrank down,

just a little, and kept staring at her glass. Was he really volunteering to date her? Or just humoring a tipsy Brenna? Was this a suggestion born out of pity? That would be just awful. Elise's throat felt knotted in embarrassment. No one as gorgeous as Rome Lozada would even look in her direction, except for the fact that her well-meaning friends were trying to coerce him into asking her out. Ugh.

"Brenna," Beth Ann said in a chiding voice. "Be nice." Elise felt Beth Ann shift in the booth, turning toward Rome. "What these two drunks aren't telling you is that Elise isn't interested in dating anyone in town. There's no one that's her type here. She's already said so, but these ladies won't take no for an answer."

Oh God! Now Beth Ann had just told Rome that he wasn't her type and she didn't like him. That was either a blessing or the worst ever.

"That so?" Rome gave a hard-sounding chuckle. "Guess Elise is too picky for the likes of me, then."

She wanted to protest, or apologize, but the words wouldn't form.

"Now, now," Brenna called, and Elise glanced over at her long enough to see her reaching out and patting Rome's tattooed arm. "Don't be sad. I'm sure you're other women's type. Just not Elise's." She leaned in and whispered loudly, "You probably talk too much."

Miranda snorted and drank again.

"You ladies sound like you're enjoying your drinks," Rome said, voice cool. "I take it you have a designated driver?"

That was her. Elise raised her hand, not looking up.

Rome made a noise of approval. "Well, I'll leave you be, then. Enjoy your drinks. See you at work tomorrow, Brenna."

"Bye, man meat," Brenna called after him. Miranda dissolved into giggles. Beth Ann only sighed at their antics.

Elise watched a droplet of condensation slide down the front of her glass, wishing she were back in her nice, safe room at the bed and breakfast. Rome Lozada, the hottest man that Elise had ever seen, thought she was a snob and too good for the men in Bluebonnet.

Yep. That clinched it. The world was definitely not fair.

Beth Ann needed a hero.
She got more than she bargained for.

FROM
JESSICA CLARE

THE CARE AND FEEDING OF AN ALPHA *Male*

A Bluebonnet Novel

Beth Ann Williamson is done with her on-again, off-again fiancé, and she's determined to show everyone that she can take care of herself. But her plans go awry when she gets stranded in the woods and has to be saved.

Survivalist Colt Waggoner is not pleased when he's sent to rescue the pampered princess, and he's even more annoyed when Beth Ann isn't grateful. He decides to teach the sexy blonde a lesson—a weekend alone in the wild. Just the two of them, in muddy, wet clothing that needs to come off...

But when Beth Ann propositions him for a one-night stand, he knows he should turn it down—because this alpha male might need more than one night to satisfy him...

Praise for *The Girl's Guide to (Man)Hunting*

"Sexy and funny."
—*USA Today*

"Clare's sizzling encounters...have definite forest-fire potential from the heat generated."
—*RT Book Reviews*

jillmyles.com
facebook.com/jillmyles
facebook.com/Love AlwaysBooks
penguin.com

M1349T0813

Risa's luck was running out . . .
Until she met a man worth his weight in gold.

FROM NATIONAL BESTSELLING AUTHOR
Jessica Clare

THE BILLIONAIRE OF BLUEBONNET

Risa Moore is content with her work as a live-in assistant to an elderly lady—until her boss passes on. Now she's stuck in the tiny town of Bluebonnet, Texas, with no job, nowhere to live, and no prospects. Leaving Bluebonnet means starting her life over from scratch, so when Risa gets the opportunity of a lifetime, it's hard to turn it down. But does her sexy new boss want something more than just an employee?

Young, hot, and fabulously wealthy, Travis Jesson has no intention of ever returning to his small Texas hometown. Then his grandmother passes away, leaving him her estate and her pet. His plans involve disposing of her things as expediently as possible...until he meets her gorgeous live-in help. And Travis finds himself proposing an entirely different sort of relationship . . .

Download this Penguin Special Novella!

jessica-clare.com
facebook.com/LoveAlwaysBooks
penguin.com

M1234T1212

Love is about to drive one man to his knees...

FROM *NEW YORK TIMES* BESTSELLING AUTHOR

JILL SHALVIS

Slow

Heat

When bad-boy Major League catcher Wade O'Riley is
ordered to improve his image, he finds himself falling
for his pretend girlfriend, tough and sexy publicist
Samantha McNead. But if he really wants to win her
love, it will mean stealing a few bases...

PRAISE FOR JILL SHALVIS

"Shalvis writes with humor, heart, and sizzling heat!"
—Carly Phillips

"Shalvis will make you laugh and fall in love."
—Rachel Gibson

jillshalvis.com
facebook.com/jillshalvis
facebook.com/LoveAlwaysBooks
penguin.com

M1354T0813

LOVE
ROMANCE
NOVELS?

For news on all your favorite romance authors,
sneak peeks into the newest releases, book
giveaways, and much more—

"Like" Love Always on Facebook!
LoveAlwaysBooks

M1063G0212